THESE ARE ONLY WORDS

+ + + + + + + + +

THESE ARE ONLY WORDS

+ + + + + + + + +

SIMON R.BIGGAM

First published 2006
by CHROMA, an imprint of
Black & White Publishing Ltd
99 Giles Street,
Edinburgh, EH6 6BZ

ISBN 1 84502 069 3

A CIP catalogue record for this book
is available from the British Library

The publisher acknowledges
subsidy from the Scottish Arts Council towards
the publication of this volume.

 Scottish
Arts Council

Design by Tilley&Tilley

Typeset by RefineCatch Limited, Bungay, Suffolk

Printed and bound by
Creative Print and Design Group Ltd

ACKNOWLEDGEMENTS

Thanks to

May Biggam for everything.

Rachael Tonge for all her support over the years and
helping me (finally) make time to write.

Edmund Dalziel who helped with research
when time was running out and who didn't mind when
I decided to only use a little.

Graham Watson, Jane Feore, and Brian Kidd
for their encouragement and enthusiasm.

Everyone at Black & White
for their passion over this new fiction imprint
(special thanks to Patricia
for her detailed reading).

Finally enormous gratitude to Gillian
whose faith, encouragement and dedication
made the whole process a pleasure.
She made it happen.

FOR RACHAEL

PART ONE

DEVELOPING

It is still.
The ball hangs in the air.
Yellow and red against a blue, blue sky.
Peter is jumping for the ball.
Sand trails through the air from the beach to his bare feet.
He is tanned. He is muscled.
He wears sunglasses held on with an elastic strap.
He takes every opportunity to show his body off to his friends.
John is sitting on a lounger.
He squints in the sun. He is wearing a baggy T-shirt.
His face sunburn red.
He hides his white flabby flesh from his friends.
He must hate Peter's muscle-hugging bronze skin. He must.
Wendy is running towards Peter.
She wants the ball. She is always competing with him.
Matching pink bikini. She is as sun kissed as Peter.
She has a perfect body.
Tight. Trim. Athletic.
Perfect breasts.
She is no prude – she goes topless when she can.
Brian is kneeling beside Abby.
He is rubbing cream on to her back.
A fold in the towel hides her face.
Brian loves Abby. She thinks of him as a friend.
They have slept together.
Stephen is playing with the ball too.
He is tanned, he is fit, he is just like Peter.
He wears tight trunks, when the others all wear baggy shorts.
He likes leaving nothing to the imagination.
This is what she sees.
This is a frozen moment.

EXPOSURE

Every few moments I glance at the minute hand of the clock above the tills and the second hand of my watch. I can hardly believe it but I have managed to endure a morning of torturous waiting.

I can't stop thinking about seeing Sarah. Kissing and touching. Making up for these long days and nights apart. I am counting the seconds until she is here. I have to see her. I need to see her. I feel like a schoolboy on the promise of his first kiss just after the four o'clock bell.

12.05 and 16 seconds
I have artfully distracted myself for a couple of hours making small talk with colleagues and customers, poring over prints and planning my afternoon. I've worked hard to keep my excitement in check and it has almost worked. But I'm still feeling that buzz you get before something exciting happens.

12.06 and 2 seconds
I work on what is usually called the pharmacy floor. You know the kind of thing – ointments and lotions, condoms and hair products. But the section that I really work in is the photographic one. That sounds quite fancy. Me sharing my huge knowledge of cameras and photography with eager customers. But the reality is that I just develop your snappy snaps.

What would you like – one-hour service or overnight service?
Sorry, it has to be dropped off before four.
What size of prints would you like?
I can make your print into a jigsaw or tablemats or coasters – or put it on to a mug, if you like.
I am so versatile.

12.07 and 14 seconds
She takes lunch at around noon every day. If she's punctual, she'll leave her office at two minutes past twelve. I can make it up to her office in a few minutes if I jog so I'm estimating it'll take her about ten minutes. Sometimes, she'll stop upstairs to buy a sandwich but, today, I'm pretty sure she'll come straight down to see me first. She'll have lots of goodies for me.

Plastic curtain.
Water in rivulets on the surface.
Smooth skin.
She is bending over.
The curve of her breast.
Half turned away.
She is trying to cover herself.
She is not quick enough.
Water hangs in the air.
One arm trying to cover her breasts.
Tattoo of a bird near the small of her back.
One leg lifting and bending slightly to hide between her legs.
Breast.
Nipple.

Buttock.
Back.
Legs.
Face.
Water.
Look of shock and surprise.
You can almost hear her shout of annoyance.
Naked.
This is a frozen moment.

12.08 and 10 seconds
Four or five minutes until I see her. Two weeks away from me. It has felt much longer.

We'll have a quick catch up over lunch, have a laugh, hopefully a smooch, then dream our afternoons away thinking about what we'll get up to tonight.

It has only been a few months but I'm completely smitten.

12.09 and 17 seconds
I'm still at the developing machine and I really need to be front and centre at the tills so she'll find me easily. I stop what I'm doing and head over to Anne. She's with a customer and I wait until she finishes. I just hate the kind of customer service you get in most places – being made to feel that you are in the wrong for daring to interrupt a staff conversation about what is happening at the weekend or who is sleeping with whom.

I tell Anne, *I've finished all the pending print jobs so I can take over your till for a while. Euan will be back from his break in a couple of minutes if we get busy.* She is relieved at my offer – typical manager preferring to wander about looking important rather than slum it at a till point. She leaves quickly, nice comfy office to go to, far away from customers.

Stand and wait.

12.10 and 45 seconds
I'm willing her to come now. I stare at every customer as they glide into the basement, escalator smooth. My eyes burn through each one into the person behind. Not her. Not her. Not her. Too early anyway. Can't stop myself. I yearn to see her. I ache to touch her. Not her. Not her. Not her. Just a sea of unfamiliar faces – not her green eyes, not her strawberry-blonde hair, not her freckles, not her dimples. Oh, hurry up.

12.11 and 25 seconds
There she is.

My heart is in my throat.

I'm trembling.

Control yourself.

She is early. Well, of course she is – she is just as eager to be with me as I am to be with her. We're a perfect fit.

She looks so beautiful.

I realise just how much I've been missing her when I see that face. Those lips touching mine. It becomes a movie. She's walking in slow motion – her skirt billows about her perfect legs as she nears. Cut to close-up on my face, eyes widen. Cut to her smile as she sees me. Roeg cut to skin pressed against skin. Cut to my returned smile. Cut to her flicking her hair. Roeg cut to tongue on skin. She reaches the counter. She leans over it and pulls me towards her, lips meet. Roeg cut to shuddering climax. She pulls back. *I've missed you.* Then the crowds fade to black, just Tony and Maria seeing each other across the dance floor. We're all that's important.

Fuck. A problem.

Customer heading towards me. If I serve this person, then I might get caught up. Sarah might get bored and not want to wait. Can't afford to miss her. I make pretence of dropping my pen and disappear behind the counter. I wait for a couple of moments, taking calming breaths, willing things to go my way for once. Please. Please. Go away. Let me be free for Sarah.

Can't stay down any longer. I steel myself for disappointment and straighten. Thank you. The customer, faced with an empty space, has turned and headed towards another till. It is going to work out. Beauty still coming towards me.

She hasn't caught my eye yet and I'm living for that look, for the spark to jump between us, for the sweetest smile ever known.

Lunch, coffee shop, maybe just a walk. She'll tell me about her holiday, all the fun she had. *Have you missed me?* She looks as if I have asked an outrageous question. *Of course I missed you, silly. I love being with you. I can't imagine my life without you. I love you deeply.* The jealousy I feel towards the friends she went with melts under those words. We'll meet again after work. We'll go for a drink. We'll see a movie. We'll go for a meal. No, we'll go directly to her flat, make up for all those lonely nights. I take her hand, inhale her fragrance, her voice trickles into my ear. She holds me close, her warmth against my chest, breath on my neck, lips close. Smooth skin, green-green eyes, hair bleached by the sun. She kisses me. Soft. Warm. She looks into my eyes. I pull her shirt from her shoulder.

She is almost at the till.

I half turn away so that she'll think she's surprised me – a silly joke but she'll love it. She loves my sense of humour, the little games couples play. I close my eyes and wait for the words I long to hear.

Excuse me?

I turn as if I didn't think anyone was there. Her smile shines, tiny wrinkles at the sides of her eyes. You only see them with a genuine smile.

Yes, can I help you? We tease each other.

I'd like to put these in for a one-hour service. Words I've been dreaming about for days, this moment rehearsed over and over. I knew she wouldn't be able to wait until tomorrow to get the photographs back.

Of course.

I hold out my hands and she places seven rolls of film in them. Her fingertips brush against my palm. The touch goes straight to my heart.

Is there any chance you could do them quickly? I need to be back at work in less than an hour.

She should know I would do anything for her.

That'll be no problem.

Interaction between us. I love this. I'll make use of this opportunity to start a conversation.

Have you been on holiday? I ask innocently.

She gives me a 'How did you know that?' look. Tanned face and shoulders, health and vigour pouring from her. But that tan – oh, that tan. Not the orange hue of the girls at the cosmetics counters but a real tan on skin that takes it well. No sign of bikini strap lines at her shoulders. Topless bathing. Thong swimming costume. She likes to be golden all over. I could faint.

She just reeks of sunshine and sea.

Oh, I just guessed, I shrug at her.

She smiles back realising that her body gives it away. *I've been to Lanzarote with some friends.*

I put her films on the counter. Seven rolls. She must have had a great time. Wanted to record every minute of it. So many glorious photos in front of me, burned on to negative. Two hundred and fifty-two photographs of her and her friends. Eight-by-five prints. Ten thousand and eighty square inches of images.

So much to look at, so much to explore. Details and clues.

That is a lot of photographs, I say.

She nods and smiles in a 'You know me!' sort of a way and my heart flutters. I love that she is so familiar with me. I love that she recognises me from before.

I start to write on the pad of envelopes that we put the undeveloped rolls in. *One-hour service.* I check my watch and say, *I'll try and make sure they are done by ten to.*

She smiles at me. I'm lost in that face.

I start to fill in her details automatically. Name: *Sarah Bennett*. Address: leave it blank as normal.

Wave of nausea hits my stomach, grips it tightly – I can feel the panic rising in me. What the hell am I doing? How can I be so stupid? She has noticed what I am writing and she is looking confused.

I stumble and mumble through some words that sound like I've got a good memory for names.

I suppose I'm a bit of a regular, she says.

Stupid. Stupid. What an idiot mistake to make. She is still looking at me. I'm going red. She's going to suspect. She'll find out about me and make a complaint. She's going to guess. I know it.

I mumble some more, *You don't need to wait for this – I'll fill in the rest*. I tear off the receipt section from each one then had them over. She turns away.

Stupid. Stupid. Should keep my stupid mouth shut. Need to think before I do or say anything. I'd rehearsed this moment so much, had been waiting to see her for so long, that I lost focus on the details, got caught up in the moment. There is no excuse for such a sloppy mistake.

I'm annoyed with myself. Stupidity has cut short my time with her. Just think what we would have said to each other. She might have flirted with me. I could have asked her out for a coffee. We could have become friends – maybe more. Any prospect of that happening today is heading with her to the escalators. But even the sight of her retreating makes me feel good. I'll be content for another day.

She stops to look at some perfumed soaps. She lifts them up and inhales scents – rose and cinnamon, apricot and lime. Then she is gone.

Sunset.
Red sky.
Clouds look ablaze.
Silhouette figures.
Brian.
Is that Brian?
Arm round Abby.
Her head on his shoulder.
Looking into the twilight.
The sea stretching to the horizon.
Waves frozen as they roll ashore.
Bare feet on sand.
Warm breeze in the night.
Do they speak?

Whisper their thoughts to each other?
Make promises they'll hold?
Nights for love.
Nights for passion.
Setting sun reflected like a path in the water.
Romance.
Love rekindled?
I see everything she sees.
This is a frozen moment.

EXTRA SET

No time for wallowing now. Put aside those feelings of self-doubt at the failures of the day. The shop is getting busier with the lunchtime rush and I'm going to be stuck at the tills. That means I won't be able to develop the prints myself but I had never planned to. I don't want to taint the pleasure by looking at them as they come out of the machine. That rapture is for later.

I'll have to indulge in some clever subterfuge.

You see I have to make sure that I get a copy of all her prints. Every last one of them.

I mark each of the envelopes for a double set and quickly take them through to Euan in the developing area. I ask him if he'll go extra quick. *I promised a pretty girl.* He laughs and shakes his head with mock exasperation. Playing my part in this sort of patter will ensure he does them straight away. Command of the 'lads' code' wins through for me again.

I go back to the tills where a queue is building and mull over the logistical headache that the extra copies has caused. I need to get back to the prints once Euan has developed them and before they are collected. That doesn't give me much time.

Making the extra set is easy – just push the appropriate button on the machine and watch them chug on out. The problem lies in the fact that the machine makes the extra print as it processes each negative so you get the original print and the copy on top of each other. So I'll have to manually separate each set and place her copies in an envelope that I've doctored to indicate that she just wanted one set in the first place. Then I have to secrete the two hundred and fifty copies that I've make for myself without being seen.

Complicated.

This is a risky undertaking. But I have mastered ways of getting round any issues.

I have great skill in feigning an air of confidence that means I'm rarely challenged if I'm seen doing this stuff. Having made an extra copy is not a problem in itself – I can simply say I made a mistake and the matter won't be taken further. The disaster with that scenario though is that the extra set would be binned. That cannot happen.

If I'm asked what I'm doing while separating the prints, I'll say, *I promised a customer I'd do it for them*. If it is a male colleague that challenges me, I'll play the lads' card again and say that it is for a gorgeous girl. With female colleagues, I'll play the 'I'm just being a nice guy' role and they'll give a sigh that says that they wish their boyfriends were like me.

I'm well rehearsed.

I've been dreaming about these photographs for ages. I've made sure my evening is free to experience each and every detail. There is absolutely no way I'll let them go.

I have to have my own set.

I've been gathering copies of her snaps for ages.

I'm not going to stop now.

Harbour.
Low stone wall.
Boats and sails.
Sarah sits in the centre.
John and Wendy on one side.
Stranger and Peter on the other.
John and Wendy have wide smiles.
Heads together, pulling faces.
Peter is looking off to the right.
A girl has caught his eye.
The stranger is a man.
His shoulder touching Sarah.
His leg touching Sarah.
Her hand on her leg near his.
Will it reach out?
Will it take his hand?
Will they kiss?
But this is a frozen moment.

ART OF COPYING

I think of myself as a collector. Yes, that's it. You might collect stamps or little ceramic frogs or first editions or whatever. I collect these little parts of people. Snapshots of other lives. They don't have to be works of art. In fact, mostly they are not very good in photographic terms but they need to have something that draws me to them – something that speaks to me.

There is a whole world full of pictures out there and I am lucky enough to have a few of them pass through my hands so of course I'm going to make my own copies.

Getting my copies of photographs is an art all of its own. Yes, like I said, it is simple enough pushing the button and making another set or a single photograph but that is only part of the story.

The developing machine records how many prints are made and this is routinely checked against sales that use the till code for developing. Way of checking no one is giving away freebies or dipping into the till.

How do I get round this?

Like any till system, it is only as reliable as the people ringing in the sales. You see the till that we sell the photographs through is not used exclusively for the photographs. A customer can bring any product to us. This helps as the first method of avoiding detection.

There is often only one of us in the developing area at a time and it is fairly simple to put through an extra set of prints or print single photographs. The trick is to make sure that these extras do not create a discrepancy with the end-of-day reports for each department. The way to make sure that this does not happen is simply to have the till balance.

This means that I pay for most of the copies I make. I am no thief. Well, actually, very occasionally, other customers pay for some of my extra prints but only if it would be too risky to be seen putting money into the tills. I'll short change a customer here and there and use their money to balance the tills. Risky though. Some customers stand and check their change right in front of you so it's only to be used as a last resort.

Sometimes I'll just swap the photographs that I want with spares. I carry a few prints about with me for this purpose. I take some snaps with a crappy camera and hold my hand over the lens or point it at a bulb to overexpose the print. These hazy, indistinct snaps can then be popped into an envelope along with the rest of the real prints. I happily slap on one of our helpful stickers on to tell you that you don't know how to use your camera and keep the real print. Most people wouldn't even think to look at their negatives when they find the fake photograph. They know they are not really all that good at taking snaps so they don't doubt the mistake is actually their own or, more likely, they'll blame a loved one or friend for ruining what was guaranteed to be the perfect shot.

Those rare people that do look at their negatives can be easily placated with, *The machine couldn't have read the negative properly – I'll do you another copy for free.*

Occasionally, I'll be forced to take a strip of negatives from a set if I can't copy them at the shop. I'll sneak them back home and use my own darkroom. I usually return them the following day and 'find' them under the machine. Some sloppy Saturday staff not taking care will get the blame. We keep these lost negatives for a few weeks just in case they belong to one of the mad customers that want to have their terrible snaps turned into coasters and towels for a friend's Christmas.

I hate when we destroy unclaimed negatives. It feels like killing a bit of someone's life.

Technology has changed things in the last couple of years, and, from my point of view, it's not a change for the good. Digital cameras mean that there are thousands and thousands of interesting images that don't come close to a developing booth like ours. Just USB your camera to a computer and download it into iPhoto.

There must be millions of photos trapped in memory cards. Never being printed. Just waiting to be purged to make space for another set that will suffer the same fate.

This is sacrilege. Photos should be seen. They need to be fixed to paper to give them meaning. They need to be tangible. Not just a stream of pixels.

I am not surprised by the boom in digital photography. Cameras, phones, MP3 players – they make it so easy to take images.

We need our snaps.

We all have our precious photo albums. Marking our passage through life. Proving that we are really alive.

Some cultures believe that photos trap part of your soul. Superstition but with a kind of truth. We each leave something in our photographs.

It is interesting to note that new photo technology is instantly seen as wonderful for those that like to take the odd saucy snap.

Polaroids meant that you could take a fuzzy shot of your girlie on all fours on your candlewick bedspread without the fear of the chemist calling the police because you didn't need to put them in to be developed. Digital cameras now mean that you can take a sharp photo of your girlie on all fours on the duvet, without the fear of someone like me calling the police because you don't need to put them in to be developed.

It is quite amazing but we do get the odd customer that tries to innocently slip the odd saucy shot through. They probably think that, because we use machines now, we don't inspect the contents of the prints as they roll out. Leads to a dilemma. Let them pass or refuse to develop them. I tend to let them pass. People need their fun.

The real trick to avoid detection is to make sure that you don't take too much. Difficult when you get a good run of photographs. I've had to let some goodies pass because I thought it would arouse suspicion if I took them.

I am blessed in another way. Saturday staff. They are all nice kids – perhaps some not exactly bright. They are just trying to earn some money while they are at school, trying to do their best, oblivious that they are cursed. Yes, the secret that all those Saturday boys and girls don't know is that permanent staff blame anything that goes wrong on them. If there are problems with prints – Saturday staff. If the tills don't balance – Saturday staff. If some important shelf stacking is unfinished – Saturday staff. Those poor mites don't realise it but they get their colleagues off the hook all the time.

The girls are lying on the floor.
They are laughing.
You can see Abby's pierced navel.
Silver hoop disappearing inside her.
Wendy has a sun tattoo round her belly button.
Black circle of flames.
Sarah is laughing hard.
Her head is thrown back.
Louise is still wearing her bikini.
Fresh from the beach.
Ankle bracelet.
Bottles around them.
Having fun.
No sign of the boys.
This is a frozen moment.

COLLECTION

There is a bit of a lull at the till and I go to the developing area for a few minutes. Euan has put the prints and copies in the tray ready to be collected. He's busy at the machine.

I open the first set out and begin to separate them into two piles. One for me, one for her; one for me, one for her. Keep the prints face down so that I don't spoil the joy of looking at them later.

When I finish, I return her copies to the pouch and stash mine in another. I have to do this with each of the seven sets.

I try hard not to look around to see if I'm being watched. Surreptitious glances are a red flag that you are up to no good. Try to look as if I'm doing nothing out of the ordinary, pre-prepared reasons ready to leap out if anyone wanders over.

It is almost time for Sarah to pick up the prints. She'll be prompt so I have only got a couple of minutes to finish.

There – done.

Each of her sets neatly back in their pouches. Now put them in the doctored envelopes that show just one copy was asked for. I've had to score out the tick for 'duplicate set' which isn't ideal but the envelope number still needs to match the tear-offs she has. It won't matter at all as long as Euan doesn't end up serving her. Now that would be a bit of a disaster.

I drop the envelopes back into the collecting tray and stick my copies in a bag with my name on it and hide them at the back of a cupboard. So many steps – each must be perfect or the game is up. No going back once you have started. Once the bullet leaves it is never coming back.

She arrives.

It is like slow motion again. Watching too many movies. I make sure I am nowhere near the tills. I long to speak to her again but my earlier mistakes are still raw and I know I would just mumble and mutter and make things worse.

I watch as she pays for them. I watch as she turns to leave. I have the urge to follow her upstairs. I just know that she'll be too excited to wait until she gets back to her office. She'll stop just outside the shop and be compelled to look through them all. Just once, just quickly.

I want to be with her when she does that – see her delight as she relives each moment.

Thinking about it makes me want to go to the cupboard and rip open my envelopes – to hell with being seen, to hell with the consequences.

But I don't. Of course I don't. Save them for tonight. Everything is planned for tonight.

Intense glare from the sun.
Her hand shading her eyes.
Barren landscape.
Beautiful desolation.
Volcanic.
Like the surface of Mars.
She is wearing a T-shirt and shorts.
Top tight against her chest.
Walking boots.
Legs and arms bronze.
Hairs bleaching towards gold.
Stranger with her.
The man from the harbour.

Dark hair.
Broad shoulders.
Handsome.
He could be with her by chance.
This is a frozen moment.

I get to go for lunch at half one. I take the bag with my copies out of the cupboard and go up to the staffroom. No one is interested in what I might have so I've no problems taking them to my locker and putting them into my bag. I've made some alterations to my bag for the sneaky smuggling of snaps – a concealed pocket.

The shop operates a policy of bag searches for all staff. Most managers have the sense to be embarrassed about the whole thing – they'll only have a cursory peep into every bag. But some see it as their solemn duty to protect the company from thieving colleagues. Nothing quite like trust.

I suppose a lot of shop theft is actually down to staff but bag searches are a joke – if you really want to steal something and not be discovered, you'd stick it down your pants.

Staffroom chat today is all about Marion's latest love failure. Her romances are the staple subject of conversation with the girls from cosmetics and body care. They are going to take Marion on a special girlie night out to cheer her up. Some of the lads are protesting that the plan is a bit exclusive and are suggesting a mixed night out.

I eat my sandwiches as the debate rages, face buried in a magazine as I daydream about the photographs in my bag. I'm trying not to anticipate the details too much. I don't want to imagine something that is not there. I'll be disappointed.

I hear my name being called. It has been decided that tonight will be a group night out – lots of jokes being voiced about Marion getting back on the horse again. Now I'm being asked if I would like to come.

I do try to go to a few work nights out – not because I am particularly interested in my colleagues but to keep up appearances. I don't want them to see anything more than a work acquaintance when they look at me, don't want to give them any reason to think I'm out of the ordinary.

Sorry. I'm busy tonight.

There is no way that I am going to give up my night for something this trivial.

You're no fun. You've not come out in ages.

I'll be at Pat's leaving do but I just can't get out of this tonight.

The conversation shifts away from me. They seem satisfied or maybe they were just asking me because I happened to be in the staffroom. Would they have made the effort to find me on the shop floor?

VIEW FROM THE WINDOW AT LE GRAS

In 1760, Charles François Tiphaigne de la Roche published what we would call a science-fiction novel. In one passage, he described a canvas coated with a special sticky substance. This canvas would capture, like a mirror, any scene you pointed it at. If you left it for a little while, the image would adhere to the sticky canvas and eventually dry. You would be left with a perfect picture. It is considered to be the first description of the process of photography.

Sixty-six years later Joseph Nicéphore Niépce, using a pewter plate coated with bitumen of Judea, took an image known as *View from the Window at Le Gras*. He used a camera obscura and exposed the plate for eight hours. He didn't call it a photograph but a heliograph – a sun drawing. It is in a collection at the University of Texas after being found by chance in London in the 1950s. It is considered to be the first fixed image.

Grainy. Buildings and sky. Cave painting for the mechanical world.

Take a moment to think about it – the first time that a real part of the world has been captured and preserved. Not a drawing, not a painting, not a description – a perfect permanent record. A real space-time event frozen forever.

It changed the world.

LIGHT WRITING

On a good day, I'll see a couple of hundred snaps. In a week it could be a thousand.

Just a couple of years ago, it would be hundreds a day and thousands a week. Those days are becoming a memory. Soon self-service digital photo booths will make this part of my job redundant. The digital revolution means you can do it all yourself – lets you happily snap without the chance of them being seen by me.

There are the film die-hards, though – people like Sarah that still hold on to the old ways. They are a dying breed. I have to cherish them while I still can.

For the moment, it is still photographs day in, day out. The nature of the job means that we have to take a quick look at each print to make sure it is in good condition. We also cast a critical eye over the content of the snaps too and sticker them if necessary. If your snap is too dark or over exposed, we slap on a sticker. Out of focus or too much 'red eye', slap on a sticker. Not on every photograph but on enough to let you know you've done something wrong.

It does seem a bit harsh because you believe that you're a reasonable photographer and then we shatter your delusions by slapping on a sticker that politely tells you that you are actually crap.

It is for our protection too. The number of customers that have come back to complain about the poor quality of their prints: *You've developed these too dark.* Did you actually use your flash? *I can't see my mother's face in this one.* The sun is directly behind her head. *The picture is all blurry.* Try focusing the camera.

You see, most of the problems that happen with photographs occur at the time the shutter snaps open – when you are in control. The results are your own fault. Light, film speed, aperture, exposure – you ignore them all.

But there is one simple problem that dwarfs the others.

I don't want to patronise but there is a simple and effective rule you should follow when you're using your snappy little shooter. Before you push the little button to commit a celluloid crime, before you jinx each of your negatives, keep your finger away from the lens!

Simple.

Rarely done.

I've seen whole rolls of holiday snaps ruined by that wandering finger.

Your lovely holiday in Rome. You take your snappy camera and plenty of film. You even ask what is the best film speed you should take. You want to ensure you get perfect shots.

There you are soaking up the rays, the atmosphere, the culture. You feel the urge to commit this moment forever to film memory. You pass that brightly coloured snapper to your girlfriend/boyfriend. *Take a picture of me, dear.*

Snap
The Coliseum.

Snap
Tiny Roman backstreets.

Snap
Your partner at the Vatican.

Snap
Both of you posing by a gladiator.

You spend your entire holiday taking photos. You are so excited to see them when you get home that you rush to the one-hour photo lab the first chance you get.

Think of the fun stories you'll have for your friends as you proudly pass your snaps around and how, in years to come, you'll dust off those old albums and relive your youth.

When you collect them, you can't resist taking a quick little peek.

What is that?

Those guys at the photo place must have been mucking around when they developed that one. Try the next one. *Just the same. There must be something wrong with the machine that they use, a piece of fluff in it or a smudge on the lens.* But the next photo is fine. Next obscured, next obscured, next . . . *What the hell is that thing? It's a finger, a finger over the lens. Bloody hell, I'll kill him/her.* But, hold on, your partner is in that shot, face half obscured by a blurred pink lump.

All of these beautiful memories ruined by a bloody great finger. You could argue, in a moment of philosophical insight, that it is profound in a way – the hand of man makes a mark on the world.

Yes, that's kind of nice.

But really it's 'cos you're crap at point and snap.

Flames.
Light stretching out as far as it can.
Until it is defeated by the night.
Beach bonfire.
Shine of tinfoil.
Half-eaten baked potatoes.
Stephen has his arm round Louise.
Keeping her warm.
Toes near the fire.
They are sitting on a rug.
Peter sits on a crate washed up on the shore.
Empty bottles in the sand.
Brian pokes the fire with a stick.
The others must be walking in the dark.
At the water's edge.
Fire in the distance.
This is a frozen moment.

THE AGE OF MECHANICAL REPRODUCTION

The snaps I develop for the rest of the day just don't interest me. I suppose that, on any other day, I would find the odd one that I wanted but I am dulled by the possibilities contained within these glossies. I'd normally randomly copy some, just in case, but I can't be bothered.

I am often horrified by the lack of ability most people seem to have when it comes to taking a photograph. It can't be made any easier for you these days with fully automatic cameras. You don't actually need to be able to do much. I am not asking for award-wining shots – just the odd one that is framed nicely or shows a hint of skill. Just use a little of your imagination.

I expect too much. A really good photographer would most likely have a darkroom of their own. No Cartier-Bressons or Man Rays would slum it with a developing booth so I am left with party snaps and holiday snaps and bad wedding snaps. And all the pointless shots people take when they're rushing to finish the film. With some of the crap that I see, you would think that every photograph taken is just to get to the end of the roll.

There are actually lots of interesting things that you can do once you have a good camera. If you master some of the basics, it'll help you on your way. You could even end up with an interesting shot.

Aperture – it sounds like a scary word but it's just the thing you use to control the amount of light that gets into your camera. Why is this important? Well, it is the light falling on your film that makes the photo. Simple.

In your camera, there are some metal blades that come together and alter the size of the hole that lets the light in. Are you following? You're not too clear about this, are you? How to explain? Got it. You remember in the movie *Alien* when Dallas is hunting the creature in the ventilation system? As he passes a junction, it closes behind him? Well, the way that the junction closes is exactly the same way the aperture works. Little bits of overlapping metal that make the hole in the middle bigger or smaller.

Now, the more difficult bit. The aperture is denoted by numbers such as 1.8 or 5.6 or 16 etc. If you are writing them down, put the letter f in front so that it is f1.8. The higher the number, the smaller the hole is and the less light gets in. The lower the f-number is, the bigger the hole. Memorise this. I know that seems back to front but trust me.

The aperture controls light getting on to the film but it also lets you control how much of what you are looking at is in sharp focus. It is called depth of field. Stay with me – it will be over in a moment. I won't tell you too much about it just now but, if you have a large f-number, a small hole, then you have a greater depth of field. That means the more you'll have in focus. Simple.

There – that wasn't so bad.

PENCIL OF NATURE

August 1835. Lacock Abbey, Wiltshire. South Gallery. William Henry Fox Talbot using a camera obscura takes an image of the Oriel Window. It becomes the earliest paper negative that survives. It is a cruder process than the daguerreotype but is refined over the following years. By 1840, the calotype process has reduced exposure times to a few minutes. Talbot's eager patenting and control of his processing techniques help hold back photographic advances in Britain.

DAGUERREOTYPE

The bus journey home is the best sort. I'm too preoccupied with the evening of pleasure ahead of me to pay much attention to my travelling companions or the rattling ride. If journeys are bad in the morning, they are usually much worse at night. Grumpy faces have changed to weary, hollow, grey ones. People too tired to enjoy the fact that they have escaped tedium for another day.

The tap-tap of text messages being written usually builds a slow-burn anger but I'm trying to let nothing get to me. Forget all this. Focus on tonight.

The heavy rain all afternoon means steamed up windows and gently steaming people. Wet clothes on warm bodies have a special odour all of their own and, in the confinement of a bus, you can get a taste of days gone by, before soap and personal hygiene became popular.

Woman sitting beside me squirms in her seat. Elbow digs into me. Smell like damp straw in my nostrils.

The reality of the journey is beginning to creep in past my defences. The constant pressure of anticipation is beginning to wane. It is no surprise – I've been thinking about the photographs all afternoon. I can feel their weight in my rucksack.

Not too much longer. But the bus and the people and the journey surround me. It is hard to stay focused. The collective weariness and grief over wasted lives seep through my pores and begin to saturate me. I'm slowly becoming just like my travelling companions. Tainted with their hopelessness. Overflowing with despair.

Need to break out of these thoughts. Take control. I know what to do.

I put my hand into my pocket and ease my wallet open. Behind the credit cards and loyalty cards is a laminated photograph. I don't bring it out – I don't want anyone else to see it. I run my fingers along the edges, picture every detail. Every curve. Every texture. It calms me. It focuses me. I think of poor Hélène. She stands in the rain.

Hélène stands sheltering from the rain. Wet nights usually mean less trade so more reason to be out making sure she finds at least one person willing to buy her time. She needs to eat. She needs to pay her rent. Just a few minutes more.

She has got her eye on a possible customer. He has been standing in an alley across the street for fifteen minutes. He has made as if to cross over to her twice now but, each time, he has stopped himself, drawn back into the shadows to stare.

Hélène is used to these hesitations. Just another husband feeling guilty that he needs to look elsewhere for the services that his wife should provide. She knows that he will feel bad for doing this but that guilt is not enough to stop him eventually crossing over to her – it is not enough to stop him coming back next week for more. She knows that men like him visit the same woman again and again, building a relationship, giving their infidelities meaning.

She wishes he would hurry up and decide. She is cold and she is wet and she has eaten nothing since noon. She wishes more than anything that she could just go home. Curl under a blanket and sleep. Free herself, just for a few hours, from her life. But she knows that would be weakness. She knows that it would be self-indulgent. She knows she will stay here and wait for this man to get his courage. She knows she will take his money, lift her skirt. If not him, there will be another along soon enough.

He is still deciding what to do.

Poor man, must be his first time.

Hélène wonders what he will ask for. If it is his first time with a woman like her, then he will be nervous and it will be just the usual way – up an alley or back to her room with him on top. It will be quick too. Perhaps he will be generous and she will be able to wash herself out when he leaves and not need to go back into the night.

She knows that, if he comes back, he will get bolder. When they become comfortable with you is the time you have to be wary. Then they want something that no respectable wife would want to give. Many nights sore and bruised taught her that truth.

This one looks nice though. She saw his face momentarily as another attempt to cross over brought him into the light. A pretty, fresh face. His expression a mix of passion and embarrassment He must be around twenty-five years. Shame that such a pretty man has to come here for what he needs. He should have the pick of the ladies. Or maybe he is a virgin. That might be nice on such a miserable night. It could be fun teaching him the joys and the hidden pleasures. Those ones are always keen to show their gratitude with extra coins. Happy to be made men.

Now he has gathered his resolve. He is crossing the road. He walks directly to her. He tells her he has been watching her. Her tells her that she is beautiful, just what he has been looking for. Hélène smiles at him and touches his arm. She has heard these words so many times before.

She asks what he would like.

He tells her he is called Henri. She smiles at him again.

She asks Henri what he would like, knowing that he will not have given his real name. He tells her he wants her to sit for him. He tells her that he will pay her. She thinks that maybe he is a man that just likes to watch. He tells her he wants to take her image. As he speaks, she sees his eyes are filled with fire and passion. He tells her that the images he makes will keep her young forever.

The person beside me squirms in her seat again and I'm back in the bus.

I take my hand from my pocket and try to peer through the foggy windows. One more stop.

THE RITUAL OF LOOKING

I go into the foyer of the tower block. Customary gossips are there – different ones from this morning. Blank-faced group wait by the lift, like me just home from work. The lift is slowly climbing up the building and I can't be bothered waiting. I don't want to be crammed in that little box with them, bodies forced against me.

I take the stairs.

Long way up to my floor but my eagerness eats up the steps.

I reach my front door. I feel the sweat prickling on my back. New record for getting upstairs. I automatically pause for a moment as I take out my key and listen for noises coming from next door.

He is shouting at her as usual – it could be about anything but tonight it is about her new boyfriend and that she's out to all hours *like a whore.* He likes to call her a whore. *A whore like your mother.* She is feebly trying to retaliate but her father has twenty years of bitterness on his side. In a moment, she'll give up trying and slam her bedroom door, cry into her pillow. She needs to leave him.

I have been neglecting them a bit lately, I know. I promise myself that, over the coming days, I'll take some time and dedicate it to them.

I don't rush through the door and rip the photos from my bag and thumb my way through the shots like you'd expect. Where would the fun be in that?

Need to take your time with a thing like this. The anticipation is a huge part of the joy. I'm not one for delaying pleasure unnaturally but everything has its own pace and I've got the timing of this one perfectly. Got the ritual honed to perfection.

I unpack my rucksack and put the envelopes with the prints on the lounge table then strip off my work clothes and have a shower. Keep it quick and functional. Dress in baggy bottoms and sweatshirt.

Dinner. Pasta and red pesto. Seems to be my meal of choice at the moment – quick and easy. Make sure it is al dente – nothing worse than soggy pasta. I decide not to have a glass of wine with my food – need to keep my mind clear.

I don't rush dinner.

Everything has to be just right.

I wash the dirty dishes once I finish and flick on the kettle.

I gather everything I'll need for the sessions as it boils.

Pad and pen to note details and clues – two hundred odd photographs will give me a wealth of information to sift through over the next few days but it is important to record these first impressions.

Magnifying glass for the detail.

White cotton gloves so that I don't smudge the prints.

Little bit of advice, while I wait for my tea, on taking care of your prints – even the happy snappy crappy ones. You know that you'll be excited when you get your photos. You'll be eager to show them off to your friends. You'll take them down the pub with you and pass them around. Creases, greasy fingerprints, spilled beer. Not so good. You'll have a look at them again in a few months and have to rip them apart, all sticky and smudged. So why not get a pocket photo album?

Everything is ready on my table. I get my cup of tea. I can be trusted with fluids around photos.

The ritual of looking at new photographs. Everything has to be perfect – can't sully the experience with haste.

I sit on the floor with my back leaning against the couch, legs under the glass coffee table, toes wriggling with the thrill.

I take my gloves and pull them on.

Somewhere in the city, Sarah is doing something similar, sharing these images with her friends.

I wish I was there.

With a reverence almost bordering on the religious, I take the first envelope and lift the flap. I arrange the photographs so that the blank side faces up.

A random factor exists in what I'm doing. I have no way to tell, without looking, where this particular set comes in the holiday. It could be the first set of photos she took or the last set. It could start with a roll that she hadn't quite finished yet and so the first images I look at might have nothing to do with the holiday. Once I have inspected every set, I'll have all the information I need to place each snap chronologically. For the moment it is pot luck. Not as satisfying as watching the story unfold as it happened. Nothing I can do about that unless I peek.

I take that first sweet stack of snaps and lay them on the table. Pause for a moment, my hands hovering over the first print. Enjoy the tremor in my fingers, the slight dizziness from my racing heart.

Not just the first photo I'll see of her holiday but the first new photograph I've had from her in a few weeks. I've been in a state of excitement ever since I realised that she was going on holiday again. She, of course, didn't mention her trip as part of some sweet pillow talk – I had to work it out for myself. A few weeks ago she bought some suntan lotion and new sunglasses from the shop. Circumstantial you say. But, the next day, Abby met her at work and they went shopping for new swimwear and sandals. I knew then that I must see her modelling her new cossie on an 8 x 5.

It just took a few calls to her work over the following couple of weeks to be told that she was on holiday and wouldn't be back in the office until today.

It is so easy to find that sort of information if you apply yourself. Every life can become an open book with a little bit of effort and inspiration.

Now.

No more distractions. No more stray thoughts. The culmination of weeks of fantasising under my fingers.

Time to take my pleasure.

I turn the first photo over.

Envelope one, photograph one

Most of the group are in this one – Peter, John, Brian, Abby, Stephen and Wendy (no Louise). Sarah takes the shot. This is what she sees. Typical beach scene. Blue sky. Golden sand. Multicoloured beach ball hangs in the air. Peter lunges for it leaving a trail of sand from his toes. Peter loves to work out. He takes his body very seriously. Sculptured. Perfect. Definition in every muscle. And why go to all that trouble and time if you don't show it off at every opportunity? I've got a file full of photos of him in T-shirts that are really too small – all pecs and abs. Got snaps of him at parties, just the right number of buttons undone. I think his showing off is more for the boys so they can feel a pang of jealousy every time his perfect body ripples. *This is what a real man should look like* is his taunt. Wendy reaches for the ball too. Female version of Peter. The same regime of workouts, moisturising and year-round tan. She's wearing a two-piece swimsuit more suited to posing and sunbathing than any exertions. Just enough fabric to cover her nipples and show off as much breast as possible. High-cut bottoms show hairless skin. Athletic. Trim. Very pleasant to look at. The other girls are dressed in a similar way. Slightly fuller tops, not such high-cut crotches. Guys wear oversized shorts. Perfect cover for hiding erections from rubbing suntan lotion on fit bodies and ogling the topless sunbather. Shorts – all apart from Stephen. Oh, Stephen and his Speedos. I thought they were a fashion faux pas these days, only to be seen in their rightful place at

Olympic pools. But Stephen can't be accused of subtlety with a thing like this. Crams himself into the briefest trunks he can. Means that he needs to spend less time chatting up girls – all they have to do is look at the stretched black Lycra and they're hooked. Eye goes next to poor John, wearing one of many baggy T-shirts. He's a little too fond of beer and chips and curries to go shirtless like the other lads. Would be embarrassed to let the others see his flabby body. Out of sight out of mind, he hopes. He's glad his sense of humour keeps him popular. Abby lies on a multicoloured beach towel. Brian rubs lotion on her back. I get a surge of empathy over the tragedy of it. They were a couple for a while until she ended the relationship. Now they are friends. But he still loves her. You can see the exquisite pain in his face as he touches her and tries to keep her from seeing.

A single holiday snapshot.

So much information in a frozen moment.

Envelope two, photograph five

Beach bonfire at night. The fire throws light round in a circle and is then lost in the darkness. Stephen and Louise are sitting on a rug close to the fire. Stephen is hugging her warm. Toes in warm sand near the flames. Around them, evidence of baked potatoes for supper – tinfoil fragments and discarded skins. Peter sits nearby on a crate, looking out into the darkness. (Search any beach in any part of the world and you will find wooden and plastic crates and frayed lengths of blue rope.) Brian is standing near the fire with a stick, poking the driftwood, watching the flames jump and spark. The others are nowhere to be seen. Walking in the dunes or by the water's edge, the bonfire just a faint glow in the distance.

Envelope three, photograph eighteen

The girls are lying on the floor of their room. They are all laughing – a couple of empty wine bottles beside them. Abby's pierced belly button is visible, hoop biting into flesh. Wendy has a sun tattoo round her belly button. Louise is still in her bikini, fresh from the pool. Sarah's head is thrown back, laughing so hard you can see her fillings. Good to see her in a shot. It is nice the girls are having fun together without the boys. I suppose one of them could be there, though, taking the photograph. But I think it is on timer, propped up on a pillow. There is a faint hint of posing from Abby. I think she sneakily set the camera. This photograph is from near the start of the holiday. I think this is second night. Evidence clear to see – tans have not taken yet, eyes not bloodshot from a week of booze, the girls together, not paired off with some stud from the beach. If you strain, you can almost hear their conversation.

Envelope four, various photographs

A run of silly shots. I suppose it's inevitable if you have a group of twenty-something friends on holiday together. Mix sun, surf, booze and a handy camera and you get silly season. Did you really expect every snap to be russet sunsets, the natural beauty of the surroundings, the local architecture? What you'll get is shots of mooning, drunken poses, red-eyed hangovers. More than a roll is taken up with embarrassing shots and the inevitable revenge ones. I can just see the camera being sneaked about by the girls and then being stolen by the boys. Plots and plans to get the most outrageous photos they can. It starts with the girls sneaking into the boys' room following a night of heavy drinking. The lads zedding off their excesses, easy targets for embarrassing snaps. The girls have gone from bed to bed snapping what they can. The boys in various states of undress or under covers. Mostly dribbling faces and trousers half on and half off. One shot of Stephen's buttocks, even asleep he manages to clench them for the perfect dimples. John gets special treatment. He must have done something to annoy them last night as there is a shot of him waking up as the finishing touches are put to the lipsticked letters E, S, R, A on his forehead. Bleary-eyed lunge for the camera. At some point later, the boys must have stolen the camera. The next few shots are of the girls. Wendy in the toilet, shorts at her ankles, angry face. Louise being sick with Wendy holding her hair out of the way. Abby having a snog with a spotty youth, all tongues and heavy petting.

Oh God.

There it is.

Shower.

She is in the shower.

Camera must have been pointed round the door. Aware of it just before the click of the shutter.

Heart stops.

Sarah.

A Weston nude.

A Cunningham.

A Brandt.

One hand reaching out to pull the shower curtain across her body. One of the boys must have been hiding in the room. She would have locked the door after the sneaky shot of Wendy. Look of surprise. Left arm already close to her body tries to cover her chest. She's not quick enough. Her back, half turned away leg raised hiding between. Buttocks. Tattoo near the small of her back. I didn't know she had one. Looks like a bird or a bee.

Curves.

Wet body.

I find myself wishing this photograph were black and white. It would look so good in black and white.

I was maybe expecting to see some shots of her bikinied body, but not this.

I have to take a break for a moment to regain my composure.

Envelope five, photograph twenty-three

Sarah is sitting on a low harbour wall with John, Wendy and Peter. Sarah looks tired. John and Wendy have exaggerated cheesy grins, playing to the camera. Peter isn't paying attention – he's probably spotted some pretty girl out of shot and is getting ready to go off and chat her up. There is a stranger in this photograph. He is sitting next to Sarah – his body is touching hers, elbows and legs. He knows them. He is posing with them. Could be local? I'm not sure. He looks European, he looks tanned, but that doesn't mean he is from Lanzarote. Why is he sitting so close to Sarah?

Envelope five, photograph thirty

Trip to the volcanic foothills. Sarah stands gazing across the barren landscape. It looks desolate but is undeniably beautiful. Reminds me of the images that probe took on the surface of Mars. The stranger is in this photograph too. He looks like he is a guide but I know he is not. Strange that someone would take a photograph of them together, by themselves. Can't be a holiday romance. They are not standing close in this one. They are not holding hands. They are not kissing. They are not even looking at each other. Surely it is just coincidence.

The same guy is in another few photographs. Posing for the camera as if he is their friend. Smiles directly into the lens in this one. That smile could be for Sarah, I'm sure she is taking the photograph. He is posing so she'll have a keepsake of the holiday fling, snapped in his last holiday hours. She must have met him at the hotel, at a nightclub, on the beach. He'll have chatted her up – she won't have made the first move. I knew it was something that could happen during this holiday. Why wouldn't it? She is young and fit and beautiful. Guys would be mad not to want to spend time with her. She is free to be with whomever she wants. I'm not jealous. If there was anything going on it was just a couple of nights, fumbling between the sheets. No attachments. No relationship. Just sex. That is acceptable when you are on holiday. She's entitled to have sex now and again – only natural. It is not love. It has no meaning for her. It is not love.

* * * * *

A series of shots of the girls and the boys breaking from the water. Ursula Andress or Halle Berry impersonations.

Series of shots giving a panorama of the volcanic mountains. I can picture Sarah sticking them together and putting them up in her kitchen. Lounging by the pool. Day trips. Sunsets. Sea. A close-up portrait of Sarah's face. Sports on the beach. Sunbathing – beach. Sunbathing – pool. Wendy and Abby with boys over several shots.

Peter with a variety of different girls over several shots.

The group will be together tonight sharing these moments. Laughing and joking at all the silly photos, vainly trying to stop each other seeing the ones they think they look the most ridiculous in. I'm sure there will be a few surprises in here for them.

Let me fill you in on the gang.

Peter
He's known Sarah for five years. They've snogged on a couple of occasions but nothing more. He thinks of himself as being irresistible to women. He has the 'bad-boy' persona that seems to be oddly attractive to females.

Love them and leave them is his motto.

One-night stands.

No strings.

No emotional attachments.

He wouldn't know how to go about a long-term relationship. He's never thought about trying.

His first love is himself.

His perfect weekend is working out during Saturday, drinking and clubbing in the evening, picking up someone for a shag. Same again on Sunday.

John
Doesn't believe his luck. He's the 'odd man out' in the group. He's the opposite of the other lads. He's overweight. He doesn't like sports. He doesn't see himself as 'God's gift'.

His idea of a romance is a good night in with a bottle of wine and a movie or a well-thumbed mag.

Humour is his survival technique. A gag for every occasion – keep them laughing and they won't turn on you.

Abby, sweet, sweet Abby, and Brian
I always think of them as a couple although they are no longer together. There must be a word for unrequited love that is fulfilled and then lost

again. That word would describe Brian. He carries a torch for Abby. He would lay down his life to protect her. Classic chivalry. Abby is not cruel in not returning his love. They tried, it didn't work and she moved on. They're still friends.

Wendy
Serious, sombre Wendy. She's not one for smiles and fun but she's not a humourless soul. She just keeps everything hidden. Overt emotion is a weakness. But this side of her nature is a contradiction to her openness about her body. She's the first to go topless. She has no false modesty. She's competitive, especially with Peter. She likes him a lot but her eyes are open to his womanising. She could never compete with his true love.

Stephen
One thing to say – he's well endowed. I bring it up because it's the one thing he just has to share with everyone. Tight shorts, tight swimming trunks. Body sculpted by Michelangelo. Greek hero in looks. Achilles at Troy. Nothing else to him.

Louise
The newest member of the group and the one I know least about. She has a sun tattoo around her navel and Celtic knotwork around her arm. Chinese or Japanese writing between her shoulders. She probably thinks it says 'peace' or 'love' or 'strength' but I'm sure it really means 'conned'. When I get to know her a bit better, I'll give you more details.

It takes a few hours to look through the sets a couple of times – my pad full of notes and observations.

It is getting late and I am working tomorrow so I decide not to scan or file any of the photographs tonight. I planned to do this over the next few days anyway. Tease out the joy of her snaps for as long as I can. Like I need an excuse.

I put the prints and my notes on the table in the spare room. Computer, printer and scanner in one corner, walls lined with shelves for my photo albums and files. I have a file for each of the gang and one for each set of windows. Others for special projects.

In the months Sarah has been coming to the shop, I have amassed a great deal of information from her photographs. I am a master at squeezing out every detail.

Sarah has become a special project. I treat her in a different way from the others. I'm usually happy to lose myself in the photos alone. But with Sarah I've had to go beyond the image to find out as much as I can about her. I know where she works, where she lives, which pub she and her friends regard as their local, her preferred gym, her favourite shops and cafés. Information gathered slowly over weeks and months. This is a departure from the norm. I like to have distance. I need to have my safety buffer. But I suppose there will always be exceptions to the rule. That is what makes things interesting.

She is a gift because she seems to love taking snaps. She's almost obsessive about it. I'm not complaining. If only more people were as dedicated to recording the minutiae of their lives, I wouldn't have to work so hard.

I think that is the defining reason I am so interested in her. Yes, she has a pretty face, has a gorgeous body and a smile that makes your soul ache and I'm not suggesting for a moment that those factors don't play an important part. But the world is full of pretty women and, if it was just something that superficial I was interested in, I could buy a lad mag.

It all started innocently enough. Just another pretty face dropping off some snaps to be developed. A fairly standard mixture of nights out and parties and places and posed shots of friends. But something in the shots fascinated me. There was a vibrancy to them.

They were telling me a story.

I felt as if I knew her through these images.

I hoped that she would come back again with more and was happily surprised when she brought another roll a couple of weeks later.

Then another and another.

She's been bringing photographs to me for months now.

She can't seem to help taking photographs. Every night out, every day trip, every holiday, every party – the camera is out.

Snap, snap, snap away.

This is usually the 'got a new camera' phenomenon. You get snap happy in the first couple of weeks. A few rolls later and you've got it out of your system. The camera finds its way into a drawer only to be brought out at Christmas or holidays.

Sarah is different.

Sarah wants to have a permanent record of her life.

A life in pictures.

Every mundane moment made to sparkle through her eyes.

Her passion for photographs must stretch back.

I hope it does.

I am sure it does.

She must have been using another developer before coming to me. Maybe one of the dry-cleaning/photo-booth places. There is one near where she works. I wonder why she decided to change? Bigger prints? Better quality? Whatever the reason, I am glad. It brought her to me. I wish it had been sooner.

Wouldn't it be wonderful to see her full collection of shots?

Close my eyes and I can see every print.

There are the obligatory bath shots. The naked baby crawling on a white sheepskin rug shots. Sheepskin rug – that really does betray my age. I wonder what the late-eighties equivalent would be. A multi-coloured nylon rug? Black and white geometric shapes? Day-glo pink throw?

There would be Christmas shots. Opening presents shots. The 'wow' expression fixed on her face as she sees the doll she's been praying for. The disappointed face as granny gives her another knitted cardigan, sludge-brown wool. There she is, surrounded by wrapping paper, presents strewn around her – she feels overwhelmed and loved. The joy of Christmas when you are still young enough to feel the excitement. Wonder radiates from her face.

Day trip to the zoo. She's laughing at the funny monkey. 'Yuck' face as she points to the snakes behind the glass. Penguins and polar bears. Holding on to Daddy's leg as they look at the lions. Ice cream smeared around her mouth.

Trips to the seaside. Sandcastles and leaping from dunes. Sitting in an inflatable dinghy just before an unexpected wave tips her into the water. Proudly showing off the pretty shells she found all by herself. Sleeping in the back seat of the car on the way home.

Playing in the park. Hugging that mangy dog with the floppy ears. Swirling fallen leaves with a stick. Red wellies splashing in puddles. Going high on the swings.

What I wouldn't give to look at her photo albums.

Does she arrange them chronologically or thematically?

Does she keep her favourite ones all together in one book?

Does she have a special album for all the boys she has liked?

Pretty young boy at primary school. Kissed once in the playground just after the bell on a Friday. She had been working up to it all week. He was playing it cool but his heart soared.

Spotty boys at secondary school – frothing hormones and downy hair. The smiles and tears that she would have caused. The casual dumping, the tangle of teenage love.

Somewhere in that collage of faces is there the boy she lost her virginity to? Was it a quick, unsatisfying fumble? Did they plan it for weeks, make sure it was perfect? Did that love last more than one night? Were they soul mates for years until the shine wore thin and they moved on to their next true loves?

She takes this album out now and again. Looks at the faces, wonders where they are. She doesn't see these days as lost in the past. The images keep them with her, keep her whole, connect up the different parts of her life.

She is her photographs.

End of school dance. Comely girls hiding their good looks with too much make-up. They feel sophisticated with the mascara slapped on. They feel like adults but they don't know what that means. Awkward boys at the side of the gym hall. Hating that they have to dance at all but knowing it is the only way to touch the girls.

Now she is in the rebel years. Frightening hair and black eye make-up. Goth look is in. Scruffy look is in. Glamour look is in.

Teenage parties. More boys. Smoking and drinking. Hide those ones from Mum and Dad. Being sick then being snogged. Truth or dare. Flirting with the boy of her dreams then finding him under the coats with her best friend.

She grows up in pictures. Baby to child to teenager to woman. Experiences recorded by others and now captured by herself.

All this history hidden from me. The detail in each image. The answers held within.

An hour is all I'd need. Just an hour with these photographs.

I know that is a lie. Once I'd had a peek I would want more. I would want it all. I would immerse myself in them, experience every moment. I would be part of them – I would be in every shot.

I have tried to make sure that I haven't missed any of her photographs since she started coming to the store. I'm almost positive I haven't. She has regular days for dropping them off and I make sure that I am either at the till or at the machine to process them. I'm going to have to start taking my holidays when she takes hers just to ensure I won't miss a visit.

I couldn't bear to miss a single photo, not now.

There is one problem with her snaps. As the photographer, she is only in a few of them. She'll appear now and again in group shots or if a friend grabs the camera or if she takes a self-portrait.

It is a loss.

I only have sixty-three photographs of her out of the hundreds of copies I have made, not counting today's photos. Sixty-three images of silly faces, exaggerated poses, dancing in clubs, drinking and cheering with her friends, birthdays and parties, a few sunbathing, a couple swimming. Now I've got the shower shot too.

I look at my photo albums. Dozens of them line the walls. Thousands of images. You could pick any one of them up and just by flicking through them you would have a greater understanding of life. The camera never lies it is said. A bit of a cliché but photographs capture a kind of truth. No matter how much you doctor them you cannot remove this essential part of their nature.

They hide nothing from me.

I put the envelopes on the table. It is cluttered with negatives and prints. I use this room to dry negatives. One day, I'll buy a bigger house and I'll have a proper darkroom. Just now, I make do with using the bathroom and the hall as my darkroom. It is not ideal but there is running water to wash the prints. I set up the enlarger in the hall. It means I have draft excluders on all the doors to stop light getting in and a heavy curtain at the front door for the same reason. I have a red bulb permanently in the hall lamp – very sexy to some I am sure but it means I don't have to bugger about with changing bulbs every time I want to develop some photographs.

A problem is the smell of the developing and fixing chemicals. It seems to annoy my next-door neighbour a bit. Our bathrooms back on to each other and the extractor fan doesn't seem to be very good. Maybe it connects with his.

I can smell his cigarettes when he smokes in the toilet – he can smell the chemicals when I'm using mine as a darkroom. I don't complain – he does complain. Fucker.

IMPRINT OF NATURE

1839 France. Louis Daguerre reveals a new photographic process. Using copper plates coated with silver iodide, images could be fixed with exposures of twenty minutes.

The plates became known as daguerreotypes and became a craze in Europe. But many thought that capturing a perfect image of creation was blasphemous.

The images recorded on the plates were extremely detailed but each image was unique – copies could not be made.

The picture was a mirror image.

WHAT I DO

Time for bed but I'm feeling at a bit of a loose end after the photo session. I'm not sure if I'll be able to settle yet so I head back to the lounge and switch off the lights. I'm looking for a distraction, something to take my mind into a different place.

I wander to the window with a chair and set it down next to one of my cameras. I keep it here most of the time on a tripod. I have a telephoto lens on this particular camera so it needs something to keep it steady.

I'll just have a quick look round tonight – see if I can get a glimpse of something interesting. It is late and most people will be in bed or will have their curtains closed but there is bound to be something that catches my eye.

The telephoto lens is not all that useful for quick scans. It is too cumbersome to move about quickly so I use binoculars for this sort of watching. If I see something I want to get closer to, then I'll switch to the more powerful lens and also have the option of taking a photo.

My flat is the perfect place for watching. I can see right across the city. Hundred of flats, thousands of windows. Obviously I can only concentrate on a limited number – the ones that are at the right angle for me to look in.

You are confused.

I suppose I should tell you what I do. Tell you everything so that you understand.

I think you have already put some bits and pieces together, jumped to a couple of erroneous conclusions already so I'll set the record straight.

Time to let you into my world.

Don't worry. It is nothing sinister. I don't feel the need to confess to you. I'm not seeking absolution – I simply want you to understand and that, in turn, will let you revise the incognisant judgements that you've made.

I like to watch people.

Plain and simple.

It would be good if it was that simple. Just go to a window and look. But watching is an art and art isn't easy.

You are thinking – what's the big deal? Everyone watches everyone else all of the time – it is part of being human, it is part of learning about yourself and others, it is part of becoming more than you are. My, you are being mature about this. Yes, I agree wholeheartedly. But I don't just sit in a café and watch the world go by. I don't just scrutinise people when I'm in the park or at the beach or as I walk around. I watch people. I work at watching people. I like watching people. I go the extra mile to see the truth behind the public face that we all put on. I look into your private world and enrich myself in doing so.

Alarm bells are ringing.

Peeping Tom.

Pervert.

Stalker.

That is not me.

There are a number of people that like to secretly watch others and get a sexual thrill from the act of watching. These are people who can't form proper relationships. The lonely that, for some reason, don't think to go out to a bar or a club or don't have friends to introduce them to potential partners. For them, porn magazines and movies lose their appeal after a while because, at the end of the day, however handsome or pretty the person might be, they are performing for you. Acting. It is not real. Pornography is about the artificial. The seductive pose that is really about giving you an eyeful. The plumber popping round and getting more than he bargained for. The fit and the beautiful and the well-endowed in paper-thin excuses to have a hump.

So these guys like to get their jollies watching real people doing real things. Waiting for a peep through your curtains, to see you getting undressed, or having a shower or touching up your partner. They need something they can take home with them and picture as they grab for their grubby spasms.

That is not me.

Let me make this plain – this is not sexual. I am not some sad little loner perv wanting to have a quick tug as I glimpse a bit of bum through a window. That is not what this is about. I am a student of humanity and the best way to understand people is to watch them going about their normal business. Seeing them in all their different guises. Public artifice and private truth.

We surround ourselves in pretension. The way we dress and the words we use and the expressions on our faces – we try to control them to create an image. What we read and listen to and watch – manipulated to created the persona we think will best describe what others should see in us. Often this pose we adopt can be just as interesting as the candid self but, in the main, I am interested in they way that people are through the front door, behind the curtains.

I suppose I have a relationship of sorts with the people I watch. You can't watch someone without feeling a sense of companionship. Of course it is a one-way relationship – there is no possibility of approaching someone in the street and saying *You don't know me but I know you. I watch you through your window and I think I'd like to be your friend.*

I suppose there is the possibility that I could use the information that I have about someone to engineer a situation where I could get closer to them. I have never tried that – too many variables, too much that could go wrong. So much information that I might not actually have.

There, that wasn't so bad. I had you worried for a moment. You were thinking all sorts of bad things but you can relax now. I've told you the worst thing about me and it really isn't all that bad.

I sit at my window searching for something to take my mind from Sarah's photographs.

Most windows are dark.

Nothing.

Nothing.

Nothing.

Nothing.

Window 8A

Clara putting her violin away. Late-night practising. I watch her. After a moment she turns off the light.

Feeling happy seeing one of the regulars, I can go to bed content now.

I strip and fold my clothes neatly on to the chair beside my wardrobe. Put on my bedside lamp and turn off the main light. I slip under the duvet and take pleasure from the coolness of the sheets.

Bedtime ritual.

Check that I have my notebook open to a new page just in case I get hit by inspiration during the night.

Pile of books next to my bed, a mixture of novels and non-fiction. Books about photography and astronomy for research. I like to read something before I go to sleep – take my mind into a different place. Don't feel like reading tonight.

I've got my notes from tonight's photo session if I feel the need to check something or find some connection or other. It will take me a few days to fully process the images, find every scrap of meaning in them. Then I'll have to transfer my rough notes into my proper files.

Need to keep everything up to date.

I think I'm too drained to do anything else tonight. I'm spent after the photo marathon. It is not surprising. I've been building up to this for a couple of weeks now.

The next set that she brings me will be even better. It won't necessarily be as rewarding as this holiday set from a content point of view but it will be more fulfilling simply because I know her better after tonight's viewing.

Tired. My head throbbing with images. Still in a state of excitement.

I close my eyes and take deep calming breaths. Unless I do something, I know I'll have a restless night.

Doesn't seem to be working.

Eyes open and I'm staring at the ceiling.

I check that I have set my alarm clock. Think about flicking through a book then decide I don't want to take myself away from the images completely.

Turn off my lamp and lie back in the darkness.

Muffled noise from a television. Sound insulation wasn't a great priority when tower blocks were built. It doesn't annoy me. I am used to the background hum of my neighbours. I could easily get myself a nice tenement flat in a trendy part of the city but I prefer to stay here for the moment so I can watch the wildlife.

Try closing my eyes again. Calming counts this time. Images tumble and jump in my head. Competing for my attention.

Peter stretches for the ball.

I stand on the beach as Peter jumps. Hot sand beneath my feet. Should get to a towel as soon as I can. I quickly step on to Abby's towel bumping into Brian as I do so. *Sorry, mate*, I say. Abby squeals as the bump makes Brian squirt some cold cream on to her back.

Sarah puts her camera away and sits down on her own towel. Brian throws the suntan lotion to her and she motions for me to join her.

I kneel beside her and she hands me the lotion. She lies down on her stomach and asks me to rub the lotion into her back. I squeeze the coolness on to my hands and rub them together to warm it. She puts her hands behind her back and unfastens her bikini top. Her skin has already taken a tan and is smooth and soft. Tiny hairs turned golden by the sun. I push down on her back, feel the definition of her muscles, her ribs. Fingers flick across the tattoo in the small of her back. She moans contentedly as I massage. *That's so good*, she says.

She is so warm, she is so tender.

I finish working the cream into her back and move to her legs. High-cut bikini bottoms expose so much flesh. I start at the top and work down to her feet. She opens her legs wider so that I can reach her inner thighs too. When I finish there, she turns over. She takes the unfastened bikini top and puts it on the edge of the towel. *Now the front.* Start at her feet. Rubbing the cream into her toes and moving upwards. Ankles, shins, knees, thighs. Thumbs brush against material as I circle near her bikini line. Stomach. Navel. Bottom of her ribs. Higher. Higher. It feels like the beach is empty. Just us. Her breasts. Her neck.

She is in the shower. Someone coming in with a camera has disturbed her. She tries to cover herself.

She sees it is me. She smiles. She pulls back the curtain. I put the camera down and pull off my T-shirt and shorts. I step in. The water feels cool. She presses herself against me, arms round my back, one rubbing, the other tightening on my buttock. She moves back a little. Nipples brushing against my chest. Hands round on my chest now, moving down. *I love you*, she says, and she moves in again to kiss me.

I reach for a tissue.

HÉLÈNE

I wake with a rush of images. Fragments of faces. Flashes of colour. That damned beach ball. Thousand details. Thousand pictures.

I'm feeling groggier than normal in the morning. Turn to the clock and discover why. Thirty-six minutes before my alarm is due to go off – that's fifty-one minutes before I need to get up.

I lie back down and close my eyes. Another few minutes and I'll get up. Might drop off until the alarm shouts.

I wait. The longer I wait, the more agitated I become.

No chance of slipping back into sleep now.

I'll get up. Have a long breakfast. Maybe look at some of the photos from last night. Maybe I'll go into work early and get some more brownie points for being a star worker.

I stretch and pull open a drawer. Fingers rummage around in the dark. Notes. Objects. Then the edge of a laminated card. I take it out and switch on the bedside lamp.

Plump up my pillow and settle back down.

Photograph of Hélène.

This is one of the later shots from America – Henri keeping his hand in and selling to the American market.

Hélène holds up a square of muslin. It covers half of her face but the eyes tell me instantly that it is her. She is lit from the side – breasts in light and shadow. The muslin stops just at the top of her pubic triangle. Her legs are parted on the seat. No explicit detail but enough to have hundreds of cowboys salivating and looking for the nearest heifer.

Her eyes tell she is smiling. Unusual, in those times of long exposures, to have anything other than a severe expression. Can you imagine what it would have been like in the daguerreotype days? Heads held in place with a metal frame as the minutes ticked by so there was no movement.

Early photographs would often have the subjects facing away from the camera, partly to save blushes of recognition but mainly so that the eyes couldn't be seen. Scary effect if you have eyes blinking through a long exposure. There are even tales of photographers advertising the use of drugs to knock subjects out long enough to stop fidgeting during minutes-long exposures in strong light.

The good old days.

No – smiling faces were not wanted in smutty snaps of yesteryear. You wouldn't want eyes staring out at you. Watching what you were doing.

Nude photography is odd.

You have the explicit porn kind – all fake tits and orange tans and spread labial lips. 'Come ahead and fuck me till I'm sore' expressions on faces. The point of these photographs is to let men have a wank. They are supposed to be ridiculous and unreal. Women made fantasy props.

Then you have erotic or art nudes. Often black and white, well framed, well lit, well shot. Often less explicit but still containing enough sexual tension to stimulate.

There is a movement called 'simple nudes'. Very revealing shots of natural beauties, often in the outdoors. Nothing left to the imagination but they are not taken with dirty old men in mind.

You get a blurring of issues with photographers like Rosen. Extremely explicit shots of people having sex. Art? Porn? Artporn? Can these sorts of photographs have an honesty about them that raises them above smut?

Then you have photographs of Hélène. Taken to give the men of Europe and beyond their jollies. Taken to be erotic. No ambiguity, no pretensions. They have a function, clear and simple. But, over time, they have transformed into something different. Something more pure. Something transcendent.

I stare at the photograph of Hélène in my hand. I feel I am Henri standing in front of her, hand hovering near the lens, ready to return the cap as I count off the seconds.

I take a folder from the drawer.

My project.

My celebration.

My homage.

The pages contain Hélène and Henri's story – from that rainy day in Paris to the ruin of two lives.

Their story is simple – down-on-his-luck French artist wants to make money from the burgeoning erotic image market. Finds a prostitute to help.

There is a mythology about photographs during the erotic postcard boom at the start of the twentieth century. A presumption that the women posing were all prostitutes. That is the 'romantic' spin we adopt with hindsight. With Henri, it was the truth.

The second section contains copies of all the photographs I've managed to track down – each one ready to be recreated. That will be the difficult part.

Can I do it?

How can I do it?

Who will pose for me? You might think it would be easy these days, with sex and nudity everywhere, selling you everything from bottled water to games. But we are not just talking about a subtle shot, nice use of shadow and a well-placed flower. Henri's photographs don't know modesty.

Friends? They're usually the first call for photographers. Somehow I don't think so. I can't see myself with Marion or Alison or Beth from work – *Just pop your drawers on the floor, dear. Now, if you hold your knees up to your ears – that will be just perfect. Oh and don't worry – it is art after all.*

Could ask some pretty girl from a club. Back to my place for a snog then I reach for the reflectors and light meter. *Do you mind if a snap a couple of shots of your fanny before we start?* I can feel the palm on my face and the knee in my nuts at the thought.

Model? Better choice. Would be used to posing. Quick search on the internet would bring up some local names. Could be expensive. Might not be up for the detail that I'd be looking for.

All these are second best.

I want authenticity.

Wonder if I should try Henri's way. Find a prostitute? My own muse – my own Hélène. That just fills me with dread. I've never even thought about speaking to a prostitute, let alone paying one to pose for me. I feel a bit soiled at the prospect. God knows what diseases they'll be dripping with in these liberated times.

But she'd be professional, I suppose – used to the oddest of requests. May have done something like this before – moonlighting in some cheap skin-flick shot by that guy up the alley where she lives.

They are trained not to flinch at bizarre requests. I know they are. I hope they are. Besides probably would like the break from shagging some stranger for a while. Nice warm studio, just lie back and let the shutter do the work. No fat sweating bloke covering you in his grease, no diseased knobs near you.

Yes. Perfect. Authentic.

I'll do it.

I have to do it if I want to be true to the spirit. Get the most out of the images.

I'll do it.

Next week.

Maybe the week after.

Maybe . . .

My alarm goes off.

I decide to forgo the fifteen minutes of grace. Get up. Time to play with the day.

Hélène stood in Henri's studio. It was grimy. It was cluttered.

Long-abandoned canvases leaned on walls or lay broken in a corner.

She noticed a cot in the corner. Henri must sleep here too.

Hélène was surprised that she came here today. Yes, the man did give her a few coins, with the promise of more if she came to the studio the following day, but she was still a little surprised that she did. She was not sure if she should trust him.

The weather was bad again that day and the promise of being indoors for a couple of hours mixed with a certain curiosity led her to his door. Made her knock. Made her come inside.

Henri was pleased to see her but seemed even more nervous than he was yesterday.

He spoke quickly and jumped from one thing to another. She didn't really understand everything that he was saying but she understood when he told her he would want her sitting and standing. He blushed and looked away when he said she would be unclothed. She found that word funny. Unclothed. It sounded silly. Why not say naked?

He took her to the wooden box on the stand and explained it to her. She did not understand a thing that he said but she smiled and nodded.

She decided she was glad she came. There was a fire burning in the grate and the chill was off the air. She would also admit, if asked, that she thought Henri pretty and found his shyness endearing.

Henri said he had asked her there that day as he needed to work in daylight. He needed as much light as possible to expose the plate.

Hélène smiled her sweetest 'you can say anything to me' smile while still not understanding.

Henri brought her a robe and said that she could wear it between exposures.

Hélène removed her rain-damp clothes. She smiled as Henri made pretence of working at the box with his back to her. She could see that he was nervous.

She pulled on the robe. It had a musty smell – a man's smell.

She felt the lumps of dried paint under her feet and looked down. Colours swirled around her toes.

Henri turned to her. He avoided looking at skin that was visible because she had not fastened the robe. She did not fasten it on purpose. She wanted to see what he would do when he caught sight of her bare breasts. Wanted to see his reaction when he saw the dark hair between her legs.

Henri tried hard not to look.

Henri led her to a chair. He told her to stay completely still and not blink. He said that it might be better if she closed her eyes. He told her that exposures weren't nearly as long as they were with daguerreotypes. He talked and talked to distract himself from looking at her body.

She normally did not like the men she was with talking about things she didn't understand. They did it so that she would feel stupid. A reminder of her place in society.

Some of them just talked and talked while they poked her.

She didn't mind Henri talking. She felt that he was sharing some secret knowledge with her.

Henri asked her to remove the robe. She did so. She leaned her weight on one leg and brought the other leg up enough so she was standing on tiptoes on that foot. She put her hands on her hips and pushed her chest forward. It seemed the natural thing to do.

Henri was trying very hard not to look too closely. He told her that was a nice pose, very classical, and that he would use it later.

He asked her to sit. He asked her if she would mind opening her legs a little.

She could feel his blushes. She could see that he was trying to hide glances at her nudity. She could tell that being this close to her was arousing him.

He walked back to the wooden box on the three-legged stand. He put his head behind it and looked over the top. He told her that it was a wonderful image. He told her to be perfectly still. He removed a cap from the front of the box and, through her almost-closed eyes, she could see a glass lens.

Henri asked her to adopt different positions. Hélène had fun sitting and standing and crouching. She did not mind that she was naked. She liked her body. She liked that it was firm and round, not sagging and gnarled like some of the women she worked beside.

She had a strange feeling too. She was not sure what it was exactly but she felt that it had something to do with Henri. She liked that he watched her body. That he wanted to take images of her.

Hélène could sense that he wanted something more. More sensual. She asked if he would mind if she tried something and he agreed. She suggested he moved the box closer and then she rested her hands on the chair and planted her feet on the floor as far apart as she could facing away from him. She bent her knees slightly knowing that her cheeks would spread apart even more.

Henri took several plates of that.

Henri said that they were finished for the day.

He asked Hélène if she would come back again. He told her that he could sell the images that he took of her today and that he would earn a good amount of money from them. He said that, if she posed for him more, he would give her a share of that money.

He picked the robe from the floor and walked to her and held it out. She took hold of it but he did not let it go. He looked into her eyes. He moved his free hand towards her and stopped. She could see his hand shaking. He swallowed hard. He looked lost.

Hélène did not mind.

Hélène took his hand and placed it on her breast.

Hélène pushed him down until he was kneeling.

Hélène took the robe from his hand and let it fall.

Hélène took his other hand and put it on her breast. His hands were still.

Hélène clasped the back of his hands and pressed them firmly to her body moving them in slow circles.

Hélène moved her hands away and he continued. She let him squeeze her. She let him rub round her nipples.

Hélène did not mind.
Hélène moved her hands to unbutton his trousers.
Hélène thought about his offer.
Hélène wondered if she would come back.
Hélène reached into his open trousers.
Hélène wondered if she would ask for money.

JOY OF BUS JOURNEYS

I can see the bus pulling up to the stop as I reach the main road. I'll have to run for it. I really don't understand why they just can't stick to the timetable. More than a minute early. What would have happened if I had arrived on time? I would have seen the back of it slinking off down the road. The driver would be chuckling as he pulled away. He'd smile into the rear-view mirror as I cursed and stamped. *Score. Another poor sod late for work. If I put my foot down I'll get to the next stop early too.*

No, never ever trust a public transport timetable. Forget that extra couple of minutes in bed hugging your loved one or that calm walk to the stop. Leave early, skip the last slice of toast, don't pause to kiss the children. Buses wait for no man.

I get on just in time. The driver doesn't pay attention when I flash my pass. He pulls away before I find a seat and I sway down the passage to the only empty one. It just has to be beside an old lady.

God, I hate bus journeys – dragging on to the end of time.

A paradox of our modern age: if the bus is ahead of schedule, why does the journey itself feel like forever once it starts? Buses eat time, like supermarkets and DIY stores.

Maybe it is a morning thing. Time drags because you're not fully awake, your perceptions are still dozing on the pillow. Then again, it feels just as long at night. I suppose you are tired then too and desperate to get home. So maybe time moves at different rates depending on how tired you are. Don't remember Einstein mentioning that fact in the theory of relativity.

Unfortunately it's the best way for me to get to work.

You know what would help make the whole sorry thing easier? If everyone on the bus didn't look quite so grumpy. I know you hate your job. I know you are thinking you're going to spend the next eight hours wishing you were somewhere else. I know you've got five days of the same monotony ahead and that every evening is spent in a stupor trying to recover. But try a little smile. Hide your troubles behind a grin.

The old woman beside me scowls. They are the worst for looking grumpy. Life has chewed them up and spat them out old and bitter.

I believe that the second evil of the bus journey could be solved with a simple thing – better suspension. Just imagine the slightly happier faces that would get off – each a little more resolved to face the day ahead. There would be no clutching of stomachs and feeling dizzy because we feel like we've spent the last twenty minutes in rough seas.

I try to block the journey from my mind. I try to block the road and the driver and the passing traffic. I close my eyes and think of Sarah and think of Hélène.

SNAPS

My day at work is the sort I love. I'll spend most of it developing photographs – hours looking into other worlds. Most of what I see will be dross but I'm feeling at peace after the last couple of weeks of tension so I can indulge in some philanthropy.

It is the late spring rush. Sun chasers taking early breaks, hoping that, after a few days in the warmth, they'll come back to a gorgeous summer.

At various points throughout the year, despite these digital times, we are inundated with rolls of film. Now – when people begin to get that frisky feeling as buds open and spring flowers bloom. Summer – when people are desperate to get their photographs developed as soon as they get home. Eager to devour memories before they fade, oblivious to the fact that the image will be their memory in years to come instead of the experience. The detail lost, only the snaps will have meaning. Thirty-six little packs of trapped time all that is left of those two wonderful weeks, the best time of your life.

The end of the year is busy too. Lots of Christmas and New Year parties. Lots of family shots. Old relatives you see only once a year that your parents force you to pose with, just in case this Christmas is their last one. The final representation of someone's life. All those years, all those memories, crammed on to a few centimetres, fixed in silver salts and printed on to paper. Looking at a portrait should be an act of reverence.

People only see the surface.

Only interested in the immediate.

Christmas and work party snaps. Not a shred of art in them but good for a laugh. Same poses from set to set, just different faces, different backgrounds. Leery bosses, drunken snogs, too much thigh being shown, the painful discos, the unwanted tongue kisses under the mistletoe, the older colleague trying to fondle the office junior's bum, the boys showing full moons, the drunken girls trying to photocopy their boobs, the surprised faces of the couple caught in the cleaner's cupboard.

Every office and every shop in the country has a set of these photographs. Proudly displayed on noticeboards, just in time for the first day back after the festive break.

The rest of the year you have the standard snaps being dropped off. The weddings, the children's birthday parties, the badly framed, the poorly lit, the red-eyed, the cropped heads.

Today's snaps are mainly holiday ones. After a single summer you'd become familiar with the eight or so poses there are across hundreds of different sets. You know exactly what they are.

The human race can be wonderfully creative. We can turn our minds to any problem – grand unification theory, splitting the atom, thinking up the wheel, fixing a boiler, how to buy a new car and still save money. So why do people's brains just switch off the moment they get a camera in their hands?

Very occasionally there are exceptions. Last summer I came across a fascinating roll. A full set of thirty-six exposures of girl's bums in bikinis. The young man that brought them in was certainly dedicated. He had the usual 'lads on hols' roll but, at some point during his time in the sun, he must have decided that he wanted to record the range of bottoms he saw on holiday. The boy was creative – lots of shots at pools and beaches but many where he must have been sneaking around so that people wouldn't realise what he was doing. I wonder how many slaps he collected for his troubles.

He wasn't prejudiced. It wasn't a series of firm, tanned, cellulite-free, perfect crotch-gap shots. He showed the variety on offer. The fattest, the juiciest, the most pert, the ugliest, the whitest, the widest, the hairiest – he had them all. The thongs, the high-cuts, the all-over cover. Inventive chap.

I feel sure that such boundless enthusiasm wouldn't just stop with bums from one holiday. I pictured him photographing bikini-wrapped bottoms around the world. What a good idea. I hoped he wasn't too fixated on bums. What about Canary Island breasts? Florida stomachs? Mediterranean armpits? Australian thighs? He could make a fortune with a book of his snaps. No faces showing so he might be able to get round the permissions question.

I was hoping he would come back and bring me more images. He didn't. It is not that I just missed his next visit – I'm sure of that because his snaps were the talk of the shop and everyone was hoping he would bring some more. I think he got nervous, spread out developing across the city's photo booths. Shame. Those bottom shots are sitting lonely in my collection.

We do get our share of readers'-wives-type photographs. We use our judgement when developing them but mostly they are pretty tame. People tend to stick to digital or instant with those sorts of risky shots but I did have a series, not complete nudity, of shots of a young couple. They must have thought it was a good idea to pose for each other. Didn't even cross their minds that someone would look at them when they were developed – then, again, maybe it did.

I do love my job. I love that I get to experience strangers in a way that no one else does. Intimate. Revealing. You can get quite attached to people by the time you get to the end of a roll. They can't hide anything from me. An image can be a lie but it can never completely obscure the truth.

Back home now.

Window 3A
Malcolm is doing bench presses – beefing up those pecs and biceps. He lives on the third floor of a tenement maybe half a mile away. He is a fitness fanatic. He has one of those home gym things that he uses every night. He only wears shorts to work out in and he has a mirror somewhere in his room because his gaze is fixed as he exercises, nodding appreciatively now and again. It works for him though. He is in great shape. I've seen him running in the streets around his home too. I've got some useful workout tips from watching him.

Window 5
Ian puts his arm round Bev. She snuggles up close and takes some crisps from the bag on his stomach. TV flashes on their faces.

Window 8A
Clara is playing. Fingers working on strings, arms back and forth.

FIXING SHADOWS

Hand in my pocket. Fingers running over the round edges of the laminated photograph.
Hélène.
A distillation of time.
Fixed.

Unchanging.

Photographs become a shorthand for memory. Memories become bound to images. Images become the memories.

What hidden meaning does the image in my pocket hold? What smells and sounds and feelings did it evoke each time she saw it? I want to experience those moments. I want to live them.

THE ROOF

I have an arrangement with the caretaker. He has allowed me access to the roof, off limits to everyone else. This means I have unrestricted access to a three-hundred-and-sixty-degree panorama of the city. I can experience places I can't see from my window.

It wasn't easy to persuade him though. I had to convince him that I was a keen amateur astronomer and that the only place worth watching the sky from the city was on the roof of the tower block. He asked, 'Cos it is closer to the sky? I politely laughed at his joke and told him about light pollution. He seemed to accept this logic but still wouldn't let me up.

He said that he was concerned that a tenant, he meant me, might slip on the roof and plunge screaming *Sweet Jesus!* to the pavement twenty storeys below. He said that he could never forgive himself if that happened. He also said he would get the blame for allowing someone up in the first place. I think his real concern was that it would be down to him to hose the guts off the pavement.

Too much responsibility, he told me. He just wanted to hang the 'out of order' sign on the lift, arrange stair cleaning and recommend a plumber if you sprung a leak. In truth, he wanted to spend his time in his ground-floor flat, grumpily watching daytime TV and ignoring phone calls from tenants.

It took me a couple of weeks of persuasion and bribery to get him in the right frame of mind. I also promised him that I would teach him about astronomy and let him use my telescope whenever he wanted. It turned out that he seemed vaguely interested in stargazing so I had to dig out my childhood astronomy books to relearn the basics myself. Since then I've become quite the expert.

I brought him up to my flat to show him photographs of the constellations and planets, detail of the moon's surface and the Hubble Deep Field image. He seemed more interested in the Cunningham print on my wall.

He bored me on the many days I spent cajoling him. Bored me with tales of assorted neighbours he'd come across during the years he's been here. Tall tales of bored housewives asking him into their homes on the pretext of some handyman job needing done, the explicit details as gaudy as the porn movie plots he was ripping off.

He liked to talk about sex. He liked to talk about women's bodies. He didn't use nice words.

He had a neat little sideline in renting out his vast collection of porn mags and videos and DVDs to tenants in both the tower blocks.

He said that the student market was particularly profitable. *Those fuckin' virgins havin' wank parties 'cos they're too fuckin' gormless to get some real pussy.* He nodded sagely after he said that. *Keeps me in the black though.* Nice man.

Seemed like he made a reasonable amount of money from this sordid service. He said that I wouldn't believe some of the people that rented his stuff. Older gents, obviously, but young couples, husbands (without their wives knowing), wives (without their husbands knowing), even the old ladies on the first floor of the other block used him. He said they were very fond of hardcore anal fuck movies. I'm sure he said that to shock me.

He tried to persuade me to use his filthy little library – *First one's free and then a discount 'cos we're mates.* I think I should have removed the nude prints from my wall when he came in. He didn't see them as art.

I eventually had to agree to borrow some of his stuff just to help me get what I wanted.

He asked me down to his flat to pick some *goodies.* He pointed out *Ass Master*, telling me it was a particular favourite. *I've got DVDs now too – you get great multi-angles and perfect freeze frame.* I was able to convince him that I'd only need a video and wouldn't bother with magazines. I said *I'll leave the moist pages for the students* and he thought that was hilarious.

His flat was just as I imagined. Dark and hot and filled with smells. Old food and dirty clothes and sweat. Real seventies theme in the décor, that decade's tasteless wallpaper and carpets. Customary picture of a 'tropical' woman holding her hair. It would be retro chic if it wasn't so genuine.

His collection of pornography was vast. I couldn't believe how much he had. It seemed he arranged it thematically. Vanilla. Lesbian. Orgies. On and on. *Don't have too much poofy stuff – just enough for the old ladies and housewives to get off on. Don't mind watching one if there are a couple of blokes doin' a girl but that is all – men with men is just wrong.* He clearly thought there was something quaint about woman-on-woman action though.

I had already dismissed him as a dull, sleazy, whisky-loving, work-shy pervert by the time I went to his flat. The stale smoke, booze and his collection confirmed my judgement.

My opinion changed when he suggested tea *or something stronger?*

I wanted to say no – that I didn't want anything he'd touched near me – but I couldn't offend him at this stage of negotiations. He told me to take a look at the stuff while he made us a cuppa.

I looked at the collection. I was amused at the creativity of some of the titles – *Lord of My Ring, Two Towering Dicks, Licking Miss Daisy, Four Lesbians and a Dildo, Desperately Shaggin' Susan*. Others more to the point – *Shaven Haven, Cum, Cum II, Cum Again, Cum on my Tits*. Must have taken them hours to think up their titles.

DVDs were on a separate bookcase. He charged more for them. *'Cos of the extras*. I decided that I would take one at random, avoiding the few gay titles of course, just in case that ruined any chance of getting on the roof.

Then I noticed the door to his bedroom was open slightly. My natural instincts made me want to have a look. I moved to a position where I could see into the room but just turn my head if he came back and give the impression I was looking at his collection.

I didn't get past seeing the pictures on the wall. Centrefolds from a variety of hardcore mags – unsurprising in itself considering the rest of the flat. It was the faces that made me feel a shiver. Each one crossed with black tape.

Alarm in my head. Classic serial-offender behaviour from any profiling book. Objectification of women. Covering faces so they don't seem like people.

I'd never been this close to a psycho before. I was repulsed and fascinated.

It would be interesting to have a good rummage around his room. See if there were any other signs and clues. But I couldn't risk even peeping round the door. He'd catch me for sure.

I'd moved back to the bookcases when I heard him open his fridge door and shout through, *Milk?*

I grunted a yes.

Maybe he just didn't like looking at the faces when he was wanking. Maybe he just had a thing about that. Might not be some loony serial killer. But it is such a freaky thing to do.

No. He must be a freak.

I knew I'd have to keep a closer eye him.

He could turn into a real problem for me. Guilt by association.

He came back with tea that was too milky and we discussed the video that I chose. He told me about the best bits with what seemed like perfect recall. *I can tell you the best shots in every one of these*, he boasted as he waved his hand over the collection.

I gagged down my tea and made my excuses.

I felt that I had to watch the tape because he would be sure to ask me questions about every jab and thrust. It titillated me in the superficial way that those things do. But it didn't engage me. It was artificial, posed, acted. I prefer the real. I was right to watch it. He quizzed me closely – laughing and nodding over the descriptions.

In the end, it took a couple of bottles of whisky and a lot more sweet-talking before he let me have access to the roof.

The first few times, he came up with me and I had to explain everything we saw. He got bored after a while or didn't like the cold or something like that because he gave me my own key. I had another one cut just in case he ever wanted it back.

The roof was mine.

Access to hundreds more windows and lives.

Spoiled for choice.

Streets and streets of fresh windows. City-centre hotels. Sports centre on the other side of the park. Watching sunspots gives me the ideal opportunity to watch sunbathers in gardens during the day.

The whole city open and ready.

PATIENCE

I have become a very patient man.

Watching teaches you stillness.

Just you and your thoughts.

Waiting for something to happen. Waiting for that snatched glimpse as someone passes their window.

Reward for your diligence.

Most people don't tend to hang about at their windows just waiting for people to watch them.

Would it surprise you to discover that some people actually do? They are the ones that like a passing stranger or nosy neighbour to get an eye-ful. They love to be seen by other people. A quick flash of skin – a boob or buttock or dick. It looks so innocent to the passer-by – just someone walking to a shower, someone changing their clothes. The passer-by thinks about stopping to gawk, the thrill of stolen intimacy excites them, but guilt keeps them going.

Is it vanity that motivates them? If so, you might think that it is the bodies beautiful that indulge themselves in this way – the well-endowed wanting to show off their wares.

You can just about guarantee that a guy who doesn't mind stripping off on a beach or dropping his shorts at any excuse is pretty happy with his size.

That is not the way it is.

They are not always the most attractive, they are not always the happily proportioned. Perhaps that is the secret need – acceptance through showing. If they can gain comfort from people seeing them nude, even in this controlled way, then it lifts their confidence, proves that they have something they don't need to hide.

It is fun to watch exhibitionists over a period of time, undressing beside a window or passing it in the buff, briefly pausing to adjust that lampshade or tweak that picture frame into place. Apparently no thought that they might be seen.

We've all done it without realising at some point but these folk check out the window – a peek to see if the next audience member is passing by. But they only deal in glimpses. They would squirm if the gaze was fixed, if they knew that the watching eye scrutinised every detail.

I have to admit that I have made the odd anonymous call to the police about the persistently vain. Always males, the body-perfect ones that are doing it just to say, *I've got the perfect body and you don't*. Just a quick call saying that someone is repeatedly exposing themselves and I'm concerned that children will see them. It is enormous fun watching the police arrive at said house and question Mr Nude about his window activities. Poor neighbours will get the blame, I suppose, but those are the breaks.

Many nights, I'll sit for hours just waiting for something to happen. It is much better on the roof with the telescope because I can move around to find something interesting but it gets cold up there and bad weather isn't conducive to watching. Even when I am safely snuggled up in my flat, a miserable rainy night can ruin viewing. If the rain is being blown from the wrong direction, it makes it much more difficult to see. Snow is worse.

Despite these problems, you are almost sure to see something of interest on any given evening – even if it is not what you hoped to see or whom you hoped to see or if it only lasts a second.

I don't always gather the same information for each of my subjects. It really depends. It is fairly easy to find some basic information about them. Firstly it is a case of working out exactly where they stay and popping round to check their names.

Much of the information that I have is based on observation and I realise that I am only getting a quick peek into their lives. Maybe a few minutes here or there over a long period of time, from which I try to fill in the gaps. I know that I'll be getting it wrong some of the time but I can live with that. Besides, I am a pretty good judge of people so I must be getting some of it right some of the time. If I don't actually ever meet them, then how can they contradict my view of them? There are benefits for being so distant from them. You can't really get so disappointed with them.

People don't, on the whole, tend to do very interesting things when they are at home. My watching is of people who are doing the things that I do or that you do – the mundane everyday things that occupy us when we have time to ourselves. Yes, some people use their spare time to climb mountains, go for walks, go to the movies, meet friends and have a good time. Most of us tend to stay at home a few evenings a week, just watching TV or doing the ironing or reading a book or playing on the computer. But I find that fascinating.

I don't discriminate between people. I don't only watch pretty girls or the exhibitionists or the body perfect. I'll watch everyone that I can. The choice is often limited though. People that live in tenements, for example, tend to close their curtains when it gets dark. They know that people can see in their windows. Once people form a habit of closing curtains when they get home, or at a certain time they tend to do it that way always. So I don't get to see. The occasional lapse gives me the odd glimpse but not often enough. These homes are the ones I am really intrigued by. Not because I think that something more interesting is happening there but because I cannot see in

Consider yourself for a moment. How many times, do you think, have you looked in someone's window as you passed or looked from your window into someone else's house? You have done it – you know you have. Most of the time you don't pay much attention to what you are doing. *Nice curtains, nice wallpaper. Wouldn't that colour of paint look nice in the hall?* But, if a person is in the room, something different happens. You become fascinated. *I wonder what that person is doing?* you ask yourself. It is so innocent at first – just curiosity, that's all. That is a natural thing to feel, isn't it? So what harm would there be to watch a little longer? And, if you think that you can't be seen, well, that is even better – you can watch for even longer. *Better switch out the light though just in case I'm seen – better pull the curtains slightly to give more cover – better get the binoculars just to get a better view.*

What if you get a glimpse of a naked body? What if you see a couple at it? You'll be going back to that window every chance you get, convinced that you will see something else interesting. You'll become a slave to that window. Chances are you won't see that same thing again. You'll get bored and you'll leave, vowing not to waste any more time at it.

Most people don't go back once this happens – well, maybe the odd glance just to make sure. But you have to stop looking completely because, if there's another interesting glimpse, you're hooked again. Back to crouching by the window, hands shaking with anticipation.

I have a group that I watch regularly. There is Malcolm and Clara and Oliver and Gemma and Bev and Keith and Neil and Joe and Terri and Mary. There are others but these are my current favourites.

Window 10
Thomas sits in his chair. Staring at a television or just into space. He is wearing his brown cardigan. He is wearing his white shirt. He sits and stares.

Window 11A
Jack is doing yoga. Must look at the names of some of those positions. I must try and get fitter.

Window 6B
Oliver and Gemma are having their monthly dinner party. Neighbours and friends line up to be invited. Oliver is a wonderful cook. Gemma would like to help but she's only allowed to set the table. The kitchen is Oliver's domain.

Wine flows, food is consumed, tales are told.

NIGHT OUT

I stand in the shower for a full fifteen minutes hardly moving. The day's grime is long gone but sometimes I imagine there is a more stubborn stain that refuses to shift.

Loud hacking cough from the bathroom next door intrudes over the sound of the shower. I should reconnect the extractor fan to cover these sorts of noises but I can't stand the droning hum that it makes. Just have to listen to his coughs, listen to his flatulence, listen to his moans.

Hardly seems worth having a shower just now. When I get home tonight I'll reek of smoke and booze and sweat that has lost the sweetness of being fresh.

I turn off the shower. I step out on to the bathmat. I didn't bring a towel in with me. No point in using the hand towel over the radiator, just go to the cupboard and get a new one.

I walk naked and wet into the hall leaving toe prints on the carpet. I feel like one of the exhibitionists that I watch. If only there was a window in the hall.

Sometimes I like to give something back.

I know that sounds a bit strange. But it makes a kind of sense. If I am getting insights into people's lives, seeing them when their guard is down and they are completely natural, without dissimulation, then I believe I should return the favour – give others the chance to see something of me. So, occasionally, I won't take as much care when walking around after a shower – leave my curtains open, wander near a window, just in case someone is watching.

Maybe I am able to do it because I really know that no one is watching me, that there is safety in my exposure. I would know if someone was watching me. But just maybe I'd be unaware of someone passing their window. They'll get a quick glimpse of my naked body, feel the thrill of a voyeuristic moment, run and get their binoculars. It could happen. Fair's fair – I am just keeping the cycle going.

Now, I don't want you to get paranoid. I don't want you to buy thicker curtains and close them the moment you get home. I don't want you to put a lamp near your window so that your shadow won't be cast against the curtains. That sort of behaviour is a bit unhealthy and I'd be sad if I was the cause of that. Equally, don't forget there is an army of perverts out there with more sinister reasons for watching than my wholesome ones. Be careful but don't get paranoid.

I'm half tempted to go to the window right now and pretend to brush my hair or do some stretches – let the world look in on all my glory.

I don't. My dark mood stops me.

Just get ready.

I walk into the bedroom, finish towelling off then open my wardrobe door. I catch sight of myself in the mirror in the door. The reflection doesn't seem real. I don't feel that I am looking at myself. Short hair, white 'stranger-to-the-sun' skin, dark hair on my chest, my groin, my legs. I turn to look at my profile.

Who is he?

I could be Stephen. I could be Peter. I could be Matthew. I could be Henri.

I look at the clothes in the wardrobe.

Tonight I am going to be someone else.

Tonight I will become the person that my work colleagues think I am.

Left-hand side of the wardrobe has clothes that I don't wear. Not my clothes. Character clothes. Clothes for people that care about how they look, clothes for people that know nothing of fashion, clothes that look plain, clothes that stand out and make you pay less attention to the wearer.

Short-sleeved shirts for summer nights – the ones that real men wear on nights on the pull with the lads. Prefer to shiver from pub to pub rather than be a sissy in a jacket. Short sleeves as much a badge of honour as getting pissed, picking a fight and pissing against a wall on the way to a club. Then more drinking and some dancing. Happy now you're wearing your shirt – no cloakroom queue, nice and cool, girls able to check out your muscles. Then let one of them take you to her flat. Shirt that gives easy access when you're there, let her unbutton it before a quick shag, then easy to throw on when you've finished and want a quick getaway.

Maybe I should become that guy tonight. I could become any of the people I watch. It would be easy to slip into their personas. Maybe I could pick up strangers, have relationship-less sex and revert to myself in the morning.

Chimera.

Lycanthrope.

Maybe I should try that.

I look at the shirts – stripes, checks, one colour, tie-dyed, polka dots, paisley pattern. Which one? Which one shall I be? Which one would he wear?

Pick the blue-and-white striped shirt, the dark jeans, the plain jacket. Uniform for the night. I've worn this one before for similar nights with these people but that will help with the image I want to project.

Some actors say start with the shoes – if you get them right, then you get the character right. That is simplistic. You need a whole range of cues if you want to become a different person, reminders of who you've become. You can't afford to slip out of character.

Watch, wallet, keys.

One last look in the mirror. Yes – that is right. I look just like him now. This other version of me. The one that works in a shop, the one that wastes his time at nights out like this. I shouldn't think like that. I have to make the effort. Haven't been to the last few. This one is more special than a night on the piss. It is Pat's leaving do. I quite like Pat. Don't want to snub her. Don't want any tittle-tattle in the staffroom about me. Euan would start it.

Couple of hours of mindless chat and then I'll come home and not need to do it again for a month or two. Not much of a sacrifice. I can do it.

Turn the key. Lock the door.

It is well after seven when I leave. Everyone else settled in for the night. Dinner on laps in front of the telly.

Noise from next door. I can afford to listen for a moment or two. Raised voices again. Father still ranting on about daughter's new boyfriend. I hear the word *waster* being used a lot. Father probably wants her to meet someone with money. Who cares about love as long as he gets a few more beers out of it?

The raging stops. TV silence replaces it.

I take the stairs at an even pace. I'm not in any hurry.

Foyer is empty. I'm surprised. Maybe I'm wrong about the old gossips' rotation. Must be in their homes resting their poor bones. Sherry and medication. Ruminating over new nasty tales to tell.

I'm glad of my jacket when I leave the building. Touch of damp chill in the air. Don't mind not being a man's man tonight.

Movement at the corner of the next block catches my eye. I'm not quick enough to see who it was. Could be kids. Could be Creeping Jesus. My mind immediately jumps to images of skulking and slinking. Been listening to the gossips too much. Poor bloke – saddled with that name.

I almost collide with the caretaker.

I mumble an *Oops, sorry.*

No harm done, he smiles, all fag stained teeth and bad breath. *Seen anything interesting recently?* Don't like the way he said that.

I tell him that I've not been up on the roof for a while. *Too cloudy.*

He smiles again – a leery crack, full of innuendo. I feel unsettled. *Must go*, he says. *Got to deliver a couple of movies to the lads on the eighth floor. Night of wanking each other dry. Can't keep 'em waiting.* He slides past me.

Haven't seen him do anything too suspicious yet. But I've only been watching him when I see him, not gone out of my way for proper surveillance – should start soon. I've got a picture of his taped-up posters in my head now. Wonderful.

I'm not taking the bus tonight. I think that would finish me off. Can't take the car because I'll need something to drink to make the night go more smoothly. Got to be very careful though – fine line between having enough to dull my senses to the pointless small talk and having too much so my tongue gets loose. I'm one of those terrible drunks that waffles on and on given a chance. Too much booze would mean I'd risk coming out of character. I might end up appearing more interesting to them. I've worked very hard to ensure that they think I'm all right but a little dull. Fine for spending a short while chatting to on a night like this but not someone you would want a friendship with. Want them to forget I exist when I'm not around. That takes effort.

I blow some money on a taxi. I think of giving him an extra fiver just to keep his mouth shut. But I don't. I listen to his chitchat. He doesn't seem to care that I'm not answering him – only interested in saying his piece. I get him to drop me a few streets away so that I can walk in silence and clear my head. Try and shake off my bad mood.

Joyous night ahead of me. Bowling and chat and drinking and then probably on to a pub. Pat's idea of a good send-off. When it comes my time to leave, I think I'll just slip away. No fuss. No goodbyes. No tacky present.

I'm close to the bowling alley. A few people walking in front of me are heading there too. Fun for everyone then.

The place is in the middle of nowhere – at least that's how it feels. A wilderness of flats and the odd fast-food outlet. A good twenty minutes' walk from the city centre.

The building is the size of an aircraft hangar – split down the middle, with one side the bowling lanes, the other an enclosed bar area, a tacky burger stand, an arcade games area, shoe collection point and tills.

Some of my colleagues will have been here for more than an hour even though we were due to meet at seven. Chats with people who are already drunk when I am sober – the fun just never stops.

I go into the building and pay the entrance fee, then down a flight of steps and almost directly into the arcade area. Spaceships explode, rally cars scream round a circuit, zombies splatter open. Move towards the bar area passing through the stink of tired meat and old cooking fat.

Large group of my colleagues near the door, tables pulled together to accommodate all of them. Euan. Debbie. Mary. Angela. Ian. Marion. John I. John III. Dan. Pat. Gary. Siobhan. Ellen. Danny. Jim. Cathy. Mandy. And me.

Euan is at one end of the table holding court. Funny story for every occasion. Popular with the boys and girls from work despite laziness and ineptitude. I'm too harsh – he's not really inept, just completely uninterested in what he is doing. I sometimes get the feeling that he thinks he is above working in a shop and he can't see why he should make an effort while he is there. Interesting that, like so many others in his position, he doesn't seem to be rushing to find something better.

Debbie and Angela from cosmetics are beside him, hanging on every word, chuckling at each comment. They worship his apparent indifference. Euan is one of those people with the strange gift of being able to smile his way into girls' pants. No effort required.

All right. Here I go. Adopt the persona. Ordinariness descends on me. Blandness.

I sometimes prefer this version of me. It can be liberating to get lost in a character. This 'me' is less complicated than the real 'me', less sophisticated. He has fewer needs, fewer aspirations, fewer disappointments.

At work I don't have to play the part so much, just blunt the edges. Not much chance to chat to people when you are on the shop floor, just switch it on for the odd tea break when people involve me in their conversations.

Fun as it is to be him, I know that, after a couple of days, I'd start going crazy. I couldn't imagine being him for the rest of my life – or any of the other variations of myself that I have to be.

Pat sees me as I get close to the table. *It is so good that you made it. I was thinking you were another no-show.* She kisses me on the cheek and pulls me over to the table. She says, *I've been drinking since five.*

At the table people smile at me and nod and silently mouth greetings. They seem pleased to see me but then immediately resume their conversations. Just the reaction I want. Comforted that another one of the gang is here but no real desire to talk to me.

Pat pulls an empty chair close to her and I sit. She gets pulled back into chat with Mandy. Pat is all right. Older than most of the people at the tables. Older than most of the people in the shop. She is younger than retirement age but she's had enough of working. She has worked all her life and now, with her kids grown up and her husband retired, she wants to spend whatever time she's got left having fun. Rush a lifetime's worth of experiences into a few short years.

It just doesn't make sense to me. Wasting a whole life doing things you don't want to do so that you can, just maybe, have a little bit of time to yourself when it is almost too late. No. My job does not define me. I certainly do take pleasure in aspects of it but it is a means to an end. A convenience. It won't be for much longer.

Siobhan is on my left – another glamour puss from cosmetics. She is wearing a top with a plunging neckline showing a good amount of cleavage – Wonderbra pert. She is one of those girls that wants you to know she thinks she is sexy – all tits and mascara. Nice to see the cosmetics girls in something other than their seventies sci-fi show jumpsuits.

Siobhan is talking to John III. He's called that because there are three Johns working in the shop. He started just a month ago. He is spending much of his time trying to look as if he's not looking down Siobhan's top. Funny to watch as he keeps eye contact with her until she breaks it and then steals a sneaky peek down her top. He's trying very hard to chat her up. He is mirroring her gestures, looking like he's interested. He needn't bother. Siobhan has a reputation. Rumour has it that she gives someone a blow job on every night out – different guy each time. I haven't seen any evidence of this. Poor John III doesn't realise that he's toying with a maneater. Maybe it'll be a distraction watching her go in for the kill.

I look round the table and catch Marion's eye. She smiles at me. She has made a big effort tonight – her usual plainness covered with the right amount of make-up to make her look pretty. It's a few days after her latest heartbreak so she is probably on the prowl for a new bloke tonight. Probably end up at a club, being felt up by some drunk and back to his place for a quickie.

She gives me the sign for 'What are you drinking?'. I sign back to her that I'll get her one. *Rum and Coke*, she mouths at me. I ask Pat if she would like a drink and she is full of *Oh, no, I really shouldn't. All right, love, I'll have a gin and tonic.*

I'm glad to get away from the table. It doesn't bode well for the rest of the evening if I'm getting itchy feet so soon after arriving. Hopefully we'll start bowling soon and then I can go. Duties discharged for another few weeks. Dust shaken off this persona – ready to be put away again for another day.

When I get back to the table Anne has taken my seat. Nice to see management making the effort to slum it with the scum. I put Pat's glass down beside another full one and go to give Marion her drink. There is a free seat beside her and she suggests I sit there. I think she was keeping it free for me. We sip in silence.

Ellen has a camera at the next table taking shots of the group. I make sure my head is turned away before each flash.

I have a range of small talk opening gambits but I just don't feel like using any of them. I should try to make the effort though. It'll make the night go faster.

Euan tells me you take your own photographs.

I am taken slightly off balance by the question. I hide it and say, *I do.*

Euan says you're good. He says that you're going to have an exhibition.

I should keep my blabbing mouth shut around Euan. *Yes,* I mumble, *there is a gallery I know that you can hire and hang your own art. I did it a couple of years ago.*

Was it good?

I liked it. Got a nice review for it.

What are you doing this time?

I don't really like talking about it.

I'm sorry – I didn't mean to pry.

She seems genuinely sorry to have asked me – no trace of sarcasm. *No. You're not prying. It's . . . it's just that I think if I describe it to people, then it takes something away from taking the photographs.*

She seems satisfied by my answer but she really wants to know more. She's too polite to press any further about the exhibition. *Do you like photographs?*

I gave the shop in-joke answer. *I'm developing a liking for them.* We both laugh, knowing that it wasn't very funny but it's the polite thing to do.

She continues. *I've only got a little crappy camera. Only use it at weddings and birthdays and Christmas.*

Yeah.

Would Marion pose for me? Could she be Hélène?

I don't really know anything about photography but it seems interesting. Do you know much about it?

A bit.

Who is your favourite photographer?

There are quite a few.

If you had to name one?
Eh. Have you heard of Edward Weston?
No.
Photographer. Twentieth century. I sound like a twat.
What sort of pictures does he take?
Lots of photographs of peppers?
Peppers?
Yes. But he's best known for his photographs of women.
Famous women?
Not really. Mainly nudes.
I knew it would be smutty stuff. She realises that she might have offended me.

No, not at all. His photographs are beautiful. They are art. Nothing smutty about them at all.

And so it goes on. She's got me talking. I give her a mini-lecture on Weston and Cunningham and Stieglitz and Brandt. I tell her about the Cunningham print, *Triangles*, which I have in my lounge.

She is interested. Not just pretending. Or maybe she is just good at faking attentiveness. Maybe that is what makes her so appealing to her string of boyfriends.

It is actually nice to talk to her about photographs. I don't often get the chance. But as we speak I find it hard not to see her in some of the classic nude poses. Marion with head on knee, hands clasped around the other knee. Marion in sand dunes. Marion kneeling on a striped rug. Marion reclining. Marion leaning on the back of a chair. Almost have to shake my head to get rid of the images.

It would be nice if she posed for some shots. Could I ever work up the courage to ask her?

I suddenly realise that I'm coming across as interesting – as having hidden depths.

I have to get out of this situation. Other people might start to listen in on our conversation and wreck all those long nights spent trying hard to come across as Mr Dull.

I think maybe we should get our shoes. No one else seems ready yet but I stand anyway. I can see a flicker of disappointment in her eyes. She walks me over to the counter.

I drop my shoes on it and wait for someone to come and serve. Marion right beside me doing the same. Both of us standing on blue-tile-effect carpet in our socks. Marion's elbow just touching my arm.

I hate that smell, she says, sniffing.

The tang of disinfectant hangs over the shoe racks.

An assistant approaches. She looks bored. *Size eight and a half,* I say as she lifts my shoes. She doesn't make eye contact. She brings over a slightly threadbare pair of black and red shoes. She picks up Marion's. *Size five*. Marion sits beside me and we put on our bowling shoes – insides smooth as glass.

I wonder how many feet have been in this pair. I wonder how much sweat and watered down disinfectant has soaked into the fake leather. I wonder how long they keep shoes before they throw them away. I tie the laces – grey from thousands of fingers tugging at them.

Marion and me getting ready has encouraged everyone else to get ready. There is much hilarity as shoes are exchanged and fun is made is made of sock colours and foot size. John III, being new, gets the most attention. Siobhan helps him on with his shoes. Perfect view down her top. *You know what they say about boys with big feet,* she says to the group. John III goes red. He tries to cover his stiffy.

Marion ends up in my team but she doesn't get much more of a chance to talk with me. I'm able to slide back into the blander persona.

More booze-fuelled laughter as people enter names on to the score screen. Ivor Bigun, Mr P. Ness, Evan Apee. Such mirth.

There are oohs and aahs as people get strikes, laughter at gutterballs. Euan and Dan and John I are taking the game very seriously.

I end up beside Debbie for a while. She talks nonsense as always. The famous people she would like to meet, the singing career that is just waiting for her, how she'll be leaving the shop soon. She's one of those people that always says, *I'll be gone by Christmas,* year after year after year. She annoys me when she laughs at her own jokes. She makes fun of the way I throw. I wonder if the character I've adopted tonight would get satisfaction hitting her with a bowling ball. I decide he would.

I stand for my next go. Lift the ball and gracefully send it down the alley. I wait for the cheers and the pats on the back from my strike. I knock down five.

Another half-hour and I'll go. Another half-hour after that and I'll be in a shower. Then watching. Can't wait to get away.

I am standing in Euan's kitchen. Leaning against a worktop. I'm holding a bottle of beer taking swigs from it although I should have stopped drinking hours ago.

I'm aware my head is giving the nod-nod of the drunk.

I promised myself I would go home. I promised myself I wouldn't get pissed. I have no idea if I have let the mask slip. I've no idea if I've spoken out of turn. Have to wait until Monday to find out. See if I get funny looks. Don't care. Let them all know. Let them all see me. Let flesh peel off until I am revealed. They wouldn't understand. See me as some seedy little perv hunched double, wanking, sobbing, slobbering. One step below a molester. That is all they could see. With their closed little minds and their evil little labels. They couldn't see the art, the honour, the truth.

Head nod-nods. Difficult to focus. Not really listening to the conversations around me. Should try and pay attention. Should try and get my mind working. Remember the evening. Try and remember what you've said. Try hard. Hard. Hardy Boys and Nancy Drew. Used to watch that on Saturdays when I was a kid. I think I did. Clean-cut boys. Wholesome. Wholemeal. Lots of roughage.

Fuck. I'm jabbering.

I'm wrecked. I need to leave – if I remember how to move. Should wait a bit longer, see if I can trust my legs. Lift bottle of beer. Take a swig. Tastes harsh now. Like it hasn't been brewed. Bubbles on my tongue. Gases building in my stomach. I really need a piss. I didn't notice before but I am absolutely desperate for a piss. Need to start walking. Put the bottle on worktop. Misjudge the distance. It comes down with a thump. People turn to me thinking I'm trying to get their attention. I slink away. Walk to the hall. Are those my feet that I'm watching? Shamble-shamble out the door. Must be mine but not sure if I can feel them. Just like pins and needles.

People in hall. Try not to catch anyone's eyes. Don't want to chat. Just head for the toilet. I need a coffee. I need my bed. Debbie and Dan snogging. Tongues and heads grinding against each other. I shouldn't watch. Toilet door must be stuck. Just not moving. Open. Open damn you. Shout of, *Just wait will you?* from inside. Door is locked. I knew that.

Just have to wait. Just have to cross my legs. Tie a knot. Don't think of waterfalls.

Debbie and Dan pressed against each other. Denim on Lycra. She has hands on his arse. Rubbing. I can hear their moans, hear the slurp of their tongues.

Don't look. Don't watch.

Debbie and Dan. D and D. Dungeons and Dragons. That's right distract yourself. Smell of the lead figures in metal sweetie box. Multi-coloured. Multisided dice. 1d6, 1d4, 1d12. Roll to discover the damage.

Debbie's pulled out his shirt and is touching him. Dan's feeling her bum. Rubbing clothed crotches against each other. Close-up on mouths. Slick with saliva. Shining in the 100-watt glare. Tongues like swords. Parry, thrust, parry, riposte. Don't stare. Pressure in bladder. Really starting to hurt. Hope no one is at it in the toilet. Could be ages. Dee and Dee looking for a room. Euan won't mind. Open minded about these things. If you've got an itch, you need to scratch. Maybe got a camera in his room. Maybe he likes to watch his friends. Consummate. Coitus. Intercourse. Copulate. Penetrate. Pierce. Wound. Knife. Parting flesh. Burn of the flash.

Dee Dee go into a room. Door closes. No lock. Extra thrill of being found. Coitus interruptus.

Bathroom door opens. Woman comes out. Twenties. Don't remember her name. Euan's flatmate. She smiles a *sorry* to me. I smile back. Cue for small talk. What would I say? I need a pee. Lock the door behind me. Don't like an audience. Like if you use a urinal. Can't perform.

Green bathroom suite. Bath has collection of soaps and shampoos and conditioners lined up round the sides. Need to pee. Lift the lid. Pull down my zip. Ahh. Try not to splash. Boys always splash. Shake. Shake and vac and put the freshness back. Zip up. Wash hands at sink. Nice soap. Smells perfumed. Belongs to one of the girl flatmates. Look in mirror above the sink. Red eyes. Grey face. Stubble. Don't want to look at myself. Light headed. Need to sit. On the edge of the bath. Just for a few minutes. Move soon. Try to focus head. Room moving slightly to the left. Eyes can't seem to catch up. Close them. That's worse. Focus on the blue towel on the radiator. Did I say anything? Dum, dum, dum, dum from music in next room. Home soon. Bed. Wonder what Dee Dee are up to. Flies open, skirt up, panties at ankle. Doggie. Woof, woof. Bow-wow. Barking and biting. Howling out the lust. God I'm drunk. Brain won't stay still. Go to sink. Turn on tap. Cold water in face. Splish, splosh. Better. Check bathroom cabinet. Force of habit. Pills and toothpaste and toothbrushes and cotton wool and razors and shaving foam and mouthwash and sanitary towels. Dull, dull. Knock at the door. Don't want to move. Knock at the door. Should move. Wouldn't like to be kept waiting out there myself. Knock. Must be desperate. Open the door. John III. Says, *Hi, I'm bustin'!* Pushes past. Starts before I can close the door. Remember to wipe off Siobhan's lippy.

Back to the kitchen. Someone singing. Everyone listening. My space at the counter still free. I'll just catch my breath then go. Give my beer bottle a dirty look. Don't want another sip. Singing stops. Someone is talking. Rhythmic. It is poetry. What's going on? Poem stops. Person looks at person beside them. That person says, *This is a Leonard Cohen song.* Approving murmur. Singing begins. No. No. No! Party pieces being paraded in the kitchen. Not staying for that. Not staying here. Time to say ta-ra. Will not perform for them. Taxi home.

Wave goodbye to Euan. He makes an 'Aw, going so soon?' face. Leave the kitchen. Jacket in hall. Would be bad if Debs and Dan were rutting on the coat pile in the bedroom, dribbling sweat and goo.

Just get jacket. Don't say goodbyes.

Want to heave off this version of myself. Sick of it now. Don't want to be that little shit any more. Want to be myself with my hidden depths and secrets and desires. Complex.

Hand at my elbow. Marion. *Are you going?*

Bed is calling, I say. I think the words came out in that order.

OK. It was nice to talk with you tonight – out of work, I mean.

You too. See you at work. Open the front door.

I'd like to see some of your photos sometime, she calls as I go. I don't answer.

Cool air is a slap. Deep sobering breaths. Wonder if I should walk home. Brrrrr. Chilly. Get a taxi. Wander to the main road. Jamie, watched from the roof, lives near here. Maybe I should wander by his house.

Wait for a taxi to pass. See one. Hail it. Don't know if I've been waiting a minute or an hour.

Mumble a destination to the driver and sit back. No seat belt. Rebel. Lawbreaker. Keep my eyes closed. He doesn't want to chat. Good. Drives on. Now stops. Hand cash over. Less than I thought it would be. Step out. Not my street. I know this street. Don't try to get back into the taxi. Let it drive away. Walk to the pavement. Avoid the dog shit. Still a bit unsteady. Wonder what it would be like if I was still wearing the bowling shoes? Could tap dance or soft-shoe shuffle along the street. Need a stripy jacket and a straw boater.

Only a couple of streets. Sober enough to ask the driver to drop me here and not right outside. Wasn't even aware this is where I asked to be dropped. Must have known.

Turn a corner. I'm here.

Sarah's flat.

Lights off.

Must be in bed. Under cool sheets. Wearing nothing. Wish she would come to the window right now. Can't sleep so just look out into the night for a change of scene. Now wearing downy pyjamas. She sees me. She isn't surprised. She isn't shocked. She waves. The door buzzer sounds. Inviting me up. Flat full of her photographs. In frames on the table, hanging up, images covering the walls instead of wallpaper. I'd take out a camera. She'd say, *Afterwards, we can hold each other until we fall asleep.* Wrapped in each other. Lost in the warmth.

Want to push her buzzer – just to hear her voice. Would have to stand at the door just in case she looked out of the window. Would have to wait until I was sure she had gone. Or I could buzz and run across the street to hide in the shadows and hope she would come for a look.

That wouldn't be nice.

That is what I want.

Let her sleep.

I'll see her soon.

I'll see her soon.

SATURDAY

Something exciting is happening and I'm watching it unfold.

Got up about ten minutes ago. Headache and feeling dehydrated from last night. I still don't want to even think about what I might have said so I've decided to leave worrying about it until later.

My plan for the day was a lazy breakfast, then maybe watch a movie or read, then go out in the afternoon, have a wander with my camera. Good plan. All changed when I checked the view from the window. A little overcast but warmer than yesterday. Then I noticed a removal truck at the tenements across the road. Someone was moving into *the* flat.

Binoculars at the ready.

I've been watching two removal guys and the couple that have bought the flat since then. I know the couple. I saw them about a month ago. I just knew they would be the ones.

They were one of three couples I had watched in the evenings coming for a second viewing. I had a good feeling about them. Maybe that is just me editing my thoughts after the fact. I probably felt at the time that any of the couples would be good, as the flat had been empty for a few months. Always couples looking at new flats. Never single people. What do they do?

I hadn't paid much attention to the flat before. It was shared by some students – dirty net curtains obstructing any interesting views during the day, horrid dirty yellow curtains closed every night. Nothing interesting to see. Then they left.

The flat came on the market and the 'For Sale' signs came down a month and a half later. It must have been some developer that bought it because the flat was gutted and redecorated over the following three weeks. White paint on walls and ceilings – blank canvas. Thought the guy that bought it might be doing it up for a son or daughter but then the signs went up again.

Then I had an idea. I would make this a little project.

The flat is a couple of hundred metres away. Nothing between it and the tower block but a garden, a pavement, a road, a wider pavement, green painted railings, a strip of grass that is part of the park, another green railing, tarmac car park and then up fourteen storeys to my window.

It could be a good place to watch. I was always disappointed with the previous tenants because the windows are in the perfect position, just the right angle for watching from up here. Great potential view into the two rooms at the front. The flat below gives me a view of a thin strip of carpet by the window and the flat above has a family with young children. I don't watch houses with children – one of the rules.

I arranged a viewing on my next day off. I didn't want to share the flat with anyone else so I went for a mid-afternoon viewing. As it turned out, another guy met me and the estate agent at the door – another developer wanting to give the place a new coat of paint, stick up a couple of prints and add another ten grand to the price. I went fully prepared – digital camera and little sonic measuring gizmo. I told the agent I was viewing the property for my sister who lived down south but wanted to come back home. I said that she made me promise to take some snaps so she could get a feel for the place. The estate agent believed me.

I went disguised. Dark contact lenses and thick NHS-style glasses, hair gelled into a centre parting with a darker rinse through it – geek chic.

As soon as we were through the door, the estate agent picked me as the first victim for the tour spiel. I nodded and feigned fascination just waiting for her to go and find the other guy. He knew what he was look-ing for and didn't stay long. I had the flat almost to myself. I hoped the agent would get a call and have to step out for a few minutes – then I could feel really comfortable – but all that happened was she kept her presence discreet.

Two rooms at the front of the house – living area and bedroom – bathroom, kitchen, smaller second bedroom on the other side.

I was able to take photographs and measurements of each room. Got a nice shot from each of the front room windows of my own windows. I spent another few minutes wandering around, soaking up the atmos-phere – getting a feel for the place and the type of people it would attract.

I told the estate agent that my sister would be very interested and promised I would e-mail the photographs tonight, confirmed my false address and left.

Over the next few weeks I recorded everyone that visited when I was at home – mostly young couples, just as I thought, but some around my age. Two guys together, could be gay, could be friends. Might have been interesting. I haven't watched a gay or lesbian couple before. If it turned out they were straight then the possibility of it being a fuck pad – spicy either way.

Now a few weeks later and people are moving in.

I've got my file in front of me. Couple six it is.

Look at my notes.

FIRST VIEWING

F. Early thirties. Blonde hair. Denims. Red shirt. Waterproof jacket. Around one metre seventy. Medium build. Thirty-six D, I think. Not plump but rounded. Pretty face.

M. Early thirties. Dark hair. Black trousers. Blue shirt. No tie but looks like he works in an office. Waterproof jacket. One metre seventy-five approx. Slight build.

They seem to like the flat.

Outdoor types? Waterproofs suggest this. Holding hands in both front rooms, stop at window look back into the room, her hand in his back pocket. Still in flush of love. New couple. First flat together.

SECOND VIEWING

F. Denims. Dark shirt. Smarter jacket.

M. Dark trousers. White shirt. Waterproof jacket.

Notice wedding ring on woman's hand this time. Nice married couple.

Definitely like the flat. Have notebook with them – writing down decorating ideas? Lots of smiles and nods. Quick snog in the lounge.

Now here they are helping the movers. Don't mind getting their hands dirty. Probably into DIY and doing adventurous things with their weekends. I think I'll like watching them.

I spend the day watching them, interspersed with music and television, creating a background hum, and breaks for tea and nibbles and trips to piss. It takes most of the day to move their belongings in and then rearrange boxes once the movers leave. The right-hand set of windows as I look is to be their bedroom. Plastic wrapped mattress against the wall. Long brown boxes containing the base for a bed. Pine, stencilled on the packaging. Left-hand set of windows will be their lounge.

They make no attempt to build the bed so I am not sure if they'll stay tonight.

When I come back from a comfort break the house is in darkness and they are at the main door on street level. They are fixing something beside the buzzer. It looks like a ceremony.

They stand back and admire their handiwork. They hug. They kiss. They leave.

I wait until it is dark and go across the road.

Will and Laura Burleigh.

Window 9A
Clara sits on her wide window ledge looking out at the night, cats asleep by her feet. She takes a sip of tea. Toes wriggle against the fur.

Window 3A
Dark. Malcolm out tonight.

Window 5
Bev and Ian. Snacks in front of Saturday-night programmes.

Window 16
Joe and Neil getting ready for a night of clubbing. Fix their hair in the lounge. Check each other out, nod approvingly. Some lucky ladies tonight. As always, they pull the curtains to stop me seeing any of the fun.

SUNDAY

I am up bright and early and at the window. It looks set to be a beautiful day – already warm and I can't see any clouds. Maybe today will be the one day of summer we get this year.

My plan is to spend a while at the window watching my lovely new neighbours – see if they are doing anything interesting, get a sense of what they plan to do with their room – then maybe go out in the afternoon and take some photographs. Need to get out and take some snaps – haven't done that for a few weeks, only taken some telephoto shots and I can't really put them on display. Got an itchy trigger finger from not taking new images. Tonight. Get my dark-room equipment set up and develop some of the shots from today.

Set a chair by the window and settle down with my cereal. Binoculars on a tripod so that I've got my hands free. Camera nearby just in case I want to run off a few shots.

They must be early birds, these two. They are already hard at work by the time I settle down. They didn't stay in the flat last night – stayed with friends or family or maybe they still have their old place. Mattress still wrapped in plastic in the bedroom.

They have already emptied the room that will be their lounge. It is the obvious room for it. When I was looking round at my viewing, I thought it would be the best room for that.

They are both in the lounge. Step ladders leaning against the wall. Large table in the centre of the room covered with sheets. On top, opened paint pots, assorted brushes, a couple of trays and a roller. Looks like peach-coloured paint for this room. That'll look nice.

Laura is wearing denim dungarees – they look faded, looks like they have been used for decorating before. A white cropped top underneath, showing off her midriff. Will is wearing a light green T-shirt and dark blue shorts. Laura and Will – perfect names.

They are chatting about something. I wish I could hear what they are saying. Lots of arm movements and nods. Talking about the decorating. They seem to agree on something and Will leaves the room. Laura turns to the table and picks up paint pot, pours some of the contents into a tray.

Quickly scan to see if I can see Will. He is in the other front room. Quick move of the binoculars to get a better view. He is just inside the room and is looking around. Looks like he is thinking about where to start. I have a feeling that he's going to empty this room so they can make a start on it too. Maybe they plan to start staying here from tonight. I'll find out soon.

Back to Laura. She's moved the ladders and set them up. Now she is picking up the tray and placing it on the floor. Now she has the roller. Can't see the floor behind the table but she is obviously getting paint on the roller. Now she is climbing the ladder.

The whole flat had been painted white when I visited. Blank canvas so anyone could just move in, unpack their belongs and start living there. Laura and Will obviously want to add their own touch. Nice.

Back to Will. He's wrestling with the mattress, trying to get it through the door. I was right – decorating this room too.

Back to Laura. Firm even motion with the roller – shouldn't take her too long.

Cereal is finished. Don't think much will change in the next few minutes so I go and make a pot of tea and choose some background music for watching. I pour my cuppa and head back to the window. Maybe take a few photos – document them moving in.

Laura has moved along the wall a bit, back up the ladders. She is wearing black plimsolls, no socks. Will is gathering boxes into the middle of the bedroom, dark sweat stains under his arms, dark patch forming between his shoulder blades.

Will is hot from his exertions. He's taken off his T-shirt. I take a couple of shots of him doing this. Quite trim, quite muscular but not in a 'fanatically-working-out' sort of a way. Looks like he keeps fit but doesn't overdo it – probably more to do with not eating too much junk. I touch my belly and decide to put down my bar of chocolate. I'll do some sit-ups later.

Laura has powered through the second coat in the lounge, just putting the finishing touches to the top of the wall with a paintbrush. Will appears at the door. He looks like he is hiding behind it. He takes a sneaky look round the door and then back again. He's smiling. He waits. Laura is part of the way down the ladder. She stops and wipes her forehead with her arm and gazes back up at her handiwork. Will sneaks from behind the door. He looks like he is tiptoeing. Must have material sheets on the floor, not plastic or newspaper. He is close to her. He puts arms out and then leans forward and bites Laura's bum. She turns quickly and his arms dive in to steady her and help her down. She playfully hits him on the shoulders. They are both laughing – so silent from the distance, through panes of glass.

I want to hear you.

Laura leans forward and they kiss. It's not just a peck – it is long and it is deep. I take a shot. Kissing gets more passionate. Shutter clicks and clicks. Laura runs her hands through Will's hair. He has his hands on her back. He slides them under her top. Her hands move down his bare back. He takes his hands and puts them on her shoulders. Shutter clicks. Heart beating fast, dry throat, swallowing. I'm trying to think objectively. Will takes the straps of Laura's dungarees off her shoulder. Still kissing. He moves back slightly and begins to pull the straps down more. I'm trying to think like a documentary maker but I can feel myself stirring. I'm not sure I can believe what I am seeing although the negatives will prove it later. This sort of thing rarely happens when you are watching. You'll get to see a bit of flesh if you watch a wide range of people for long enough – you might even get to see some kissing or petting if you are in the right place at the right time. But this is singular.

Camera moving millimetres up and down so that I can follow all their actions.

They look into each other's eyes. Laura's hands on his chest, now rubbing. Will bulges in his shorts. He pushes the dungarees over her hips – pink knickers. They move together again. Passionate kisses. He moves his mouth down her chin to her throat, she moves her head so that it is pointing upwards, presenting as much of her neck as possible, she's pushed her hands into his shorts, grasping and needing. I've struck gold. His mouth finds hers, his fingers under her top, pulls it over her head and throws it on the floor, her breasts press on his chest – 36D, I was right. He's kissing her mouth again – hand moves to her chest, thumbs her nipples.

Two exposures left until I hit thirty-six. I always put a bit more film in when I load the film rolls, probably get another couple shots before I need to change. Don't want to risk it. Shot of them kissing – her hands pulling on his buttocks, his hands on hers. Quick change. Auto rewind button, hand fumbling on the floor for new roll of film. Eye still on the viewfinder. Chests pressed together. Hurry the fuck up and rewind. She is pulling his shorts down as far as she can without leaving his mouth, now he's got his thumbs round the sides of her knickers and begins to pull them down, his shorts catch on his erection, she moves her hands to the front and their bodies part a little while their mouths and tongues touch, eyes closed, no need to look down to see what they are doing, she pulls his shorts forward and he eases himself back and out, she lets go and they drop to the ground, he presses his erection against her.

New film is winding to the first frame, finger trembling above the button. They are oblivious to the curtain-less windows. They feel secure that the nearest window facing them is a couple of hundred of metres away. They are not even thinking they might be seen. They are not playing to an audience. This is real. Shutter snaps again. This is immediate.

I hold another new roll in my other hand ready for another quick change.

He pulls her knickers down. They push their groins hard together. Feel moisture on my stomach. Dark hair between her legs, camera lens moves up, he kisses her breasts and she looks at the ceiling again, his tongue on her nipples, his hands squeeze her buttocks, her hand on his chest twisting at the flesh, the other on his penis pulling forwards pushing backwards, angle still perfect for photographs – more than I would have dreamed of. He moves down now, they are still behind the table, it obscures them from mid-thigh down, only see his shoulders and head, kissing between her legs, hand moving hair aside, she's got one hand on his head the other on her stomach, camera moves to her face, silent-mouthed moan, she moves down too, no, behind the table, can't happen now, not now, can still see their heads, moving together, tongues meeting, lips meeting, he's pushing forward, they disappear, fuck no, not now, not now. I take my head away from the camera and look out the window as if that would give me a better view. Can't see much from this distance. Back to the viewfinder – nothing. Nothing. Swivel the camera to end of the table, can see the floor, can see a heel, his heel, legs slide back to reveal whole right foot and ankle and lower calf, toes tight against the floor, sole at ninety degrees, shutter clicks anyway, plimsoll lying near the open door, his heel moves backwards and forwards. I want to close my eyes and imagine what he is doing between her legs but can't afford to miss anything. I can only see a foot, a foot. You bastards, taking this away from me. Fall apart, you fucking table, cease to exist. Foot disappears behind that censor of a table – now I can see nothing. Penetration. She comes into view again, facing the opposite direction to the one when she disappeared, she is kneeling, no crouching, she's moving upwards, breasts come into view, his hands on them, she seems to be adjusting something, looking down at what she is doing, moving both arms now. She slowly moves back down, he's inside her – her face upturned again, her mouth open. I can hear her gasp as she moves up and down, controlling each beat. Her brows move together and closed eyes clench on every downward motion, breasts judder every time her descent is stopped, click-click-click, eighteen, nineteen, twenty, nipples hard, hands cupping, his thumb on her mouth, she is licking, twenty-two, twenty-three, thumb on her nipple, her mouth opens and closes, twenty-five, twenty-six, she stops, she pulls herself up a little, now he appears, lips on lips, twenty-eight, twenty-nine, thirty, my knuckles white from gripping the next roll, he moves forward pushing her back down to the floor, fuck they've gone again, nothing this time, no feet, no hands, nothing, stopped at thirty-three, I change to a new roll anyway.

Still nothing.

Still nothing.

Still nothing.

One minute, five minutes, ten minutes.

Eighteen minutes. She stands up, back to the window. She picks her dungarees from the floor and leaves the room. Click-click-click. Long back, shapely bum – not too pert, not to flabby. Camera moves to bedroom – she's not there. Kitchen or bathroom? It must be bathroom. Three minutes later he stands up, stretches half-facing the window, penis limp, heads out of the room, tight dimpled bum. He doesn't appear in the bedroom either – bathroom too. Another go in the shower, on the bathroom rug, on the hall floor, carpets burns and chafing?

They don't return for a while. I'm annoyed that I can only see into the front two rooms. I'll miss so much of their lives, only experiencing these two rooms. I want more than that.

He comes back wearing fresh pants and retrieves his clothes. She is in the bedroom, dungarees back on. No top. Breasts clearly visible. Will joins her, puts her crop top on a box. He stands behind her and pulls her close to him, hands down her dungarees on her stomach. They are looking around the room, discussing what it will look like. They spend the next three hours getting the room together. Bed built. She puts sheets and pillows and a duvet on the bed, he puts a lamp on the bedside table he brings in.

Will disappears for a while and Laura potters around the flat doing bits and pieces. Will brings home a carry-out – looks like Chinese food – they eat and watch some TV. Will set it up before he went out. They stay in the flat tonight. At ten fifty-five, they go to bed. They have no curtains. The camera clicks as Laura puts on a nightie and gets under the duvet. It clicks as Will gets in the other side a few minutes later wearing pyjama bottoms.

Click – Laura leans over to Will. Click – long kiss goodnight. Click – she turns and goes down to sleep. Click – Will picks up a book, a biography of JFK. Click – he turns out the light at eleven twenty-eight.

I peer into the darkness of the bedroom for another half-hour. I can't really see anything now the light is off. But it is good to know they are there sleeping. If I think about it, I can hear their breathing. I'm tired but I'll finish developing the prints before I go to bed. Look at them as I hang them up to dry. Relive the day.

SLEEPERS

Alarm kicks me in the head with its drone. Five forty-five a.m. Shocked awake, I remember my dream. I'm in a house alone, I feel someone else is with me but I know I am alone. I look at my palm. There is a hole in it. Rough edges. A black ant climbs out. I look deeper into the hole. I can see my bones. They are grey with black spots.

It means nothing to me.

God I hate early mornings – this one especially difficult because I chose to get up at this time.

I should be happy about today.

I drag myself into a sitting position so that I don't drift off. Tiredness has set into my body. Need something powerful to shake it off.

I become aware of my head nodding to my chest. Five fifty-nine.

Pull myself to the edge of the bed. Make myself stand. Unsteady for the first few steps.

Bathroom. Lino cold under my feet. Fill the sink with cold water. Put my face into it and hold it there as I count to ten. Only make it to five before I've had enough. That's helped.

Kitchen. Kettle on. Mug out. Coffee will help. First cup of coffee of the day is the only one worth having. Caffeine levels drop over night so this first one is the one that gives you a kick.

Lounge. Settle at the window with lenses on Laura and Will's bedroom. Still quite dark outside but street lights throw some light into the room. Enough to see they are still sleeping. Good. Thought I might have missed it.

Sky looks cloudy. Not thick, heavy ones waiting for rain to be wrung out of them. Might be a chance of some patchy sunshine later.

Still no sign of stirring yet but it's getting lighter by the minute. I wonder at what point the brain registers light levels through closed eyes and begins to wake you up. I marvel that they can sleep without curtains. Extra thick ones are what I need. Even a hint of light and I know I couldn't sleep. Without curtains, I would be up at dawn every day. That would be strange. Rise at dawn, bed at dusk. Seems unnatural.

Will they get curtains? Have they just not got round to it yet? I hope they don't. This is such an experience – I don't want it to end.

Kettle switches itself off. I make sure they are still asleep before I go to the kitchen. I was going to make instant coffee for speed and for the bitter, wake-up jolt. Now I have a bit more time, I get some proper ground coffee from the fridge. I put some of it into a filter paper and pour on hot water. Watch it drip into my mug. Much more satisfying taste. Can feel it coaxing brain cells awake with the first sip.

Drop the mug off in the lounge. Check they are still sleeping and go to the bedroom. Dressing gown off the door. Slippers from under the bed.

Back to watch.

Will sleeps on the side nearest to the window. Duvet pulled up so that I can only see his hair. Laura faces the wall.

As it gets lighter, I alternate between binoculars and the camera so that I can take some shots.

They are beginning to move position more frequently. Wakefulness creeps up on them.

I feel privileged to be watching these moments. How often do you get the chance to watch people sleep, to share such intimate moments?

I feel their peace – their restfulness invades me, calms me.

In all the days and months and years I've been watching people, I have never seen someone go to bed and fall asleep – I have never watched someone wake up this way either. I've seen people nod off and wake up while watching the box but that is different. This is new. Virgin territory. New experiences like these keep me fresh. Keep me watching.

Will turns over to face the window, duvet now down at his chest. His eyes flicker open a few times and then shut tightly against the brightening light. He turns his head slightly from the window and rubs his eyes. After a moment or two, he sits up and leans his back against the headboard. He yawns. He stretches his arms. Eyes not fully opened yet but you can see he's becoming more alert every moment.

He looks out the window at the lightening sky. He looks at the travel alarm clock at the bedside. He looks back to the window. Eyes idly scanning the tower block. What is he thinking? Is the plan of his day taking shape in his mind? He looks directly into the lens. I involuntarily move back from the camera. He can see me, just an illusion created by the angle I'm watching from. But just for a moment it feels like he is looking at me.

I wonder what he would think if he knew I was watching.

Heisenberg's Uncertainty Principle – theory of quantum physics which suggests that, by observing something, you influence its behaviour. Obviously the theory describes subatomic particles but I wonder if it applies in this situation? Does watching change the subject? Surely Will would have to know I was watching for his behaviour to change? Watching from this distance, unobserved, changes nothing.

Laura moves closer to Will and puts her head on him. Her hand comes up and strokes his chest. She moves up and gives him a long sleepy kiss on the cheek. He gives her an equally long kiss on the head and then they find each other's mouths.

Laura sits up and rubs the sleep from her eyes. She gets up – nightie crumpled. She leaves the room.

Will watches her go and then reaches for his book. He reads it until she comes back. He gets up – his time in the bathroom now. He stands on his tiptoes and stretches. He is wearing light-blue pyjama bottoms.

Laura walks over to a chest of drawers and pulls her nightie over her head and drops it on the bed. She opens the top drawer and looks in. Naked. Click-click. White knickers pulled on. Bends to put them over her feet. White bra selected and put on the bed for later. She goes to the door, unhooks a dressing gown and pulls it on. She walks out.

The bedroom is empty.

Move lens to the lounge.

It is empty.

Switch between rooms, waiting for some activity.

I wish my view wasn't so restricted. I really need to see into every room.

Laura appears in the lounge with a bowl of cereal and a mug. She sits and switches the TV on from the remote. She munches her muesli while watching the news.

Will enters the bedroom. Towel wrapped round his waist. He takes something from the side of the room I can't see and sits on the edge of the bed. He moisturises his face and neck. Puts more of the cream on his hands and applies it to his elbows and then his feet.

Laura has left the lounge.

Will stands. He dries the remaining damp patches and drops the towel to the bed. He walks naked to the wall I can't see. I think he must have drawers there. Takes a half-step back that brings his bum and back into view. He bends down and puts pants on. Still standing, he pulls on socks.

Disappears completely.

When I see him again he is buttoning a white shirt.

Laura comes into the bedroom. Hangs up dressing gown.

Will hugs her.

Will pulls on dark trousers.

Laura retrieves her bra.

Laura turns to the mirror in the corner and adjusts her breasts until they feel comfortable.

Will leaves the room.

Laura dresses in a mauve blouse and dark trousers.

Will is in the lounge with cereal.

Laura shouts something to Will and he responds.

Laura stands in front of the mirror and brushes her hair.

Will finishes his breakfast and leaves the lounge.

Laura is not in the bedroom.

Both rooms stay empty.

A few minutes later, they appear at the ground-floor door. They walk to their car. They drive away.

I remove the roll from my camera and put it with the other one from this morning.

I'll develop them tonight – add the images to Laura and Will's album.

Time for me to get ready for work.

Unwatched.

Waiting for Will and Laura to come home.

They are late tonight.

Might be shopping. Or out for dinner. Or seeing a movie.

Rooms are dark.

Have to keep watching.

When they first get in is always a good time to watch.

Have to keep watching.

Don't want to miss anything.

I'll set up a video camera tomorrow.

Will and Laura in bedroom.

Covered with duvet.

Streetlights throw yellow glow into the room.

Tops of heads appear and disappear.

Duvet moves up and down.

Finish.

Lie hugging.

Fall asleep.

Laura passed the window a few minutes ago, towel wrapped around her.

Waiting for her to come back into the picture.

Got to see what she is doing.

Got to see her doing anything.
Staring hard at the window.
Concentration.
Everything round the window disappears.
Pane of glass and what lies beyond become the world.
Head spins from the single-minded intensity of my stare.
She appears.
She's dressed.
She goes out for the day.

Window 3A
Malcolm working on his abs tonight. Three sets of fifty crunches. Three sets of cross-knee crunches.

Window 16
Joe and Neil having a meal – at the table for once.

Window 34
B&B.
    Man sits on bed, laptop beside him. Checking mail. Playing a game.

LOSS

Will and Laura have curtains.
    I watched them put them up, a churning feeling in my guts.
    They started with the lounge ones – red.
    I cursed them. I hated them. I shouted at them. But they still hung the curtains.
    I hoped that they were thinking only of complementing the colour scheme of the room with bold drapes.
    I prayed that they wouldn't move to the bedroom.
    Why would they put them in the bedroom?
    They like sleeping without them.
    I watched as Will took the ladders through and set them beside the window.
    I watched as Laura arrived with blue material.
    I watched as he hung and she passed.
    I watched as they stood back to admire their work.
    Curtains.
    Why would they put curtains up now?
    Why are they punishing me?

Maybe the curtains are decorative. They won't be closed at night – just there so the room doesn't have bare windows.

I waited all day to see what would happen.

At night, they closed me out – destroyed my pleasure.

We are separate again.

Individuals.

There is nothing good in the world any more.

Melodramatic – but it is how I feel.

I've got to know them so well over the last week. Gone deeper than I ever have before.

I liked it. I liked sharing intimacy with them, being with them when they slept and hugged, ate and loved.

It won't be like that any more.

Back to watching others again.

Window to window.

I might get a chance to see Will and Laura on summer evenings before the curtains close. Or during the day at weekends.

Crumbs.

Teases.

I can't say I won't shed a tear over this.

I can't say I won't miss them.

BORED

I've been at the window for an hour and I've seen nothing of interest. I start my rounds again, binoculars to my eyes, window to window.

Nothing.

Nothing.

Nothing.

Nothing.

Nothing.

Nothing.

Maybe I should look at some photographs. Scan and file.

Don't feel in the mood.

Hate nights like this. That 'loose-end' feeling that takes the joy out of watching or movies or reading or music.

I should do something – break the cycle. Jolt myself into a new frame of mind.

Not sure if I can be bothered though.

Got an idea.

Makes me chuckle.

Need to use the clone phone for it.

Pick the right flat for the job. Nice residential flats a few streets away. Lots of lovely windows.

Get the camera ready.

Make the call.

Telephoto fun.

There it is. Just took six minutes. Blue lights flashing, sirens blaring. It stops outside. Burly firemen get out.

Here they come.

Curtain twitchers.

People eager to see what is happening in the street. Curtains pulled back. People bleary eyed from being ripped out of sleep.

Click. Click. Shutter snaps.

Nice fast film for night shots. Red glow from yellow street lights. Lots of heavy grain in the prints. Atmospheric.

Pyjamas, boxer shorts, nighties, couple of people obviously sleep in the nude, hiding behind curtains or hastily-thrown-on dressing gowns.

Firemen decide it is a false alarm. Probably think it is some naughty children making the calls. Very bad to do that. Waste of valuable resources.

Got some good shots.

I've made my own fun tonight.

Boredom banished.

Window 10

Thomas sits in his chair. He has a cup of tea on a saucer beside him, matching plate with a couple of biscuits. He picks one up and bites it. Crumbs fall on to his brown cardigan. He doesn't notice. He takes a sip of tea. He finishes the biscuit. He finishes his tea. He takes up a newspaper then puts it down again. He looks at something out of my view. Chest shudders with a silent sigh. He stares.

AUTHENTICITY

I'm actually doing this.

It's giving me a better appreciation of Henri's first hesitant steps.

I drive past first to take a look.

Meat on the rack.

I'm looking for one that inspires me.

I don't want to be rude but some of them scare me.

Heavy make-up hiding the worst ravages of time in an unkind life. Clothes too tight for swollen bodies, flesh cut by seams. Mutton dressed as mutton.

I suppose I can take some comfort that I'm not the target audience.

If I was fifty and lonely and desperate, I would probably think they were exotic beauties, schooled in the secret arts of love.

I wonder who they are. I wonder if they are housewives sent out by husbands or lone parents who've fallen through welfare cracks. I wonder if they are junkies and drunks earning money for their next score.

Maybe I'm wrong. Maybe they are all Julia Roberts waiting for Richard Gere to take them away from all this – just good girls fallen on hard times.

I don't kiss on the lips.

I feel sick as I get closer.

Bet this is the night for a police bust. I just know it.

Honest, guys, I only wanted to take her picture.

What the hell am I doing? There must be an easier way to do this. There are websites where you can find models ready to pose in the nude. No shortage of willing girls. So why am I soliciting a complete stranger?

Authenticity.

I park and walk back to the street.

I wonder if there's a hierarchy here – if the ones under the bridge in the damp and the dark are the cheapest because you can't really see what you're getting?

Trade. Selling of goods. Commerce. The oldest transaction.

Do they have a verbal menu for you to choose from? *Today's special. Three for two. Buy one get one free.*

A guy ahead of me – wearing an overcoat, collar pulled up. I watch him approach the girls, each one with her own patch. I feel a surge of annoyance as I think he is going for the one I think will be best for me. He walks past her. Looks around nervously. Picks a different girl.

Transaction.

I feel dirty.

I don't want to be here.

Be brave.

I watch from across the street. I am Henri. I know that she can see me. Does she think I am shy? Does she think it is my first time? Will she come to my flat tomorrow and pose for me?

I close my eyes and picture crossing to her.

Can I help you, honey?

Err . . .

I would sound like a hundred other stuttering guys.

It's all right – just take your time. You're in charge here.

Very nice. Words designed to put me at ease, give me control.

She would smile at me. A friendly smile. Nothing threatening. Nothing cheesy.

Then she would speak. *Hey, gorgeous, do you want some fun?*

You are such a big boy – biggest I've ever seen.

You're the daddy.

No – that's not what she'd say. She would be subtle, alluring. She'd tease me with whispers and promises.

Then I'd say. *I was wondering if you would like a . . . a coffee? I've got, um, a proposition to, um, put to you. I know your, eh, time is valuable so I'll pay you for a ten minute chat . . . There's a café a couple of streets away.*

That sounds terrible – far too much info.

She'd think about it for a moment, wonder if I am some lonely Joe too nervous for action.

Thirty pounds.

I'd agree.

Upfront.

I'd agree and reach for my wallet.

Give it to me as we walk.

We'd walk in silence. I'd slip her three notes.

Greasy-spoon café. We'd take a table by the wall.

I'd ask her to pose for me.

Mucky pictures?

Oh, no. Photography. Art.

She'd sneer at the word. *Art? Me flashing my tits and fingering my fanny is art?*

Fuck.

That is exactly what she'd say.

This just isn't going to work.

I can't do it.

It wouldn't be like Henri's approach to Hélène.

This drab would just laugh and sneer and take the piss.

She is looking at me. Looking at another trick.

She smiles at me.

Can't do it.

I feel sick.

I go home.

WATCHING THE WORLD

Home from a long day at work.

Asked to help out in the pharmacy section. Dozens of people handing their prints over to Euan on the other side of the shop floor.

Giving them blank looks, he put them into envelopes and passed them through to be developed. Should have been him on the tills in the pharmacy, selling eczema creams and condoms and thrush pessaries.

I'm the photo expert.

I shouldn't be doing menial stuff in another department.

Don't know if I was being punished for something. Anne has her little prejudices. She can turn on a whim. Likes to let you know who wields the power on the floor. Typical small-minded bully.

I'm trying not to think about the photo gems I might have missed today. I used to worry about things like that on the days I wasn't in the store. The perfect set of photographs finally arriving and me not being there to copy them. Managed to resign myself to the fact that I couldn't do anything about it. Still, days when I'm working but kept from seeing prints make the 'might have missed something' ache even keener.

I'm distracted by yesterday's failure.

Bad move to try what Henri did. It is a different time now. That sort of stuff is just sordid these days.

Don't know how I'm going to do it.

Need some inspiration.

Need a plan.

Have a quick shower and dress. Heat some leftovers from my meal last night.

I take the tape from the video camera at my window and stick it into the video machine. Wait impatiently as it rewinds through eight hours of activity.

I sit in front of the screen with a plate on my lap and watch. Need to see the comings and goings from my window while I've been out. Might have missed something profound.

Lean on fast forward when there is no one in shot.

Need to have details.

I see the caretaker on his rounds.

I see Creeping Jesus skulking with his dog.

I watch the toing and froing of the postman, of students, of mothers with prams, of the kids bunking off school.

I started recording the world from my window last week. It has become my ritual while I eat.

Got to see everything.

Got to gather information.

Got to keep on top of things.

Hélène lives with Henri.
  They plan to marry.
  Henri has moved out of his studio and has a riverside home.

Henri has a reasonable income from his photographs. Hélène has become a much sought-after model.

Henri does not tell her that he has been asked to let her pose for other photographers. He has not told her she would be paid for her work.

Henri does not want to give up his muse.

Hélène is happy to be away from the streets.

She does not miss it.

She does not speak to the women she stood with in the rain or in the sunshine or in the moonlight. It is not that she hates them. She does not want to be reminded of those times.

She likes living with Henri.

She likes being respectable.

She likes that she can sleep in the morning. Pose in the afternoon when the light is right. Make love with Henri in the evening. Pretend she has breeding and culture in the Parisian night.

Most people think that Henri is an artist and Hélène is his muse.

Henri returns home one afternoon. He seems excited. Hélène believes that he has been given a good price for his new images. For those they have posed together. European tastes have changed. The naughty images of women posed simply do not satisfy any more. Women with women, men with women are the fashion now.

Hélène was surprised at first when Henri suggested they pose together. Henri always kept his face hidden. He told her that fashions may have changed but she would always be the star.

Hélène waits for him to tell her his news. She is happy she will be able to buy a new dress and new shoes.

Henri tells her to pack.

Henri tells her they will be leaving Paris.

Henri tells her they are going to America.

He will be a proper artist there.

Hélène will be a real lady there.

Hélène does not mind.

Hélène is not shocked by the thought of leaving her home.

Hélène wants to leave Paris.

Hélène wants to leave the life she lived behind.

Hélène never again wants to think of the cold streets, the money pressed into her palm as she hitched her skirt.

Hélène knows she will be free.

Window 10

Thomas sits in his chair. He is wearing his reading glasses. He needs them when he does the crossword. Boxes, clues too small. He worries about his eyesight. He worries about going blind. He knows he won't be able to cope. He is, as always, smart. But he'll have no visitors. I have not seen him with friends. I have not seen him with family. He is alone. A lonely old man left to wither.

FIRST WINDOW

I have to testify.

I'll tell you about an experience I had many years ago.

You'll nod your head and rub your chin and say, A*h, now I understand.* But you'd be wrong. Put away your Freud and don't open it again.

It happened when I was entering my teens. It happened at the perfect time. A little earlier and my hormonally barren body would have shrugged it off with little thought – a little later and my testosterone-filled frame would have used it as a wanking fantasy for years to come. But, between these two eras, between boy and man, was the perfect moment.

She was beauty. Nude. Curves and form.

You are disappointed. *Is that all? Just seeing a naked woman?* Of course this wasn't the first naked body I'd seen. There had been plenty in books and magazines, in films and in gym showers at school. They were different. I was removed from them in a sense. They were upfront and obvious and perfunctory.

This was thrilling and new and secret.

I was the only witness.

A private moment between the watcher and the watched.

Real.

Tangible.

I was in the back garden one summer evening, just as the light was beginning to fade and the bats were beginning to hunt. The air was still and warm. The world was peaceful.

I threw my ball up and, as I caught it, my eyes shifted focus to the top-floor window of the house that backed on to our garden. Something drew my attention. Before I saw what it was, I knew something significant was about to happen.

There she was. Standing by the window. Exposed.

She was brushing her long black hair. She was looking into a mirror.

She didn't know I was there. In the twilight. Watching

The brush moved, slowly, abstractedly. She was lost in thought. Just brushing and looking at her reflection.

It did not strike me that she was being vain. She was not admiring – only seeing, accepting.

I became complicit in her thoughts.

Some part of me said *forbidden* and made me move behind the big tree.

The view was better.

Those flowing lines.

I was transfixed.

Revealed.

Unveiled.

Her breasts.

Her flat stomach.

Her belly button.

Triangle of hair.

I didn't know what to think about that.

Although there was distance between us I could feel the touch of her skin, the moles on her chest, the curl of hair.

She became beauty.

Personification of perfection.

I was breathless.

I felt the heat of blood in my face, the roar it made in my ears.

But there were no sexual stirrings, no sudden spurt into manhood.

Time lost meaning.

I passed a lifetime as I stood being taught the meaning of beauty.

It was dark when I moved from the tree and she was long gone by then.

Rain, wind, cold, warmth – I braved them all every night for months to see her again at the window.

That was the only time I saw her there.

BEING WITH SARAH

Lunchtime again. I am living for lunch breaks with Sarah these days.

I know I shouldn't do this today. I should put it off until later in the week. Friday. Yes, do it on Friday and that will set me up for the weekend. Even better, do it on Monday, then I can think about it all next week. Start the week with something good. I'm off on Saturday and Sunday, so two days to plan it. Let the anticipation build.

Spend all morning trying not to think about it. Trying to be strong. Just so tempting.

You either have to resist these thoughts or serve them. I'll resist. I'm strong. I can do that. I am master of my desires and impulses. The rational brain rules the passionate heart. Put my mind to it, then nothing is impossible.

Who am I kidding? I know I'll do it today no matter how much time I spend pretending that I won't. I knew from the moment I woke this morning, when the idea first came into my head, that I would fail miserably if I tried to put it off for even one day. No place to hide once an idea like this grips you. Have to act on it or be in torment until you do.

Failed again.

Passion wins out.

So I'm going to see Sarah at lunchtime.

It doesn't matter that I've spent days looking at her last set of photographs, updating my notes, examining every detail.

I'm an addict that says in a blasé way that I can quit anytime.

I am a liar. I know that I can't stop, that I want everything now and now and now. Forget prolonging the pleasure, forget teasing myself with expectation, forget 'absence makes the heart grow stronger' – I want my cake and to eat it too.

I played around with the lunch rota when I got into work this morning to make sure I'll get away for the twelve-noon lunch. Proof, if you needed it, that I already knew I would give in to my desire. I'd halfheartedly tried to fool myself saying that, if I took care of lunch breaks, that would give me the option to see her or not. I could leave it until the last minute to decide, not feel pressured, just go with what felt right.

I'll have to slip away a few minutes early to make sure I reach her office before her lunch break starts but that isn't a worry. I'm allowed to be a bit more flexible with my breaks. All the unpaid overtime that I do and don't take back gives me more privileges than my work-shy, unpunctual colleagues.

It is always a gamble going to her office. I can never be sure if she will go out at lunchtime or not. I'm risking a night of gloom if I don't catch a glimpse of her. I'm gambling that, being almost fresh back from holiday, she won't want to stay in an office over lunch on a nice day. She won't be dulled yet by drudgery and routine.

Visiting her will take up most of my lunch hour but I don't mind. I get a tea break this afternoon and I can grab some chocolate or pretend health with a muesli bar on my way back to the shop.

Of course, I know where she works – I found out months ago.

I had her name of course. You have to give a name when you leave your negatives and most people use their real ones. Name – but nothing else. We used to ask for more details when people dropped off their snaps – names and addresses. An implicit threat that we would stop at nothing to track you down and make you collect your snaps. But no more. The shop just isn't that interested any more. Got all the targeted data it wants with loyalty cards, doesn't need addresses on people just after prints, would need to have us get permission to use that sort of information for promotions and stuff. So now all we ask for is a name.

It would make my life so much easier if we still did it the old way. But perhaps, if it was that easy, then the challenge of discovering things for myself would be lost.

Phone books usually help with the problem of getting more information. Occasionally a customer will just give an initial and that means having to go on a 'stake-out' if there are a few people with the same initial and surname in the book. Sitting in my car waiting for a familiar face to appear, then I have your address.

If you are ex-directory that doesn't scare me off. I'd just track you to where you work and then follow you home from there.

Sarah gave her full name. She was in the phone book. Home address found.

Having a home address is a good thing. I try to match it to the areas I can see from my window or the roof. Unfortunately, I can't see her road from my vantage points – wrong part of the city. Quite disappointing. It would be wonderful if I could look into every aspect of her life. One day I'll have that.

In cases where window watching isn't an option, it is much better to know where you work. Much easier hide in a crowd in the middle of the day and watch than skulk around outside your home at night. If I did that regularly, I think I would be entering a whole different world. Seedy. Perverted. Not for me. No, I'll stick to watching from afar – as much as I can.

So I had her name. I had her home address. Now to find where she worked. Only way was to use legwork. I planned that, the next time she dropped off some snaps, I would follow her. Timing would be everything. I could easily be caught at the tills or with an epic customer question and then I'd lose her by the time I got outside.

Every second would count.

I had to wait for a couple of weeks. Every day on tenterhooks just in case she appeared and I would have to spring into action. It is exhausting just waiting for something like that to happen.

Then she brought in a new set of snaps. I let Euan serve her. Much as I wanted to be the one she spoke to, the rewards I would get from forgoing that sweet pleasure would be greater. The moment I saw her I went to the duty manager of the day, Jackie. I told her I had been really silly and had forgotten an appointment I had with my bank. I said that the previous meeting had been cancelled and I didn't want to miss this one too. I used my *You'd be doing me a really big favour* tone, flashed big Bambi eyes and humbly waited for her permission, making her feel that she actually had some say in the matter. Jackie smiled and said, *That's no problem. Hope you get it sorted out.* So easy to sucker them.

There was no way that I could have left my jacket in a cupboard on the shop floor. That sort of thing is frowned upon. I could go out just like I was but thought I would be too recognisable. So a dash up to the staffroom. Grabbed jacket. Thundered back downstairs.

Tried basement first. She might still be there. Euan with another customer. Quick scan of the shop floor. Fuck. No sign of her. If she's gone out, I could lose her in the shopping centre. Run to the main entrance. Whizz past the make-up harpies, the too sparky security guard. Out into the shopping centre.

Can you see her? Can you see her?

It must have looked pretty odd. Me bounding out of the shop then suddenly stopping dead in my tracks, trying to look nonchalant. She was just a few metres away looking in the window of the next shop.

I noticed I was getting some odd glances. Oh, very inconspicuous.

I moved to the other side of the walkway as if I had a lofty purpose, hoping that the people that saw my performance were many steps away by now – my strangeness lost to the goldfish memory of shoppers.

Quick glance at her to see if she noticed me. No, I'm fine. Good. Still in the game.

If you have ever followed anyone, you will appreciate how difficult it is. I'm not talking about the movie way that most people are familiar with. The person you're following feels something is not quite right and glances round. The person tailing has just enough time to leap into a doorway, pull their newspaper up to hide their face, become fascinated by a shop window. That sort of behaviour would be a give-away.

The truth of it is that most people wouldn't dream that someone was following them. Have you ever thought that some sinister stranger was following you? In a busy shopping mall? If so, you're paranoid. No one thinks that they have to glance behind themselves, every few paces, just to be sure they are not being followed. Even in these sweet times of celebrity stalkers, kidnappers and serial killers, people don't think that they could possibly be the victim, the object of some loony obsession.

You need to force yourself to think that way. You need to have a reason.

Maybe you should think about it more. It is a well-established fact, discovered through serial-offender profiling, that these people have something approaching a sixth sense for spotting likely victims. It might be the way you walk or hold your shoulders. It might be the expression on your face when you think no one is looking. It might be the way you sip your coffee or tug at your ear. But there'll be something you do, some signal you send that says, *Pick me – I'm weak, I won't struggle, I absolve you from your actions.*

So be vigilant. Be confident. Walk with purpose. Show no weakness. Assume everyone is out to get you.

It is difficult to follow someone for very practical reasons. You need to be careful with your speed. You must match it closely with the person you are following. People out on lunch breaks tend to be quite erratic. Quick bursts of speed and sudden stops. Too many places to go in a short space of time. Much resolute marching from shop to shop until something interesting catches the eye. Then it is abrupt stops and the risk of bumping into them or having to walk on by. The good thing is that the determined, 'only got a short time' shopper will be even more oblivious to what is going on around them. But you must keep on your toes – it is so easy to misjudge what they are going to do and miss your opportunity.

You also can't let them get too far ahead in a place like a shopping mall – certainly not if it is busy. It is easy to lose someone in the sea of bodies, miss that quick change of direction as they remember something else to buy. Distance has its place but not in these circumstances. Shopping malls can usually help you out though. They often have upper levels. Makes it so much easier if you are following someone below you and you can watch from above without being seen. If people don't think to look behind them, then they wouldn't even comprehend looking up.

The biggest problem you'll face following someone is psychological – more to do with you than the person you're surveilling. The more you follow that person, the more you'll feel that you stand out. Watcher becomes the watched. You'll begin to think that you are being obvious and everyone round about will notice you, realise what you are up to, raise the alarm. You'll begin to imagine that people are looking at you closely, memorising your description, ready for the police line-up. You think you see mobile phones being pulled out, think you overhear calls to the police. But it is only your imagination. You need to master these fears, channel them into something positive, something powerful. The truth of the matter is that, unless you do something really stupid that attracts attention, the shopping zombies will sail right past you without a second thought. They are consumed with thoughts about that new shirt, that new dress, those trainers, that DVD, so why would they waste a moment on some stranger passing by?

Clearly there are things that you'll do that could actually attract unwanted attention. Don't stare fixedly at the person you're following. That is a bit of an 'I'm a stalker' signal. You need to make yourself ordinary, casual, part of the herd. Look in some shop windows, look at your watch now and again, eat a sandwich – anything that makes you look like a bloke out on his lunch break.

Maybe you could try smiling – stalkers tend to be intense, po-faced people. Scowl says 'up to no good', smile says 'trust me, I'm just like you'. Well, maybe a big cheesy smile would look a bit odd – maybe that is just the sort of thing that would attract a lot of attention. *Is that the police? There is a man out shopping and he's smiling. He's obviously some kind of lunatic.* No, maybe excessive smiling would be too much in a city. So keep your face neutral, banish hints of emotion – then you'll fit in.

All this is good advice if you're in a street or shopping mall. But beware – everything changes when you are in a shop. Distance becomes a big problem. Your subject might spend ages standing looking at one thing. Then wander off to look at something else before coming right back to the same spot, picking up the item of clothing and spending another five minutes thinking, *Should I or shouldn't I?* Not so good for you because you're either rooted in one place or having to make the pretence of being interested in something yourself. Such pretending can put you on the radar of shop assistants.

Customer service can be put into two camps. Well, of course, there is a whole range but they are just variations on the two basic types. Firstly, you have the 'couldn't care less about you' members of staff, the ones that are actually bothered when customers interrupt them with stupid questions. They are the perfect ones. They'll do everything they can to completely ignore what you are doing, just in case they have to help you. Then there are the dangerous ones – the vigilant ones waiting to pounce. Eyes constantly scanning the shop floor, interrogating every gesture that potentially says, *I could use a little help.* Then they've got you – they're in for the kill, smothering you with customer service. It is that breed that will notice you acting suspiciously.

Then you have store security. You will naturally be quite apprehensive following someone into a shop. You'll probably have to wander around in an erratic fashion, suddenly breaking off to look intently at something, with occasional glances here and there making sure that no one has spotted you. You won't be surprised to learn that your efforts make you look like a shoplifter. Suddenly you'll be the one being followed. You'll make a hasty retreat while your description is radioed from shop to shop. Forget the imagined paranoia – eyes will be on you now and you won't be able to show your face in those shops for ages for fear of being stopped.

Occasionally you do get the odd break. Changing rooms. Groups of displaced men milling around waiting for their loved ones to appear modelling that new trouser suit. It is easy to pretend you are there for the same reason. Just adopt a slightly bored and irritated expression, tut, sigh, look at your watch as if that will hurry things along. You can even share some brotherly camaraderie by nodding knowingly at the other waiting blokes. As your subject moves off into another section of the store, you can gradually move further away from the changing area looking vacantly at items as you go. Shop staff will completely ignore you if they think you are a slightly pissed-off husband.

Word of warning – if you do brave surveillance in a shop, take extreme care if you end up in the lingerie department. Whatever you do, don't pretend you are shopping for a present for your partner. It might appear to be the perfect cover but I can assure you that you'll spend fifteen minutes with a shop assistant answering all sorts of questions about cup sizes and favourite colours. You'll leave that shop, having missed the person you were tailing, with £50 worth of impractical novelty lingerie for your imaginary girlfriend because you didn't want to appear cheap. But, then again, you might find that exciting – a new world of possibilities might open up as you get back to your lonely flat and try the goodies on.

The best recommendation that I can give is that, if your subject goes into a store, find the most likely exit they'll take, go to it and wait. It may mean losing them but you'll be safe from harm.

Fortunately, Sarah was in a hurry the day I found out where she worked – all of her shopping done in the centre. The good thing about the centre is that most shops only have one entrance so I was able to hang around outside and wait for her.

I needed to hang back – she wasn't some stranger that I was following. She would recognise me from the shop. I didn't flatter myself that she would have found me memorable but I had made some small talk each time I served her and things like that tend to stick in the mind. A chance meeting outside a shop would be a happy coincidence – I work here after all so it wouldn't be that strange. She would smile and I would smile, then we'd go our different ways. If she saw me again, that would look a little odd but I could cover that with a *You're everywhere I go today.* After that second encounter, I would be forced to give up – it would look really bad if she saw me again. She'd be thinking I was some sort of weirdo and she would never again bring her photographs right to me.

That is the golden rule – if you think you have been spotted, you must give up. YOU MUST GIVE UP. You will ruin everything. You need to put a hold on any activity for at least a couple of weeks. Then slowly build up again, making sure you don't compromise yourself.

I didn't want to take any chances that day. It was too important to have to delay until the next time she came into the store. Didn't think I could manage to keep a lid on the level of tension I was feeling.

She left the shopping centre with a purposeful stride that suggested she was heading straight back to work. Only quarter to one – that meant that she had either a reasonable way to walk or that she wanted a few minutes of peace before the afternoon started.

Amended rules for following someone outside. Out in the world people aren't bunched as tightly together – well, perhaps in the city centre at weekends they are but weekdays aren't as bad. Don't bother in a busy street on a Saturday afternoon unless you like difficult challenges and heaps of frustration. The walking masses dictate the path you can take and you're bound to lose sight of your subject as they realise they've forgotten something and double back to the shop they've just visited.

Out on the streets, you still have to pay attention to your distance. Again, not too close in case you are spotted and not so far that you're not sure what door they end up going into. However, outside, following does mean that you can hang back a little more than usual and that people pay even less attention to what you are doing. No need to show off your acting skills with the props that make you look ordinary.

I usually prefer to walk on the opposite side of the street – gives better sight lines and it is more difficult to be noticed.

It took about nine minutes to get to her office on the other side of the city centre and a little way from the busy main roads. Quite a nice walk.

Large stand-alone building, eight storeys high – type of building that is home to a number of different companies. Bit more investigation needed to find the one she works for. I would have to hang around for a bit. I don't mind the extra work. If it was easy, then it wouldn't be so enjoyable.

I stopped opposite her building and pulled out my mobile phone. Pretended I was taking a call. Mobile phones. The perfect cover for something like this. People use phones all the time, nobody pays attention, just another guy arranging to meet his girlfriend or talking over that memo. I can spend a few minutes pretending to talk and can switch to pretending to text if I get bored.

I watched her stop by a group of people in the foyer waiting for the lift. She's fit so I assumed that she didn't work on the first couple of floors. Some people seem to have an aversion to going up one flight of stairs but not her. I'm sure of that.

Ideally, I'd wait for her to get into the lift then head into the foyer and take a note of all the stops it made. The lift would be full so there'd probably be a few stops but it might help me narrow things down. Unfortunately the building has a commissionaire so I didn't risk hanging about inside. Too many possible questions and I didn't feel up to bluffing my way through it.

Lift doors opened. She got in.

Needed to get a better position. No chance of her seeing me so I risked getting closer. Stopped by the main entrance and glanced at my watch. Looked up and down the street as if I was looking for someone.

Being closer made me feel like I was up to the task of going inside, telling the commissionaire that I was meeting someone for lunch or that I had an appointment. But then what would I have done? Stopped off at every floor to see if I could spot her? Stupid idea. Too close. Too much exposure.

Instead, I smoothly put my phone away and replaced it with my Dictaphone, moved for a better view of the ground floor and pretended I was speaking into my phone again. Took a note of every company listed – it would just be a case of getting the company names from the phone book. I continued the pretence for a few moments longer, looked at my watch again, final look up and down the street as if I'd been stood up, then headed back to work with a bound in my step.

Seven phone calls in and I got a *Hold on – I'll put you through*, when I asked to speak to Sarah. I was a bit naughty and waited until she answered. *Hello, Sarah speaking, how can I help you?* I put the phone down. That is how I found out where she worked

Today I'm back at her office when I should be denying myself the pleasure of a glimpse.

I know I shouldn't do this today. I should put it off until later in the week. Friday.

No sign of her yet – hope I've arrived before she's left. Had to run all the way just to make sure. Just a matter of waiting now – see if luck is on my side today.

No way of knowing if she'll come out or not. What if she has broken with tradition and taken an extra early lunch? Could have missed her by ten minutes – could have missed her by one.

Doubts.

Maybe she did bring some sandwiches. Maybe a work colleague is getting her something. Maybe she grabbed a tin of soup as she rushed out the door this morning. Maybe she has brought leftovers from dinner last night. Maybe she has been asked to finish something important and has to stay in over lunch.

Please come out. Please come out.

Hope she wants to stretch her legs for a while. Come out for a change of scene. Might want to buy something new to cheer herself up. Might want to meet someone. Might go to the gym.

Wouldn't be so good if she went to the gym. On the odd lunchtime, she goes for a swim or a workout at a health club. She likes to swim at least once a week. She often meets the others at a sports centre on a Thursday. I've been there too. Sat in the café watching them swim. Followed them to their local afterwards. Sat outside and watched.

If she goes to the gym today, I'll only have her for a few minutes. Can't go in. Women only. Would mean I was too close anyway. Might panic if I bumped into her.

Please go for a walk today. Wander about some shops. Give me a full hour of fun.

I try to be philosophical about it. If I see her, great – even if it is just for a few minutes. If she doesn't come out, then I've got photo sorting tonight and I'll try again tomorrow. No. Don't want this to become some sort of lunchtime ritual.

If I don't see her today, then I'll wait until next week. I can wait that long, surely? I'll distract myself over the weekend at my window. Weekends are good for watching the city. Lots of people out and about, lots of people having special nights in. Maybe I'll pop to the roof and 'watch the stars'. Gibbous moon on Sunday.

I take out my mobile phone and become inconspicuous.

I try not to stand in the same place – don't want to be a regular at this street corner. People mostly ignore me but, if I'm here often enough, then recognition will spark in people's brains.

Sometimes I wait in a side street a little distance away. She has to pass it if she takes the most direct route to the city centre.

Always got to be thinking and planning. Think about every option, every outcome. Always ten steps ahead. Anticipating all the possibilities, a plan for each one.

People start to come out of her building. The commissionaire nods and smiles at some of them, makes small talk.

No sign of her yet. Lift should be back on the ground floor soon. There it is. Doors open. Some faces familiar from all the times I've been here.

There she is.

Heart thumps.

Wearing blue trousers, black jacket. Checks her watch at the door then heads towards the city centre quickly.

What does that mean? She's clearly hurrying somewhere. Maybe just desperate to get to some shops. Maybe she is going for a swim after all.

What are you up to today? What adventure is ahead for us?

I wait for a few moments before following her. No need to be so close. Stay on this side of the street. Quick glance around as if I'm looking at traffic. All clear. No worries.

I can't help but stare at her bum as we walk. I can see the shower shot in my mind. It is like I can see through to her flesh.

Can't get distracted by the photograph. Nude body under those clothes. Makes me think of Hélène. Sarah as Hélène. Her face looking out from those poses.

Focus.

Need wits about me.

She has a definite plan for her lunch hour. She is marching with intent, somewhere to go. Health club, some aerobics then that swim? If she's heading there, then I won't wait until she is finished. She cuts things too fine when she goes there. Waits until the last minute then dashes back to her office. Waiting would make me late back and I'd risk losing some of my brownie points. Need them for potential emergencies.

At least I've seen her for a while. That's something. It'll sound a bit odd, I know, but I feel much happier now that I've seen her. Seeing her in the flesh. Animated.

I'm quite looking forward to my afternoon now. Who knows what interesting photographs I might get a chance to look at? Could find something really special and, if not, I'm bound to at least see some interesting ones.

Amazing that a few minutes with her can raise the spirits so much. Yes, tonight I'll go through the photographs again. Spend some time at the window.

Life is good.

Approaching the turn off to the gym. Last few seconds. Torn between following her to the door and leaving her here. Decide. Quickly. Make up your mind.

She doesn't take the turn. No gym today. Oh thank you, thank you.

Where is she going then?

I think I've completely misread her haste. She's probably just going for a sandwich. She likes those Port Salut baguettes. I've become rather fond of them too.

This is such a good day. I'm getting to spend even more time with her. Might risk following her into shops. Even risk having to buy a teddy or two.

She suddenly turns and stops at the kerb. Traffic stopping her from crossing. I have to stop too – can't risk passing her. Pull out my phone and again pretend I'm making a call – buy enough time for her to cross. One-way traffic so she won't look in my direction.

Shouldn't take the risk. I'll cross to her side of the street so I end up opposite again once she's over.

Go now. Not much of a break in traffic but I can make it. Hope no one hits their horn at me. *Toot, toot!* might make her look.

Made it.

Stop and continue my bogus conversation.

It would make more sense if she crossed a bit further down the road. She could wait for the filter light to go on then cross easily. Then it hits me. There is a café opposite where she's standing. She's meeting someone.

Don't think she'd go out for lunch by herself. Must be meeting someone.

Throat tightens, cheeks flush.

Who is she meeting? A man? No can't be. If it is, it'll be one of the guys. Peter or Stephen. Maybe John. Just one of the guys taking her out for lunch. Innocent enough. They are just friends. No romance between them.

Maybe it is a get-together with the whole gang. Probably not – they tend to do that in the evening.

Maybe it is something private. Not for everyone's ears. One of the guys needs some relationship advice. Maybe Brian asking about Abby. Maybe he wants to marry her – maybe he is that smitten. She'll know the right thing to say. She'll have the answer.

What if it is another man? Not one of the group.

She has other male friends.

It won't be a work colleague. They'd have left together – unless they are trying to keep a secret affair from their workmates. Then why go to this café? It is on the main route from her office to the shops. They'd risk being seen.

I might recognise the person if I see them. I'm quite familiar with people in her photographs. Good with faces, terrible with names. See people all the time that I recognise from photographs.

Not as easy to work out relationship dynamics when people appear in the odd photographs. Acquaintances, friends?

Might be someone new. Someone I haven't got a photograph of. Could be tricky. Don't like being in the dark, not having any clues. Don't like not being able to go home and dig out relevant images.

Flash of sitting on a harbour wall.

Flash of standing at Fire Mountain.

Her head leaning slightly towards his.

Arms touching.

Bare legs touching.

Skin to skin.

That guy. The guy from the holiday.

I know it – she's meeting him.

Did they share a cocktail at the bar before he suggested that they go to his room? Clichés and less-than-subtle persuasion pouring from his lips. Seducing and pleading eyes. Too much to drink. She's unsteady on her feet. Takes his guiding hand. Follows his lead. She's not too bothered – only a bit of fun.

Did they meet in a club? Beats pounding in their chests. Shouting to be heard. Both taken over by the music. The closeness of another body. Hypnotic swaying. Intoxicating rhythms. Back to a room. Hands clasping tightly. Sweat on skin. Hard kisses.

I had resigned myself to the fact that they might have spent a night together. Sex. But that was all. No more depth to it than that. Sex. She's single. She can do what she wants. Don't grudge her some pleasure. But it was only supposed to be a holiday shag. Just a hump and then forgotten. But here she is meeting him for lunch. More than a casual fuck. She could have met someone from anywhere in the world but she had to meet someone from the same city.

But it can't be right, can it? There would have been more photographs of them together – more photographs of him if there really was something more between them. Her need to document her life means that, if it was more than a shag, there would be image after image of him. I know her.

Could be they met right at the end of his holiday – spent just one night together. But surely that wouldn't have been enough? She couldn't have fallen for him in that length of time. Don't believe in love at first sight.

But he gave a phone number. She promised to call. Now they are meeting for the first time since she got back. No. He's been here for days. They've spent every night together. They woke beside each other this morning. Held each other as dawn was breaking. Hands entwined. Warmth. Didn't want to part and promised they'd meet again at lunch. New love is like that. Can't be apart too long without feeling that ache.

He's been with her all this time and I've been oblivious to it. He was probably waiting outside the shop when she dropped off her photographs.

Should have gone to her flat that night – I might have sensed she was not alone.

I've neglected her the last couple of weeks – got too consumed by photographs and with Will and Laura.

I'm paying the price.

Just can't believe he lives here too. That would certainly explain the instant connection between them.

But holidays are supposed to be something out of the ordinary. You're supposed to avoid reminders of home.

What if he's from somewhere else? What if he's so besotted by her that he's travelled all the way here to spend time with her? Just arrived so they've not spent the last few nights together. That sounds better. Can't be right. How would he know about this place? She'd have met him at the station, at the airport. Must have arrived in the last few days. Nights together.

Better if he is from far away. Long-distance relationships never work. A few weeks of rushing to be with each other and then gradual drift towards complacency. Telephone break-up. Tears and regret. But it is for the best. It was doomed.

I need to accept the situation. She's been in relationships before. I'm a realist. I understand these things. I have no jealousy.

Just my luck that she met someone on this holiday.

She's at the door of the café. I'll know in a few seconds. Misery just about to start.

She's inside. She's looking around for him.

Please don't be right. Please don't be right. Fingers crossed.

Anyone else but him. Anyone else but him.

Holiday romances get under the skin. She'll be smitten for ages.

She's spotted someone.

A little wave.

Can't see well from here. Move to better position. Don't care if I'm seen. Don't care if I blow my cover. I've got to know who it is. Got to see who it is.

If traffic hadn't started again, I would be across the road. I'd be at the window.

Can see her near a table. Can just see her bending down for a kiss hello.

Everything within me stops. Time stretches.

Please don't be him.

Not a kiss on the mouth – more a peck on the cheek. No yearning embrace. No passionate clinches.

It is a girl. Thank god. It is a girl.

Looks about the same age as Sarah. Pretty. Not sure I recognise her. View still not good. Definitely not one of the gang.

I'll cross over and pass the window. Quick look. It'll be fine. No harm done. If I don't get a good look at this friend, I'll be worried all day.

Relief that it is not him.

No engagement. No marriage. No love. It is not him.

At worst, he was just some quick fuck on holiday.

I think I misread the signs. He probably put his hand on her leg and she naturally leaned in just as the shutter opened – all feelings from his side alone. After the photograph was taken, she would have smiled politely and moved away, making it clear that she just wasn't interested.

He was persistent. Went on the same trip to the mountains the following day. Tried to get close to her. The camera caught the moment again.

No, nothing in those images. She didn't spend any more time with him. She doesn't even remember him now.

I'm at the window of the café. Phone at my ear. They are talking. No reason to look up at me. Still safe.

Girl looks more familiar. I'm sure I've seen her in a photograph. University friend, school chum, ex-work colleague – just can't place her yet.

I'll look through my collection tonight. Find the face. Might have made some notes about her.

They are laughing. Catching up. I smile. Could have been a lot worse. Could have been disastrous.

I think they'll probably stay in the café for the rest of the lunch break. No point in hanging around. I feel confident that I can leave – she won't be meeting anyone else now. I could cross the road again and watch for a bit but I don't think I'll be able to see very much so I decide to head back to the shop. I'll have an enjoyable afternoon and look forward to my mission tonight. Another piece in the puzzle of her life.

At least I got to see her for a while. Maybe take a quick run by her flat at the weekend. Maybe check out the sports centre.

Last look and then I'll go. Imprint the image.

Sarah has her handbag on the table. She is taking something out. Oh god. Recognise the envelope. Know what she is doing.

Photographs.

She's taking out a wallet full of photographs. Must be the ones from the holiday. She lifts the flap. Takes the bundle out. Friend looks at them expectantly. The first print is passed over. They talk about it. They laugh. The next print is passed.

Before I realise what I am doing, I have my hat out of my pocket and on my head and I'm heading to the door.

This is a mistake. Hat won't disguise you enough. But she is looking at the photographs. She is talking about the photographs – describing why she took them, what is going on in them. If I'm in the café, I can hear what she is saying. Can't miss this opportunity.

So she might recognise me. It could be a coincidence. It is not such a fantastical idea that someone you know from a shop might also come into the same café at lunchtime.

If I'm seen, I'll keep a low profile for the next few weeks – a price I am more than willing to pay. Think of the details I could get from her conversation, the insights, the fact checking. Yes, it is worth the risk, worth the potential sacrifices. It is worth anything.

I'm in the café. I'm heading toward where they sit. Next booth along is free. Blessed coincidence. I can sit with my back to them less than half a metre from them. Cap on, head in a newspaper and I won't be recognised. All that I have to do is make it to the booth without being seen.

If she catches my eye, we'll laugh about it. *Small world*. She's showing off her photographs when in walks the man who developed them. It would make us laugh. She'd ask me to join them. Tell me directly about the images.

Let's just get to the empty booth and stop thinking about the what-ifs. Sit down and eavesdrop on the most important conversation in the world.

I can do this. Just got to stay calm and look away as I pass. One foot in front of the other. Try not to stumble, try not to fall on your face and look up to see a shocked look of recognition.

My face must be scarlet – I must look like a red, sweaty, shambling loon. Must stand out a mile. Everyone will be looking at me in a moment. They'll be able to read my expression, find me out. Can feel the sweat running down my back, hands clammy, holding my breath.

Almost at her booth. Take a little detour round the tables in the centre of the café, look at the counter, pretend I'm looking at the cakes. Pretend I'm someone else.

Don't look at me. Don't see me.

I am sitting in the next booth.

I force myself to turn and look at her.

I haven't been noticed. She is too engrossed in her chat, too happy talking about the photographs. Part of her joy in taking pictures is sharing them.

I'm safe for the moment. I can relax a little. Sitting in the booth with my paper, I become anonymous again. She might glance my way but she'll see nothing.

I can hear her beautiful voice but I don't concentrate on the words yet. I need to scan the café quickly – look for potential problems.

Beginning to get busy with the lunchtime rush. I'll probably be asked if I'll share my table. Ordinarily, I wouldn't be too pleased but, under the circumstances, I'm desperate for someone to join me. Better if I'm not sitting alone. Less noticeable. Just as long as they don't try to chat to me. Keep my newspaper up, adopt a scowl, grunt dismissively if there is any chitchat. Just make sure I don't look as if I'm spying.

Toilets are at the far end of the shop. She'll have to pass me to get to them. Could be difficult but don't waste time planning for it – improvise if it happens.

No one looking at me.

I can't believe that I am sitting here. I am actually doing this.

I've broken so many of my rules. Rules that are there to protect me, stop me from doing things like this and getting too close.

Thou shalt not follow her into a café.

Thou shalt not sit beside her.

Concentrate on her words now. Block out the noise of the till bleeping, other people talking, coffee mugs hitting tables.

So good to hear her voice again. She doesn't have much of an accent but, if you listen closely, you can tell she is local – that tiny inflection almost imperceptibly forming around her words.

I take out my Moleskine and open it to a new page. Don't want to miss anything important. I'll use key words to help me remember everything she describes.

Can't be sure how many photographs they have looked through but I hope it is not too many. They are talking about a pretty sunset but I can think of six photographs that feature sunsets.

Think about this logically – she would start with the first set of prints. Most people get quite uptight if the order is mixed up too much so all I have to worry about is if they have been reversed or not. You know the thing, you let someone see your pics and they lay them down face up so the set is back to front.

That's a silly one. Who is he?

That's Scott, Sarah replies. *He was at the party at New Year. Got very drunk and spent the night singing.*

I don't remember much from the party – I was well gone by the time I got there.

Scott. She said the name Scott.

I need to know what photograph it is. Silly one? That could be one of any number of photographs. Silly photos – there are loads of them, everyone pulling stupid faces, rude gestures, full moons.

The friend just asked about one person in the photograph but I can't assume that there is only one person in the snap.

Scott. Scott. Scott. Which one is he? Which one is Scott? I write the name down in my notebook and write the word silly beside it.

Scott.

He is one of them. He is one of the group. Is he Peter? Is he Stephen? It might be John. Let's face it – he could be any of the guys.

I am suddenly struck with doubt. In a strange way, I think that this might not be such a good idea. I have lived with these identities for the past few months. I have kept my distance and purposely avoided finding out too much about them – except Sarah. Now here I am about to find things out. I'm a little scared by that thought.

I'm being stupid. How could I possibly not want to find out accurate information about them from her? These are real people and now I can give them real names. This is quite thrilling on so many levels.

A waitress comes up and interrupts my reverie to take my order. I'll have some lunch. It will help make me look the part. This might be one of those places that ask you to leave if you only order a coffee during the lunchtime rush.

I'll make myself an ordinary customer.

I'll have a cappuccino, a cheese and tomato toastie and a blueberry muffin, please.

As she leaves with the order, I lean back in the booth, notebook in front of me. Look like an author waiting for my muse. It brings me that little bit closer to Sarah and her friend.

More photographs are passed. Little laughs and a couple of words I can't make out.

I wish she were one of those bores that droned on about every snap. I want to hear her say, *This is so and so . . . That is when we went to . . . Look at me in this one . . .*

She is not one of those people. I might only get scraps.

Should I risk turning round and having a peek? Try to get a better idea of where they are in the sets so that anything I do hear marries roughly with where I think they are.

What if she turns her head at exactly that moment? What if she catches sight of me? She'll see my eyes. She'll recognise me.

Should just keep my head down. Not risk anything. Following her here is excitement enough. Should protect myself as much as I can when I am so vulnerable.

But this is wonderful. The feeling of power I have. The feeling of control. I should have done this ages ago.

I want to know everything. I want to hear every word. Know all that can be known.

Fuck it, I'm going to risk peeking. Make it nonchalant.

She passes another photograph. Her friend looks at it for a moment and puts it on the pile in front of her.

That one is a group shot over dinner on the third night.

I've worked out the chronology of the holiday from the photographs – have a plan of it on the wall in my study.

I know these sets back to front.

Next image is of them in the bar that night.

Next image . . . Something is wrong. Not the right photo. She must have mixed them up. Should be Abby and Sarah in the toilet. Sarah worse for wear at the mirror. Abby having a pee. Candid shot the boys took. The start of the 'set-up' shots. Next shot is wrong too and the next. Then it is the boys the following morning. Drunk in bed. Back in sequence again. Why are some missing?

I chuckle to myself. The vanity. Sarah has taken out all the embarrassing shots of herself and the girls. Some of them are not completely flattering but I think she looks great in every shot. I hadn't imagined that she would be so self-conscious. I hadn't thought that she would censor herself out of her snaps. I feel a tiny bit disappointed. Maybe I'm being silly but this just doesn't fit with my idea of Sarah.

They are laughing at the fun shots of the boys. She hasn't taken out a single one of those pictures. There should be one of Louise sniffing her knickers next. It is gone.

I know the shower shot won't be included. They pass where it should be.

Peter on a bed with his arms wrapped round a teddy bear. Not his bear of course – another set-up to make him look a bit sissy.

That's a good one, the friend says.

You can see Peter's bum in that shot. Sheets expertly pulled aside to give a good view. Even asleep he seems to be clenching his cheeks to give the perfect dimple.

The friend is lingering over it. *Good arse,* she says.

She doesn't know that Peter is a 'love 'em once and leave 'em' guy. She doesn't realise that all she could ever be to him is another notch on the bedpost. But she's mesmerised by his tight bum and well-muscled body. Good physique wins over personality again. She doesn't know that all his hours in the gym are just perfecting a weapon to use against silly girls like her.

Do you mind if we share your table?

What?

I turn back to my table and see a couple standing beside it. The woman asks again.

I tell them that it is fine. Might make me look as if I am with friends. Help the illusion some more.

I ignore them as they sit and I half-turn to Sarah's booth again.

I like that one, says Sarah. Her friend says, *Matt and Joan,* trying to remember the names.

Yeah.

Matt and Joan.

I know that shot. Sunset. Abby and Brian. I can't believe what I've just heard.

Matt and Joan. Abby doesn't look like a Joan. Matt sounds good for Brian though. Yes. He could be a Matt. The name fits the face.

Matt and Joan.

Brian and Abby.

I am giddy with excitement. I simply wouldn't have believed you this morning if you told me that, by lunchtime, my world would have been changed.

I want Sarah to turn to me and give me everything I now need.

Tell me about your desires, your dreams, your fears, your hopes, your pains, your comforts, your joys, your secrets. I want to take the photographs and fill them with detail. Fill them with truth.

Tell me everything.

Lunch arrives but I hardly notice.

My head reels from the implications of hearing those two names. Matt and Joan.

Matt, Joan and Scott – new names for familiar faces.

Oh, my God! Abby and Brian are dead. Their lives are over. Everything I believed about them has gone. Every detail revealed a lie.

All gone.

There is something different now.

Pay attention to Sarah. Want to find out more.

They are talking but it is difficult to hear because the people at my table are talking too, drowning out all those precious revelations. I want to turn to them and scream at them to be quiet. Don't they know what is happening? Can't they appreciate that this is profound?

They yammer on and on and I can only hear odd words. Nothing interesting.

And then it is over.

The photographs are packed away into their envelopes. Sarah and the friend stand. They talk about meeting in a couple of weeks. They go to the counter. They pay for their lunch. They leave. They stand outside the window for a moment, lean together for a kiss and then they go.

My lunch is untouched.

I sit and take it all in.

Getting late.

Should leave.

I wait a moment longer and then get up. No one will make the connection between Sarah and me. Pay the bill. Get out into the fresh air – great greedy lungfuls.

Almost one o'clock so I'll have to run back to work. I don't mind because it means I have to concentrate on avoiding colliding with people and not think about what has just happened.

No one mentions that I am a few minutes late.

Marion smiles at me in the staffroom as I dump my coat. She has noticed that I'm flushed and sweating. I don't wait for a comment.

Quickly into the toilet. Splash water on my face, unbutton my shirt and rub a damp paper towel under my arms. Shake the open shirt to create a cooling draft.

I look at my face in the mirror. *Matt*, I say. I look for any signs of change. *Scott. Joan.* The same face stares back. It is still me – I'm still here.

It is much more difficult to keep lunchtime off my mind during the afternoon. The shop isn't so busy. My colleagues have been put on tidy duty – someone from head office making a store visit tomorrow. I'm left in the developing area, mopping up the leftovers. Nothing worth spending my time on – not one interesting image in all the rolls of film that pass through my hands.

Details of my spying slip into my thoughts. The different names. I try to focus on the scant details I overhead about the holiday. Hints and teases. I really wish I had been there with them. Ridiculous but just think what that would have been like. Louise falling on the volcano, Sarah going snorkelling and feeling sick. Joan and Matt on the beach. Joan and Matt. Not Abby and Brian.

Joan. Matt. Scott. Mutated. Abby becomes Joan. She looks the same. She is not the same.

I'm not even sure who Scott is yet. Could be Peter. Could be Stephen. Could be John. I'm not convinced that I can identify which one when I look through the albums tonight. So little to work on. Tiny tantalising titbits that are going to keep me on edge for days. I'll have to work on a plan to find out more.

It is such a strange thing – these sudden revelations. I'm not entirely sure how I should process them – what implications they will have. Could be the pebble that starts the landslide.

I have been close to people before – got to know a bit about them before moving on – but these people are different. They've been filtered through Sarah's eyes and that's made them special. I am closer to these people than I would have thought possible. Closer than all the people I watch from the flat.

This changes everything.

I could simply ignore what I found out today. Keep everything as it was. I was happy with that. Part of me is beginning to regret having followed her. I should know better. I should work on resisting these sorts of urges. I want everything straight away, no thought for the consequences. I need to develop the impartial spectator, treat every situation with cold logic – be objective, removed. But how can I do that when my passion is aroused? Those feelings can suffocate reason.

Spontaneity is the source of creativity, the source of personal development. It is also exhilarating.

No. Can't regret what has happened. Can't change it. I'll have to adapt. Can't be safe and still forever. No evolution in that.

I should look on this as a joyful occurrence. A collision of possible fates that has started me on a different path.

Despite my acceptance of this new reality I am still feeling unsettled when I get home. I shower and eat quickly, using mindless early evening TV to stop me from thinking. After a while, I decide to brave the photo albums.

First things first. I search for an image of the friend that Sarah met. Try parties/nightclubs/pubs. There she is – five or six shots with her at a nightclub. The usual gang aren't there – all new people. Hugging and mugging for the camera. Must be a college get-together. I'm surprised some of the regulars aren't there. I felt sure she knows some through college. Maybe they are people from work that have moved on – none of the others work in her office. Maybe they are childhood chums.

I brave the recent holiday photographs. Go directly to Abby and Brian in that sunset snap. Have to get used to new names. Joan and Matt in the sunset shot.

I flick through the album. Stephen. Louise. Wendy. Peter. John. Sarah. Joan. Matt.

All different. Transubstantiation. Conversion of image to flesh. Paper to meat. Real people leaving this 2D world. Maybe that is the way it should be.

I think that I am a little scared of being disappointed. I have spent so long getting glimpses and images of people and filling in the rest that to actually know all about a person is a little daunting. The people that I have created won't turn out to be unsatisfying. Won't have annoying habits. Won't have funny voices. Won't say things that I disagree with. Perhaps this is exactly what I need.

I need to find out more to be sure. I need to get a handle on the reality. What do I know that can help me?

I know the pub where they hang out. I've got some photographs of the inside from Sarah's snaps. I got the location by following her from her flat one night. I also know that some of the guys meet up at a sports centre for five-a-side. I know that some of the girls use the same centre for swimming on a regular basis.

Plan of action is to check out the pub and the sports centre. Might take a couple of weeks but I should be able to find out where they all live, where they work, their real names. Then I can decide if surveillance should be stepped up.

I'll probably have to put Henri and Hélène on hold for a while. I get a flood of relief at this thought. Not sure I feel mentally up to walking the streets to find a whore that I can persuade to pose for me.

I'll start with the pub.

I imagine that I am there. They see me. Instant recognition – faces breaking into smiles. They wave me over to join them. I point to the bar to ask if they want a drink. Peter gets up and comes over to me. *I'll get this one in,* he says and pushes me towards the others. They greet me warmly, shaking my hand – peck on the cheek from the girls closest to me. They ask how I am, how work is, how my pictures are coming along.

We spend an hour or so chatting and drinking and having fun. The group are going to Peter's flat for food and they ask me if I want to come. I tell them that I should really go, that I have up to be early the next day, but they won't hear of it. *How could we have a party tonight knowing that you're going home?*

Peter's flat is nice. He keeps it simple, lots of uncluttered rooms, hardly any pictures. Furniture is modern and unfussy. I like his place – just the way I would decorate a flat like his.

The food is good – Peter certainly knows his way around the kitchen. Wendy helps him.

Over dinner, they get me to tell them stories about some of the funniest photographs I have developed. They laugh at my tales. They want to hear about my exhibition. They are enthralled as I tell them about Hélène and Henri.

Later, Sarah takes me aside. She wants me to tell her more about my photographs. She says she is really fascinated by what I have been saying. She would love to see them. She tells me that she wants to know more about photography, that she wants to develop her own pictures. *Could you teach me?* I tell her I would love to and suggest she comes to my flat and I'll show her how it is all done. She jokes that I'll have to go slow so that she can take it all in. I tell her that it is not too difficult, especially black and white. She says that she has always thought that black-and-white photos are a bit arty but I tell her that they are usually the best.

She tells me that she would like to pose for me, be my muse, just like Hélène.

The party continues. We are all having fun. Sarah shyly takes out her camera. *I almost feel embarrassed to take pictures with you here,* she says, *you're the talented one.* I tell her that her photographs are good. They capture the dynamics of the relationships within the group. They reveal so much about her friends' characters and lives. They give such a sense of life and fun that she should never stop taking them. I make her promise that, if I teach her more, she will never stop taking her snappy shots. She laughs. She promises. She raises the camera.

Flash

Peter is pouring a glass of wine.
Wendy is holding her glass up for him.
John has fallen asleep in the couch.
His shirt has popped open.
Well-rounded stomach exposed.
Stephen is playing on a PlayStation.
His back to the rest of us.
He loves his games.
Matt, Joan and Louise sit beside me.
Joan has her hand on my knee.
Louise has her head on my chest.

Matt has his hand on my shoulder.
We are a family.
We are all smiling at the camera.
This is what she sees.
This is a frozen moment.

Time passes.

Flash
I am sitting on a balcony in shorts.
Bare feet on terracotta tiles.
Towel over my shoulders.
Skin wet from the pool.
Matt, Peter and Wendy are sitting round the table too.
We are having lunch.
The sun reflects on the pool below.
The others are splashing in the water.
The sky is blue.
Mallorca in summer.
A village near the coast.
All my friends are here.
I am with them.
One of them.
This is what she sees.
This is a frozen moment

I have to go to the pub. I want to talk to them, find out everything, rewrite the file.

I can't do it. Of course I can't. It doesn't work that way. There will be no hugs, no 'long-lost friend' routine. No talking. I'll sit in the background. I'll be quiet. I'll just listen. Unnoticed. They will reveal themselves in conversations. That is what I need to do.

So risky. Could be seen. Exposed. Too immediate. Too close. No comfort zone. Need that distance. But I need to know more.

Might just be a couple of them there. They won't know who I am. Just a bloke having a drink. Waiting for his date. Having a pint before he meets the lads. I'll blend into the background. Who would give me a second glance?

That is settled. I'll go. Just for twenty minutes. Just for a short while. See what it is like then I'll leave. That will be enough. I won't risk it again for a bit. I'll have enough to last me.

That's settled

If I go, I'll probably stand outside for half an hour, trying to work up the courage to go in, and then I'll lose my nerve and come home. Despair and self-loathing are my weakness.

But I can be brave. I can be bold. I can conquer my fear. Fear is the little death that kills you slowly.

Yes, I'll go. Just for ten minutes. I won't be recognised. No risk.

I'll go.

Just for a few minutes.

That is it decided.

I find the album that has the most photographs of the pub in it – to get my bearings for tomorrow.

I'll risk it.

I'll go to the pub.

SITTING WHERE THEY SIT

Seven o'clock exactly. I've been sitting in my car for fifty-eight minutes. Pub diagonally across the road.

No sign of any of the gang going in. I am wondering if anyone will come. I'm wondering if Sarah will appear. I'm scared she might see me.

I'm trying to find excuses not to go in. I'm trying to work up some courage. Shouldn't feel this nervous when I know they are not inside. Won't be recognised. Got to keep saying that over and over to convince myself.

I'll just pop in, maybe order a quick drink, stay for a while and then leave. If it gets too much when I'm in there, I can just go. No problem. No pressure.

So why am I still sitting here?

I'm going to be closer to the group than I have been before. Of course, I'm apprehensive.

Be brave. Nothing is going to happen. Nothing to be scared of.

I lock the car door and walk towards the pub.

Eyes scan right and left for familiar faces. Keep them peeled for sight of Sarah. She's the danger tonight.

Have to walk straight in when I get to the door. Can't hang about ruminating. Have to look like I know what I'm doing.

I've been practising my 'looking for friends' glances so that I can check the place out as soon as I am through the door. Got it so it looks convincing.

I decide the only thing to do if I see Sarah is to pretend not to recognise her. Leave all the recognition to her. If she challenges me, I'll act dumb and then slowly remember who she is. That will look natural. That will keep me safe.

Push open the door.

Distinctive pub smell. Stale beer and old smoke. Smell of men that haven't washed before leaving the building site.

Fourteen people in the pub. I know where every one of them sits or stands.

Walk to the bar.

Conversations, laughter, satellite TV tuned to a sports channel, quiz-machine buttons being pounded by eager fingers, glass on teeth, glass on wood, coins jingle-jangle in pockets.

No one I recognise.

No one to recognise me.

Gone for low-key disguise today. Baseball cap, jewellery and glasses. Don't want to look as if I am in disguise. Sarah would see through it but other people will only remember the things I can change. They'll remember the chunky gold necklace that I'll bin after tonight. It was cheap. A fake.

Using a 'wide-boy' sort of persona tonight. Another me to add to the list. Bit cocky but not so much that I'd end up pissing someone off. People will see me as a bit of an arrogant twat, that's all. Nothing out of the ordinary in a place like this.

The bar looks exactly as it does in Sarah's photographs. I've studied every frame I have.

I order a pint and slap some coins on the bar. I tell myself I'm not in a saloon. As I wait for it to be pulled, I can legitimately check the room out again. Five tables and booths empty. The booth the gang seem to use most often is free. Two guys at the quiz machine, competing more against each other than the machine. Three couples at different tables. Group of five men, big boots and concrete dust on their trousers. Two men standing at the bar. Barmaid placing my pint on the counter. Plus me, that is seventeen now.

Barmaid takes my coins. I hold out my hand for the change but she puts it on the bar and raises an eyebrow at me. Makes a point. Fair enough. Persona working.

I pick up the glass and head straight for *their* booth. Where else would I go?

I sit where they sit. I run my hands over the material. Sarah has sat here. Coarse fabric worn smooth. Sarah in a skirt, in shorts, in trousers.

I look around.

This is what they see when they sit here.

This is what they experience.

I feel what they would feel. I slide into their thoughts. I hear the conversations imagined from photographs. I add my own voice to theirs.

I could be one of them.

I take out my phone and pretend to check for messages and then reply to the imaginary ones I've got. I'm taking photographs with it. Click-clicks covered by the noise of the pub. I'll download them later. Call them something like 'Pub through Sarah's Eyes'.

I stay for half an hour, soaking up the atmosphere, while keeping a wary eye on the door. Nine more people come in – all new faces.

I could really fit in here. I could be comfortable.

I leave most of my pint and walk back to the car.

Next time, maybe I'll have some company.

Next time, maybe I'll get closer.

CREEPING JESUS

Look out of the window before I leave for the day.

Looks like nothing is happening out in the world, but I see everything.

Woman pushing a pram, slight bulge in her top tells me that she is pregnant again, partner so eager to begin his rutting he forgets to take precautions.

Man is in a car parked by the roadside, windows up despite the building heat of the day. He holds the wheel tightly, as if he is driving.

Man walks from the next block towards the broken railings that provide a shortcut to the park. He has an old, mangy dog at his side. He calls it Sorrow.

He is Creeping Jesus – he was named this by one of the busybody gossips that lives on the sixth floor. Kindly Mrs Armstrong. Widowed thirteen years and counting. She is one of those women that treats you like you are a long-lost relative but, the moment you pass by, the whetstone is out, the blade is sharpened. She and her cronies hold court in the foyer with their shopping bags and their headscarves and poisonous tongues.

No one is safe from their chatter.

Do they talk about me?

Nice boy. Keeps himself to himself. Watches the stars. Does something with chemicals in his flat. Photographs he says. Must be lonely. Needs a girlfriend to bring him out of his shell. But he's nice and quiet.

Nice and quiet. Damned by three words. Everyone knows it's the nice and quiet ones that go to work with an AK-47, rat-tat-tat their colleagues. It is the nice and quiet ones that that go to the bell tower with a rifle.

The name Creeping Jesus stuck.

People don't care what his real one is. They call him Creeping Jesus to strip him of identity, to make it easy to fit him to all their prejudices. They call him Creeping Jesus because he is scruffy, because he is different, because he isn't all there.

Children shout *pee-doh* at him when he passes – it's a new word that they've learned and think gives them power. He just waves his hands and rants at them then tells Sorrow to ignore the taunts.

A few hundred years ago people like him would have been blamed for crops failing or infants dying or diseases spreading. He'd have been pricked by the witch-finders until they found the spot where the devil hid. Then he'd have been murdered, people believing that doing this would kill the evil luck too. Of course, they'd be wrong.

Things have hardly changed. These days his type are the reason there is so much crime, so many drugs in schools, so much sleaze in the media. He becomes pervert. He becomes pusher. He becomes leper.

We all need a sacrificial lamb, a focus for our rage. It is good to have him close where we can keep an eye on him. Mob justice if something goes wrong. We don't need to care if we are right. The oblation will take away any taint.

Creeping Jesus ducks down and goes through the gap in the railings. His dog plods behind.

I set my cameras.

I go to work.

TOES IN THE POOL

I start my hunt for more information at the sports centre. From Sarah-watching, I know that members of the gang use this centre. Squash or badminton, swimming and health suite, the occasional game of five-a-side (boys only).

I've had to join the sports centre and come here every evening to make sure I see some of the group. There is a photo of me on my membership card. Another image of me in the world. The majority of likenesses that exist of me are official ones. It is impossible to exist these days without your face being stuck on something. I don't like that. I don't like the kind of longevity that gives me.

Tonight is the third evening of my stake-out. I arrived just after six. That seems like the most likely time they'd come – just after work and before dinner. You don't want an hour of frantic activity or swimming on a full stomach.

I try to spend most of my time wandering about, dropping into the fitness suite and having a go on the treadmills or the bikes. Then off to watch the badminton and squash courts, followed by a trip to the café area from where you can see the swimming pool.

I've been staying for a couple of hours or so. I don't believe they would come much after eight-thirty, though I know, if I didn't make contact soon, I'd have to revise my timings.

No need – tonight I am in luck.

Four of the group arrive together. Stephen, Matt (once Brian), Louise, Joan (once Abby).

Famine then feast.

I loiter in the foyer pretending to be absorbed by the noticeboard but paying no attention to the changes to kendo and step class start times. I hear the boys paying for their booked squash court and then swimming while the girls pay for swimming only.

That makes my decision for me. I can't hang about the squash court, too exposed. Time to go for a dip. Brought swimming gear with me just in case, and changing gives me an excuse to follow Matt and Stephen into the locker room.

See the ease with which I can adapt to the situation? I am not at all fazed by being this close to members of the gang. I've spent ages thinking about how I would feel when I got close, how I would react and how I would cover those reactions.

I am in perfect control.

The boys go to the aisle next to the one my locker is in. Matt sits on the bench in the centre of the aisle and takes off his shoes. Stephen puts his jacket into a free locker.

Some other people are dotted around the room. Various states of undress. Murmur of conversations. Steam curls from the shower area.

It all reminds me of gym time at school. The same smell. Sweaty clothes and sweaty bodies, damp towels and the clash of strong deodorants, the overpowering disinfectant.

I pull off my trainers and socks and put them in my locker. Tiles cold on my feet. T-shirt and shorts stowed too. I hesitate with my pants. Don't think I've ever felt comfortable stripping off in front of people. It was always an ordeal at school. All the random teasing that went on. I feared I would be the next victim. *He's got a small dick. He's got none. Look at donkey boy! Look at the stiffy!* Gym teacher standing at the entrance to the communal showers – girls had individual cubicles of course – making sure everyone washed. Looked like he was inspecting everyone, holding the image until he got home.

Got to be brave. No one is going to try to humiliate anyone here – we're all mature. Take them down and stow them. Pull on my trunks – more like baggy shorts but with tighter elastic. I'm sure Stephen will have his Speedos with him – don't think I have the balls for that sort of fashion statement.

I've brought swimming goggles and a cap with me – contingency if Sarah appears. Good disguise. Would look like a twat but that wouldn't be out of place here. I leave the cap and put the goggles round my neck, they'll be enough.

I loiter a little longer. I take the towels from my bag and arrange them for easy access after my swim. I make the act last ages. Want to hear any chat from the next aisle.

Matt appears and walks for the door. *Come on, Dave, we've missed five minutes already.*

Double revelation – a name and a voice. It is the first time I've heard Matt speak. Sounds different from the way I had imagined it – all of the group sound a lot like me when I imagine conversations.

So Stephen is Dave.

David.

Dave.

I think my name for him fits better but probably just familiarity with it.

Dave seems such a short name for Stephen.

Dave (Stephen) runs after Matt.

I go out the door that leads to the pool area.

Splish-splash through the disinfectant footbath.

Scan the pool and poolside.

Girls aren't here yet. Seems that girls take longer to get changed in every situation.

I walk towards the shallow end where the showers and sauna cubicle are. Eagle-eyed pool attendant ready to pounce if I tried to get in without stepping under a shower first. Would it make much difference? I saw a news report that said asthmatics can have attacks when they swim because of the mixture of chlorine, sweat and urine that you find in every pool. Makes you just want to leap right in.

As I approach the shower, I hear a hiss from the sauna. Water hits hot rocks. Saunas are supposed to be really good for you. Deeply cleanse the skin – trapped dirt and toxins are flushed out. Give you a cardiovascular workout too. Haven't had one in years.

I spend a few moments under the shower and walk to the pool. On one side people are swimming lengths. The other side is for the splashers.

I sit on the edge and dangle my legs in the water. Nice temperature. Not too cold, just above tepid. I put on my goggles.

I drop in and under the water. Sound muffles and becomes eerie. My goggles give me a perfect view. Legs and arms thrashing through the water. The fat legs and bums of people standing with their kids. Skin looking pale and sickly from under here, like a blue filter.

I bob my head above the surface and tread water for a while.

Louise and Joan walk towards the showers.

Both wear one-piece costumes. Was hoping that at least one of them would be wearing a two-piece – much more flattering.

I start a length and am on my way back when the girls come in.

Maybe I could accidentally collide with one of them, apologise profusely and that will get a conversation going. *How can I make it up to you?* I'll say. *Let me buy you a drink.* That's terrible – sounds like the worst sort of chat-up line.

Would be better if it was Sarah. Cutting across her path, our bodies collide. Arms round each other to steady ourselves, feet touch as we reach for the bottom. We are both embarrassed, not sure whose fault it is. We keep on saying sorry, each trying to take the blame. We laugh about it. She recognises me. *Is this your local centre?* I ask. We end up in the café.

I don't bump into Louise or Joan. Might get asked to leave if I did. But I do swim beside them for a while. Louise is the stronger swimmer. If Wendy was here, she'd have done five lengths to my one.

We swim together.

I'm assuming that Dave – Dave. New name. Got to get used to it – that Dave and Matt will be playing squash until their hour is up.

It's been about twenty-five minutes since they went in.

I'm knackered. I don't consider myself unfit but a few lengths' swimming and you really know you should get more exercise. Don't think I'll last a full hour.

I tread water again and watch the girls. I sink below the surface for a better view. Thighs ripple against the water as they push themselves forward. Bubbles trailing from their feet. Louise has the fitter body, smaller breasts and bum, maybe hovering around the too thin mark but she looks tidy. Joan is a bit bigger, more flesh on the bone but not fat. Nice round breasts.

I bob out of the water. Shouldn't stare for too long. Wonder how embarrassing it would be to get an erection in a swimming pool. Not really the done thing. Difficult to disguise.

I butterfly to the steps at the shallow end and pull myself out. Body feels heavy as I break the surface and then feels light again. Satisfying splosh as the water falls away from me.

I go to the pool showers and wash away the chlorine water. If that news report was correct I'm washing away traces of my fellow swimmers' sweat and piss too. How lovely.

I watch the girls as I shower.

I'll go back to the changing room, dry off and get into my shorts and T-shirt again. Best not to get dressed to go until Dave and Matt finish their game. They are planning a swim too. Don't think I'll manage any more time in the pool. Wouldn't be able to hear anything anyway.

Wade slowly through the antiseptic foot pool. Don't want to catch anything nasty from other people's feet. Of course, I probably undo all the good by walking to my locker barefoot.

Towel myself off and dress in my sports gear.

I wander to the squash courts.

Dave and Matt still playing a hard game. Running backwards and forwards to slam the ball against the wall. God they're fit. I'd be on all fours gasping by now if I was playing against them.

A while until they finish.

I stroll to the balcony overlooking the pool. I watch the swimmers. No Louise or Joan. Bugger. Must have missed them. Maybe they've got something else planned because the boys still need to have a swim. Perhaps they won't wait for them. Probably in the showers now, lathering up.

I watch the pool for a few more minutes. Good swimmers race by the less confident ones. Family with two children at the shallow end. Must be family time for the pool. I can see more getting ready to go in.

I go back to the changing rooms and sit on the bench in my aisle and wait for the boys. Another couple of squash players appear in my aisle and get undressed. They are chatting about their game. I hope they go away before Matt and Dave come in. Always my luck, having loud people hanging round when I need to hear. They wander past me with their shampoo and their soap.

Dave and Matt come in. They talk about the game. Dave won.

Fancy jumping into the sauna before we swim? asks Matt.

Dave says, *That sounds great.*

Sauna. Up close. Hear every word. Can't let that opportunity slip by.

I undress as quickly as I can. Want to get to the sauna before them. Swimming trunks disgustingly cold and wet when I pull them on. Grab the hand towel I brought – can use it to put over my head if I want anonymity.

I pass them while they are still undressing and go to the pool area. Wet feet again.

There is a man in the sauna when I enter. Heat takes my breath away as I close the door. Skin tingles as pores open.

The man nods me a hello as I settle down on the upper wooden platform. His skin glistens with sweat.

The wood is hot under my legs. I breathe through my nose and it feels like it is burning. Forgot about that. Breathe with the mouth slightly open so the hot air doesn't hurt your lips.

The noise from the pool seems distant.

I'm not used to this sort of heat. I'm shining with sweat. Hope they come soon. Not sure if I'll last long.

I close my eyes and can feel the heat from them on my eyelids. Got an overwhelming urge to wipe the sweat from my forehead but I suppose there's no point.

The door opens. A glorious blast of cool air as Matt and Dave come in.

They sit on the lower level. Nods and raised eyebrows as a greeting.

They made eye contact with me. We make a connection. Something to build on. Heart flutter. Could be the effect of the sauna.

Dave picks up the ladle and pours some water on the stones. They sizzle. Steam pours from them.

Now this really is heat.

Apparently we are not doing this authentically. The proper Finnish way is to be nude. It would be seen as odd that we are all dressed in swimming gear. Fortunately modesty forbids.

Good to see that Stephen, sorry Dave, is wearing his Speedos. I would be disappointed if he wasn't. Bet he waxes his bikini line. Only hair that I can see is on his head, arms and legs. He must wax or shave the rest of his body. Matt has hair everywhere – so does the other guy. Dave probably thinks it interferes with his muscle definition, creates drag when he is swimming. Vanity boy.

Funny – I would have thought Dave and Peter would be the ones always out together. Body fascism making a bond between them. Maybe there is a competitive thing between them. Peter would win on the six-pack front though. Peter is probably jealous of Dave's big dick though. Some sort of balance between them then.

They chat.

The talk about their game. They talk about work, they mention names. Sandra. Neil. Mark. I think they must be work colleagues. The chat is not particularly revealing, same as a hundred other conversations I've heard.

The other man stands and leaves. I get another cooling blast of air and realise that I'm not long for this world if I stay in the heat.

So how are things going with Chris? Matt's voice.

It is going good. Still feels a bit strange because we've known each other for so long.

They are quiet.

Much as I'd love to hear what Dave has to say on his seemingly new girlfriend, I can't wait any longer. I need to get out before I collapse.

I summon all my will and move from the top bench. Wood underfoot is hot. Feel that sweet breeze as I open the door. I want to stand here forever but don't want angry shouts of *Shut the door!*

Third time tonight that I'm under the pool showers. Feels so good to be cool again. The grime just washing way. I put my face in the spray and let it wash around my mouth. I'm going to down a litre of water the moment I get home.

I go back to the changing room and sit with the wet hand towel over my head.

Probably a good thing to pace yourself with saunas, build your tolerance up over a few visits. Bit stupid of me, really, after all the swimming. I'll know for next time.

I go for a proper shower. Feel a pang of embarrassment when I walk in. Four guys already there. I go to the nearest showerhead and turn it on. Got to look straight ahead or concentrate on yourself. Bad etiquette to eye up other men in the shower. Just like urinals. Against the code to compare yourself with other men. It is a myth that we all have a peek and give each other approving or sympathetic nods.

I dry myself and am dressing when Dave and Matt head for the showers. Promise I wasn't looking. Dave just walked right out in front of me. Trunks not exaggerating his size.

I order an orange juice in the café. Overpriced bottled rubbish not freshly squeezed.

Louise and Joan there. Waiting for the boys.

A few minutes pass and then they arrive. I almost jump up and shout my surprise when Dave leans down and kisses Louise. Didn't see that coming. When did this happen? Didn't see any sign of it in the holiday snaps. Maybe it blossomed there. I'll have to double-check each one when I get home. I'll be annoyed with myself if I overlooked any clues. Penny drops. Louise is Chris. Bugger. Lucky boy.

I follow them discreetly out of the building. They stop on the path into the car park. I have no option but to pass. Avoid their eyes.

They are saying goodbye. They talk about meeting up later in the week.

I sit in my car and watch them. Kisses for the girls as they part. Boys just nod goodbyes. Dave and Chris (Louise) leave together. Matt and Joan have their own cars.

No choice but to follow Dave and Chris. Should hopefully lead back to one of their flats. Maybe they'll go out for a meal first. Fingers crossed that they don't. I could do with taking it easy for the rest of the night.

An hour later I've got my albums out, checking for signs.

Dave and Chris. David and Christine? They went back to Dave's flat.

Got the name from the buzzer. Pretty obvious she would be staying the night so I decided not to wait.

Three nights' work and I have two names and an address.

Bit more work and I'll have info on all of them.

Check the windows before I go to bed.

Will and Laura's curtains are closed.

Malcolm must be out. His flat dark.

Clara is practising. I put on a solo violin compilation as I watch her. She is playing just for me.

OBJECTIF

It is going to be such a good day today. I'm going to see if I can see Sarah at the office and tonight it is a trip to the pub. Most of the gang will be there but Sarah is meeting some other people.

I'll be drinking in the pub with no fear of recognition other than maybe a couple of the boys noticing that I go the same sports centre. Instant connection. If we build on that, then there can be an introduction to Sarah. We'll all laugh and say, *What a small world it is!* when Sarah says, *Oh, my God – you're the guy that develops my photographs!*

Accepted.

I'll have burrowed my way right to the heart of this little gang. I'll be part of the picture.

Sarah has been a bit neglected the last few weeks while I've been finding out about the others. I've got a file thick with notes and photographs. Felt like paparazzi as I snapped away from my car. I could go on *Mastermind*, specialist subject Sarah and chums.

But I've missed Sarah. Only managed to sit outside the flat a couple of times and have missed her at lunch for days. It has had to be this way. I need to know them, become part of the group, so they introduce me to her. That is the only way the plans will work. I have to be their friend first.

Sarah is the point to all this. She was the beginning and she will be the end.

She'll try to hide her feelings at first. But we'll both know that she's fallen in love me with me. Then it will all happen. It will be us decorating our flat, it will be us having sex with the curtains open, it will be us with the camera. Sarah posing. Sarah as Hélène.

I don't ask if I can leave a few minutes early at lunch today. They owe me and I'm not going to grovel and feel like they are doing me a big favour when I'm just asking for what is mine. I leave ten minutes early, just to make sure I get to her office in plenty of time.

It has been a bit of a disappointing week for meeting Sarah at lunchtime. This is the fourth day I've tried. It was pouring on Tuesday so I didn't think she would be going out. Wednesday, no sign. Thursday, a day when she often has a wander, no sign. I'm hoping fourth time lucky but there is always next Monday.

Commissionaire in the foyer, reading a newspaper.

I settle into my spot and put on my headphones. I'm not actually listening to anything but it is part of the illusion. Should be listening to 'Music to Watch Girls By'.

Lunchtime surge starts to exit the building. Not in first batch. Lift doors close, called upstairs. Wait. Wait. Doors open, six people. Sarah.

Beige swishy skirt, white top, sandals, hair tied back, sunglasses. She just has a handbag with her so she is not going for a step class.

As always, I let her get a little way ahead then set off. Slip my sunglasses on. Shades are good. People can't see your eyes so you can be facing one thing but actually looking at something else. Wrap around are best for that – especially mirrored ones. Guys use that knowledge to walk about on a hot day and ogle cleavage without getting a slap.

Sarah is walking with purposeful strides again today. Think she is going to visit a few shops. Being so determined tends to keep the mind focused on your goal so I feel I can get a little closer today.

She looks good in that skirt – tight round her bum, stops just above the knee.

It would be really good if they went swimming at the weekend. I'd like to see her in her cossie again. Image of the shower shot comes into my head.

She is clothes shopping. She marches from shop to shop, looking at items, holding them up to her body and not being convinced. Might be a new dress for tonight.

Department store. She's found a couple of things that she likes. She's going to try them on.

She turns.

Momentary pause.

Did she see me?

Did she recognise me?

No. Couldn't have. If she was suspicious, she would have been staring. It was just a glance. Probably looking for an assistant.

I'm safe. I know that the rules say that, if there is a chance that you have been seen, then you should go but I think I'm OK. No, I'm positive. No need to go. I've missed being with Sarah like this and I'm not going to let one little glance ruin the rest of this hour with her.

I walk around some displays to get a better look at the entrance to the changing rooms. Sarah has just gone in. If stores were a bit more enlightened, there would be unisex changing rooms and I could pretend to try on a shirt or something. Be in the next cubicle. Be close to her as she stands in her underwear, looking at herself in the mirror.

Shop assistant hovering nearby. She hasn't seen me yet. I move away before she can pounce on me with her *Can I help you sir?*

I wander away from the changing area, looking like I'm shopping for my spouse. Nice tops. Nice skirts. Would she like that?

Every so often I end up in a position where I can see if Sarah has finished yet. It would be nice for her to come out and ask the assistant for an opinion. Would be nice to see her dressing up for me.

Now that is a nice dress. I wonder if she'll see it and go and try it on. It would really suit her – pretty little flowers. Hopefully she'll pass this way and it will catch her eye.

Changing area check.

Sarah is there.

Sarah is looking right at me.

Shop assistant speaks to her. She turns from me and hands over a card.

She turns back and looks at me.

Right at me.

She is staring right at me.

This can't be happening. How could she recognise me? I'm always careful. I take every precaution.

She turns to type in her card number.

I move further away. Different position. Test her. See what she does.

She finishes with the number. She retrieves her card. She waits for her receipt to print.

She turns her head. Looks to where I was. Can see that she is frowning. Her eyes scan the shop floor. I'm half hidden behind a display.

Eyes pass by.

Stop.

Come back.

She is looking at me again.

Time to leave. Need to get away from here as fast as I can.

When she turns to collect her bag and receipt I go for the nearest exit. It leads into the mall.

I run to the escalators and push past people to get up to the next level. I have to be sure.

I go to the edge of the balcony and look at the shop door. I wait. If she comes out that one, it'll suggest she chose it because it was the most likely one I used.

She comes out. She stops. She looks around.

She is looking for me.

I slowly take a few steps back from the balcony railing before she thinks to look up here.

I go up to the next level and then to the shopping centre car park.

Need to leave as soon as I can but can't risk using the exits. She might be waiting for me.

Head down the ramps between moving cars until I reach the bottom. Machine operated barriers so no one to ask what I'm doing.

Sprint back to work with a plan.

I tell Anne I'm feeling really sick when I get back, *funny tummy*, going to take the afternoon off if she doesn't mind.

Back to the flat to work out what to do.

By late afternoon I've got it in perspective. There could have been a whole range of reasons why she was looking at me. She might have thought I was a friend. She might have recognised me following her but not actually recognised that it was me – the man from the photo place.

Probably made things worse by disappearing. Should have taken off my shades and put on my jacket and baseball cap and become someone different. Then I could have watched exactly what she did.

Maybe I should have held my ground to see if she walked up to me. If she accused me of following her, I could have said that she was wrong – that I was waiting for my sister and I thought that I recognised her from somewhere so was looking at her to work out where I knew her face from. I'd say I realised it is from the shop.

The problem would be solved.

Might have worked out even better. Direct approach might have been better all round. The ice would be broken between us. She'd apologise and we'd get talking.

Shouldn't have run. That was bad.

Nearly six now. Soon be time for me to go if I plan to go to the pub tonight. Not sure if I should after today's adventure. It's started to rain too.

I shouldn't let this afternoon put me off going.

Sarah won't be there so I can go along see what happens. Then I'll decide over the weekend what to do in the long term.

I'm going tonight – it might give me more options.

That is decided.

I go and get changed.

ONE OF THE GANG

Sitting in the pub. Beer in my hand. Cheer and laughter all around. The cares of the day seem far behind me.

No one has made any comment that I am by myself. Anyone that has noticed thinks that I'm waiting for my date to show. But I wouldn't care if they thought I was some lonely guy trying to feel part of something bigger than him.

Most of the gang are here. I've got used to the new names now, even if I still don't think they are as good as my names for them.

Dave. Big dick Dave, bad of me to define the guy by the size of his penis but, come on really, that much is just a waste. Dave has his arm round Chris. Must admit I'm still flabbergasted by that one. Didn't think they would be the ones to get together. I had my heart set on Brian and Abby or Matt and Joan.

Then there is Craig who was John. He is the most elusive of the bunch. Isn't as sporty as the others so the only time I've seen him is in a pub or meal setting. I've only got close enough to hear him say, *Another two spring rolls, please.* Not exactly enough to give me keen insights into his personality. He remains the person that has stayed closest to the character that evolved from the photographs. I'm comfortable enough now to face the inevitable changes to that character the more I find out about him.

Then comes Rose who was Wendy. I think I made the biggest mistake with her character. I thought she was the painfully serious one. Yes, there are a few photographs of her smiling and laughing but mostly she just looks like she is frowning. I think it might be an unconscious photo face. My first-hand observations have led me to revisions – she seems to be a lively, up-for-fun sort of a girl. She certainly would win the prize for fittest – tightest tush out of the females in the group. Her body is hard. I'm not saying that she is not womanly. She's just fit. She's got a new bloke now. Not with him tonight. Just started going out with him three weeks ago. They are still in that starry-eyed, want-to-spend-every-moment-with-you phase. So he must be working or away or something tonight.

Funny the things people find attractive in someone. I wouldn't have said Rose's guy, his name is Kevin, looks attractive enough for someone like Wendy. But there must be something about him that she loves. I suppose that is the sort of thing that gives every ordinary-looking guy the hope that some pretty girl might fall for him – seeing Rose out with Kevin.

Unfortunately no sporty Scott – the Peter of times past. Another enigmatic one. Body beautiful is a religion to him, doesn't slum it with the plebs working out in a public gym, private all the way. He does make exception with the biweekly five-a-side. Must just love when he is on the skins side. Don't think there is an ounce of fat on him. I think he is with his new girlfriend tonight. Serial shagger.

Abby is the other no-show – apart from Sarah, of course. But I'm not thinking about Sarah tonight.

So there we have it. Most of the group, out for fun, out for a party and tonight just might be the night that I get a step closer. I'm just waiting for one of the lads to see me. Matt or Dave. I've said hello to them on three occasions at the sports centre. Last time I got a *How you doing?* from Dave. It was just an automatic pleasantry – he didn't actually wait for a response – but it was a definite movement in the right direction.

If no one notices me soon, I might make sure I end up at the bar ordering a drink when they next go up. Bit of engineering the situation to my advantage wouldn't be cheating.

No.

Sarah.

Sarah has just walked in.

Can't just follow my preservation instinct and jump up and run out of the pub. *Look at the trouble running got you into before.* But can't just sit here and wait for her to see me.

The fear that I'm feeling is telling me that I know, deep down inside, that she probably did see me today. That I've been deluding myself that she didn't because of the implication it could have on my plans for the future. Problem with Sarah means problem with the group.

Why the hell is she here anyway? The information I had gleaned from eavesdropping clearly suggested that she couldn't make it tonight. That is what I get for listening to Dave.

Things are going to end badly for me tonight. I just know it.

Why didn't I be sensible and stay at home? Why did I have to be a stupid, blasé little cunt and expose myself to this much potential danger? If she saw me today and she sees me in here, I am sunk. Unmasked. It would be the end of the world. Let's not mince words, I'd be totally fucked.

What should I do?

I'm beginning to panic.

Need to calm down and be focused. Need to be a problem solver not a problem builder. Oh, just fuck off with your clichés, this is serious.

If I keep my head down, I'll look suspicious. Worse, if she sees me looking furtive, then that would convince her that I am up to no good, that I am some scary little stalker.

Maybe I should laugh the whole thing off. Bluff my way out of it. I could tell her that I am absolutely head over heels with her and I was going to tell her in the department store today but I chickened out. Might work. Do you think?

Best thing is to stay put for a moment and then make my escape if she goes to the bar or the toilet or sits with her back to me.

She might not even stay for long at all. Maybe Dave got it half right and she is meeting people tonight but fancied a quick five minutes with the gang beforehand.

I should have stayed at home. Even the remotest possibility of her appearing here tonight should have kept me away. Especially after today. I've broken, no, completely disregarded, the most important commandment about watching people. If you think you've been seen, keep a low profile for at least two weeks. It has been about seven hours.

What the hell was I thinking? This isn't a game. This is as real as it gets. It could end so fucking badly for me. This could very well be the end.

I'm praying she doesn't stay. *Please just be here to say hi. Just be passing through. Don't stay. Don't fucking stay.*

She takes off her coat. Disaster. She's going to be staying for a while. No. No. No.

Breathe.

I have to breathe.

If I can brave it for a moment . . . wait until she is settled, she won't notice me passing their table. If luck is on my side, just once . . . then I'll be fine. Put on the baseball cap (should have brought glasses), stay out of her eye line, make it to the door, then out, the car, home, safety.

Why did I come this far into the pub? Should always stay near the door so you can get out quickly. What the hell was I thinking when I sat down with their table between me and the door? Yes, obviously I wanted to use that to my advantage tonight because the men's loo means Dave or Matt would have to pass me and I was madly thinking they might stop for a chat. What am I thinking? I have lost my brain completely.

I am a rat in a trap.

Why has nothing quite like this happened before? Because I follow the rules. Because I am sensible and level headed and work hard to make sure my fantasies don't take too much of a hold.

I promise I will not do anything this stupid again. I promise I'll never get this sloppy again. If I get out of here without anything happening, I promise I will be so good in the future.

Stick to photos, you idiot. None of this trouble with photos. Just stick with Hélène. Real thing only lets you down.

They are budging up to make a space for her. John, Craig, who-fucking-ever, is moving right round. A space is created looking in my direction.

Got to take action. Got to get my body to work.

She puts her coat on the seat.

Time for me to go.

She is facing away from me.
She turns.
Her eyes.
She's turning.
Those eyes.
She's turning.
All the fear I'm feeling is on my face.
Her eyes.
Can't happen.
Can't be the end.
Those eyes
See.
Me.

Look on her face. She's got a vague recollection of my face. Eyes meeting eyes. The images passing through her optic nerve – initial pattern recognition. Familiar face. Biochemical impulses travel to memory centres. Compare the image with all the other. Her face is changing. Neutral to a slight frown. Images compared. Connection made. Positive identification. There is a match. Recognition. Eyebrows furrow. Implications. Realisation comes. Fuck – I am a dead man.

Crash back to real time – the last nanosecond rewinds and then plays again.

She sees me.

She recognises me.

She realises I was following her today.

She's telling her friends. She's got very animated now.

There is nothing inside me any more. Just a hole. A deep hole that my guts are accelerating into. I'm waiting for the impact. I'm waiting for it to shock me into action.

Nausea of falling.

You don't die on the way down – you just wait to hit something hard.

She is talking to them. She is telling them about me. I can't hear the words but she's saying she saw me today. She's telling them everything. The photos. The knowing her name and where she lives. Outside her office. The café. Her flat. The streets. The shops. A flood of half-remembered images and feelings that something is not quite right and I am part of every one of them.

I've fucked up and now I get to pay the price. I knew it would catch up with me one day. For every beginning, there is an end. For everything received, there must be something given. Time to pay in full.

She is looking at me. She is talking to them about me and her eyes are burning through me, seeking out my soul. Immolation.

Can't stay here. Can't face those eyes any more. Piercing. Searing. Accusing.

Can't pass them. They could reach out and grab me, hold me, pin me down.

On my feet.

I push the toilet door open.

Smell of beery piss and blue chemical blocks in each urinal.

No one in here with me.

I lean against the door and then decide that isn't a good idea. Don't want someone to have to force their way in. Don't want the whole pub's attention on the toilet.

Maybe they didn't see me come in. Maybe Sarah had turned to the others to say something. She'd look back and, like in a movie, I'd just have vanished.

Why am I still trying to kid myself?

I'm stupid. Should have just gone straight for the door, suffered the consequences if they caught up with me. But I've come to the toilet instead. Make the situation worse, why don't you? Now I'm trapped even more and, if they come in, there would be no witnesses. Craig would stand guard while the others beat me to death.

Should go into a cubicle and lock the door. Good idea – they are really sturdy things, good strong locks. They'd kick it open in a second.

Window. Try the window, Drop into an alley, make my escape. Windows are tiny and barred.

Trapped.

Door opens.

I spin to face it.

Fight or flight.

Yeah, right.

Cower or beg.

Man looking at me. He is surprised. I'm just standing staring at him. Fists clenched. Look of panic on my face. Must think I'm a loon. He walks to the urinals. He keeps on turning his head to that he can keep an eye on me.

I go to the sink and turn on the tap, like he surprised me on the way there.

Need him to leave so I can decide what to do.

Hurry up and finish pissing, you fat bastard.

Look in the mirror to see what he is doing. I smile because he's shaking himself off which means he'll go soon. I catch his eye. He's watching me over his shoulder. He thinks I'm a pervert. Pulls up his zip and leaves.

Now wash your hands.

Can't stay here all night. Matt or Craig or Dave is bound to need a piss.

I have to go. Get out of the pub. Get to the car. Drive into the night and don't look back.

Nothing else for it. Have to face the fear. Just have to walk out of here. Keep my eyes fixed on the door. Don't look at them. Don't acknowledge anything they say to me. Get out and then it will be fine.

Only take a few seconds and then I'm free.

Nothing to be scared of.

Put on the cap. Pull the front down as far as I can. Hunch up my shoulders. Turn my jacket inside out. Different colour might throw them off the scent.

Walk to the toilet door. Too pumped with adrenaline to turn back now. Have to see it through.

Here goes.

Door opens, walking through the pub, head down, marching for the door.

Half expected the pub to be silent when I came out. Everyone looking. But it is just as it was.

Every last bit of will used to stop me from running.

Don't look as I pass the table.

Don't listen to anything that might be said.

Out the door.

Drizzle hits my face.

Puddles splash with each step.

Don't run. Not yet. Don't look guilty.

Feels good to be out.

Oppressive weight already lifting.

No eyes on me. No accusing stares. No whispers. No pointing. No outcast, unclean.

Should I turn to see if I'm being followed?

Too scared to in case I am. But need to. Have to be sure.

Glance over my shoulder.

No one.

I think I've made it.

That could have been a really tricky situation. I tell myself that I could have handled it even though a few moments ago I was panicking in the toilets.

You really need to face a crisis before you know how you'll handle it.

I am so looking forward to getting home. To curling up and shutting out the world.

Tonight means that . . . No – don't think of the negative consequences. Not yet. I'll have plenty of time to brood.

Car is parked in the next street. Just get in and drive away. Don't pause to catch your breath.

Hand on my shoulder.

Hang on, mate.

Didn't hear them coming.

Pulled roughly round.

Dave. Matt. Craig.

Girls didn't want to witness this.

Dave is holding me by the shoulder. Dave is the one that spoke.

What the fuck are you doing?

Say nothing.

You think you could just run off? Do you think we'd just let you go?

Say nothing.

Do you? Violent push on my shoulder. I manage to keep my balance.

Matt says, *Take it easy.*

Take it easy? Dave says it in a way that means that he isn't going to take it easy. *Our friend says you've been following her today. She says you freak her out when she drops off photographs.* He pauses for a reaction. *Nothing to say? Have you been following our friend, you freak?*

My legs are going weak. I don't think I want to be here.

God, I recognise this guy from the sports centre.

Thanks, Matt.

Dave has me by the collar now. *I thought I knew his face. What the fuck are you up to, you little prick?* Beer breath and spittle hits my face.

He pushes me backwards and I hit the car. I can feel the rain from it soaking into my trousers.

Let's just call the police, says Matt

They won't do a thing, says Craig.

Dave is just looking at me. I can see hate in his eyes. This just isn't going to end well.

I'm going to say this just once. Violence brings out gangster clichés. *Keep the fuck away from our friend. Keep the fuck away from all of us if you know what is good for you. Do you understand?* The fists holding my collar push against my throat.

Matt puts his hand on Dave's shoulder. *Let's just call the police. Just let him go and we'll call the police. Or you'll be the one that's done.*

I feel Dave's grip relax.

You can't call the police. You can't.

Dave brings his head forward. His forehead butts against mine. *We know where you work. OK?* Grip on my collar tightens again. *OK?*

I nod. There is no way I could even mumble just now.

He lets me go. I see Matt taking a note of my licence number. Great.

Fucking pervert, Dave spits at me.

They back off. Matt hasn't mentioned the police again.

But Dave hasn't had enough. I can see it in his eyes. Something's snapped inside.

He rushes at me so quickly I haven't even got time to cower. Fist connects with my stomach and the wind is knocked out of me. I struggle to breathe. I've doubled over but he's pulling me up again. Fist hammers home. Lower this time, right in the guts. I'm falling toward the pavement. Black from the rain. Streetlights reflected by the water. I think the fall saves me from a broken jaw as his fist punched at the side of my head.

I remember fights from the playground. Angry faces and clenched fists and little punches and kicks.

I know it is strange but I feel like a hero as I hit the road.

Must have cut something. Can taste the blood in my mouth. My skull aches, my teeth ache.

I'm vaguely aware of Matt and Craig trying to hold Dave back. I might have heard Matt saying, *What did you do that for? We could have called the police. You fucking idiot! Now what?*

I think he's got the message. Dave lunges back at me, feet flailing. Trainer connects with my chest then shoulder. *Haven't you? Haven't you?*

Legs move away. Figures struggling down the street, moving away. Angry words and shouts back at me.

The aches and pain really begin as I lie on the wet street.

No passing stranger rushes over to help me up, say they saw everything, ask if I need a witness.

I'm already thinking of the consequences. I'll take some photographs when I get back home, before I clean myself up. Evidence. Insurance. Dave's temper might have saved me. They won't want to call the police now. Not after kicking the shit out of me.

I try to move. Every part of me feels battered and bruised.

I lean against the wheel of my car.

I touch my face, nose is bleeding, can feel a lump on my head already. I think I must have bitten my cheek. I put a finger in my mouth to feel for loose teeth from the fall.

I need to go home. Lick my wounds. Take time to let the bitterness and humiliation pass.

Then it hits me like another blow. My time with Sarah and her friends is over. I'll never see another one of her photographs. I'll never be part of the group.

The weeks and months of work. The dreams and the hopes. They mean nothing now.

I am alone again.

I feel the tears coming. They mix with the blood and the rain and the dirt on my cheeks.

PART TWO

THE JUDAS HOLE

I have been in a strange sort of limbo in the weeks since I went face down in the rain.

Visited many troubling emotions and outstayed my welcome.

Fear.

Fear that they would tell someone at work. Fear that they would risk their own freedom and call the police. Fear that one day, when I'm least expecting it, they'll come and finish the job.

Shame.

Shame that I had been found out. Shame that I had been so stupid as to ignore the simple rules designed to stop exactly this sort of thing happening.

Humiliation.

Rage.

Despair took hold of me.

I've lost months of work.

I've lost Sarah.

No way that I can ever see her again.

Consequences of my actions.

But she betrayed me by seeing me.

As much her fault as mine. She might as well have been with the boys, throwing punches too.

Her fault.

No way out of the pit I was in. No hope. Only self-loathing.

Nothing mattered.

No watching.

No windows.

Then.

It got better.

I realised I had made a fundamental mistake. What happened was inevitable when I started to mix the world I created with the real world.

You see, images can only take you so far and then you have to accept that the journey has come to an end. You can still be happy at that point if you just accept that you've reached a limit.

But you can move beyond that point. Find something more tangible.

I had become content with glimpses. Half-lives. Half-truths.

Reality could only smash my fragile imaginings.

Stone-cold truth.

Only one way it could end.

I made a mistake.

My methodology was wrong.

To truly understand someone – to really know them – you have to become part of them. Slide into their life and experience it with them.

In the refining fire of my humiliation, I was left with that perfect truth. I knew what I had to do.

Every gesture, every word, every moment need to be seen.

Still images. Glimpses through windows. What truths lie there?

Henri saw that lesson. Taking the image wasn't enough for him. He had to become part of the story – he had to become part of Hélène.

Clarity.

Purpose.

I need to find someone new.

I decide to choose someone I know. That way, I can familiarise myself with the technology without having the extra pressure of working with a stranger. I'll take that shortcut. Just this once.

I'm in no rush.

I can be methodical.

The obvious choice is someone from work, someone I can track through shift rotas.

I've narrowed it down to three possibilities.

Marion.

Debbie.

Ellen.

Each one has advantages. Each one has disadvantages.

There are certain criteria that have to be met:

- Subject needs to live alone – having a partner would make the experience much more interesting but less chance of being discovered if single female.
- Ideally, subject will live in a flat I can see from the tower block. Allows multiple surveillance.
- Flat available to rent nearby.

Ellen, a very promising candidate, dismissed herself almost immediately by handing in her notice.

Debbie fits the requirements well. I plan that it should be her. I spend several days imagining what it would be like but there is something nagging in my mind. I'm not sure why but it doesn't feel right. Then enlightenment. Debbie just isn't interesting enough.

Really only one person it can be. She lives in a top-floor flat so access to a loft. Three properties available in the street parallel to hers – unfortunately her flat can't be seen from home.

Now I can perfect the skills I need.

Now I have my test case.

It is going to be Marion.

Hélène is thinking about they day they arrived.

She is thinking about the approach to New York harbour and seeing the newly erected Statue of Liberty, the way it dominated the view. She had not seen anything like it before. It made her smile and feel content – a gift to America from France. She knew that the American people would open their hearts and arms to her. She knew that she would be happy here in the Land of the Free.

Hélène turns from the window and sips her tea. She has learned how to hold a cup properly, she has learned how to dress and behave properly. People see her as the daughter of a well-to-do French family and she does nothing to make them think otherwise.

Those first days in New York were full of splendour. The buildings and the people and the diversity of culture and language. She thought she had found heaven on earth.

New York was too expensive to stay long. They moved further and further out of the city and then headed west. A series of small towns as Henri slowly worked his way to glory.

At first she was very lonely. Henri worked hard trying to be a 'legitimate' artist. She would find herself alone for days, scared of company, feeling inferior because of her language difficulties. She found some Americans unforgiving in their attitudes.

Friends were few and those that she made were always left behind.

Conversations were stilted in each new boarding house. The only English words she knew were the ones used by sailors and soldiers and they would not do in polite society.

Hélène found it amusing that people could not tell that her accent was coarse and common. They only heard the lilt and the vowels and many thought she was exotic. For some, France was the epitome of culture and art. They spent no time thinking that there was as much squalor there as here.

Hélène was unhappy with their itinerant life. She had expected to be living an adventure from the moment they had stepped on the boat. She loved the weeks of the crossing. Watching the sea and the weather, the passion in their cabin, the promise of a bright tomorrow.

Henri's money started to run low after six months. His extravagance with new acquaintances, that he believed would be some help to him, was legendary. But the drinks and the food and the hospitality returned little and his purse became light.

Henri came to their room one night in an excited state. They had only been in this boarding house for three days. He told Hélène that he had rented a room across town to serve as a studio for one week. After that, he would not be able to afford to keep it on.

Henri said that he would like her to pose for him again. He said that he had heard from an acquaintance that America was a market eager to buy his work.

For weeks they had heard stories of the boom in erotic postcards back in Europe. Many of his old friends were making money from this business. There was talk that his early images of Hélène would be perfect for this blossoming market.

Henri knew that there would be risk trying to sell his photographs in repressed America. But he also knew the rewards could be great here for the same reason. He would have to be careful.

The following day, Henri opened the shutters and light flooded into the second-floor room that would be his studio. It was dusty and one side was piled with stored furniture. Hélène was reminded of a similar room all those years ago.

Hélène let the robe fall from her shoulders slowly, watching the effect it had on Henri.

Hélène knew the excitement would help him produce better work.

Hélène felt happy as she stood naked in front of the lens.

Hélène felt a freedom she had not felt in years.

Her joy was infectious and soon Henri was smiling and laughing.

Afterwards they made love. Footprints and angels on the dusty floor.

One month later the money started to trickle in.

Hélène's English improved over the next three years.

VOYEURISM RULES

Technology for spying on your cheating spouse.

That is how domestic surveillance equipment is advertised. Well, they can't really say equipment to spy on neighbours and strangers.

So spying on you partner is OK. It is wholesome. But, best of all, it is acceptable.

The stuff you can buy, especially from America, is unbelievable. Mini cameras, infrared cameras, cameras built into music centres and televisions. All manner of watching devices cleverly disguised as household items.

Surveillance is easy.

Surveillance is big business.

Someone could be watching you right now and you wouldn't be aware of it. Same thing as being followed – you don't expect it so you don't look for the telltale signs.

Voyeurism rules.

Economically, socially, politically.

Voyeurism is entertainment.

Voyeurism is education.

Voyeurism is commonplace.

We dress it up in different guises so that we don't give the appearance of being slavering perverts.

But we are.

Big Brother isn't watching us. We are doing it ourselves. Everyday. All day.

Curtain twitching is tame compared to what most people go in for these days. Junkie tolerance leading us to crave bigger hits.

You are all voyeurs.

I'm able to buy a load of interesting equipment on the internet. I don't buy in bulk. Different items from different suppliers. Spread across America. A new state for every purchase.

Buying in this way increases the number of threads that lead back to me. But who would spend the time trying to gather these disparate clues?

Ah, the internet is bountiful. You just need to reach in and grab fistfuls of treasure.

I've gone a bit over the top with my purchases. Run up a hefty bill.

It is work so I can justify the expense to myself. Savings depleting though.

Mini cameras to be hidden in cornice work.

Microphones to transmit conversations.

Night-vision cameras for 'lights-out' viewing.

Keystroke plug for computer surveillance.

Electronic lock pick.

The last one is a bit of an extravagance. Couldn't resist it when I saw it. It makes picking locks easier but you still need patience and skill. It's not like the cop shows where you stick your gizmo in a keyhole and, *voilà*, it unlocks. I plan to buy a pile of locks from the hardware store when it arrives and practise.

You can go to extremes if you want to keep tabs on your spouse. Buy semen-testing kits. Get a garment that the light of your life has been wearing, the one she's just taken off after a 'late night at the office', unpack your testing kit and find out if she's been sloppy with her boss's juices. It seems you can detect traces for up to two years.

Check if your wife or husband is cheating with another man. Check if your children are still virgins.

I'm not making this stuff up. I don't need to – any surveillance device you can think of is already available, packed up neatly in a box, just waiting for you to hit a few keys, get your credit card and wait for the doorbell to go.

I'm most interested in the cameras.

There are, however, difficulties you need to be aware of. Some of which can render your new toys useless:

i **Size** – most cameras are small but you need to be able to conceal them in a place where they won't be noticed – more difficult than you might think. You see, we are all oblivious to the detail in our homes, until something changes. Our perceptions work on pattern recognition. Same old pattern and we don't notice a thing. If a detail changes, alarm bells go off. You'll have to drill some holes and hide as much of the mechanism as possible – well, that is what I would do. This means you need time and access.

ii **Range** – most surveillance cameras and audio equipment have a limited transmission range and there is potential signal interference from other electromagnetic sources. Signal boosting is the answer but degradation can still happen.

I've done my research. I've solved the problems. Got my contingency plans.

Just sit back and wait for the postie to bring me my presents.

SPY CHIC

There is a certain cop-movie romance about using a hired van with a row of monitors, parking it outside Marion's flat within range of the equipment and settling down to watch.

Give it a moment of thought and the enchanting spy chic of the situation will vanish with the reality of stiff backs, cold nights and no comfort.

If I'm doing this, I'm doing it in style.

One of the benefits of choosing Marion is that the street behind hers has two flats for rent and one for sale. The flat for sale is out of the question. There would be a paper trail leading to me. One of the rental flats has a better view of Marion's across adjoining back gardens but it is a three-bedroom one and significantly more money. I settle for the partially furnished two-bedroom flat. Sight lines aren't great but I don't think reception will be a problem.

I've already got a deal on some monitors and video machines so I can watch and tape at the same time. Don't want to miss a detail.

Going to be a bit tight on the money front. I've already spent a lot on equipment. Add to that the rental cars I've had to use and the three-month lease on the flat and I'm close to my financial limits. Might have to rein in spending on photographic supplies for a while – sacrifices have to be made.

The flat is a treat. Much nicer in many ways than home. It isn't such a box. Décor is neutral. Furniture minimalist. It opens up so many possibilities that I hadn't considered before. Dinner parties. Friends round for a coffee. Fuck pad. As long as I keep the spare bedroom door locked I can entertain as I please. I'll have to break the 'no cosmetic changes' terms of the lease and fit one.

Could even use one of the rooms as a studio. Just think of all the shots I could get. Could buy some old furniture and create an authentic feel for some of the Hélène shots.

Can't wait to move in.

Can't wait to start watching.

Just need to get into Marion's flat.

KEYS

When Marion is on the tills, I take a comfort break. The toilets are opposite the staff area door so I am able to peek in as I pass. Staff lockers are by the door then the coat rails and the staffroom beyond. I thought I had timed things quite well, just after the main run of morning breaks when there is hardly anyone up here, but I can hear some voices from the staffroom.

The best time would be late-night opening when Marion and I sometimes work together. Staffroom is usually quiet and it would be easy to get the keys then. But what would I do with them once I had them? The key shop would be closed and I can't just take a putty impression and drop it off the next day. I'm planning to learn how to do this. It is on my list.

There are three people in the room, Debbie and Angela and Fiona from the make-up counters. All immaculate in their collarless white coats and cinnamon-coloured, fake tans. I tend to pass pleasantries with the make-up girls and not much else. They stick to their own kind. The three in the staffroom are the younger ones. All heartbreakers in their twenties but made up like the crones they work with.

I go into the toilet, lock the door and press my ear against it. Timing is everything now. I've a few minutes before I am due back but the first lunches will start soon and I won't have much of a chance to try this again later. All I need is for the girls to leave before anyone else comes. If they stay, I'll have to go to plan B.

I hear the scrape of chairs and chitchat as they leave. They are already planning their weekend and it is only Tuesday.

I take a quick peek out. The door leading to the stairs closes behind them.

Time to move.

I dash across the corridor. Make straight for the coats.

We've not had much trouble with staff thefts for the last year or so. We went through an awful time before that when someone was delving into people's pockets. The culprit was never discovered and everyone felt very uneasy with each other. There was talk of installing a camera in the staffroom but that didn't come to anything. That sort of thing does happen though. I have heard lots of stories – like the couple sacked from the cash office in a store down south because they were caught on camera shagging on the takings.

While the slippery-fingered thief was going about their business, Anne insisted that everyone use their lockers. We're supposed to anyway. For a while after the thefts, everyone religiously put all their valuables away but, as time passed, most got lax in their habits again. Marion was no exception. She always leaves her handbag on the coat hook under her jacket. It is always easy to spot her coat because of the tatty fake-fur collar.

I arrived late this morning. I had to make sure that Marion was in before me and, with her punctuality issues, I couldn't take any chances. Marion was rushing to the shop floor when I arrived. She had the sheepish look the habitually late always have.

I put my jacket beside her coat. Ready for this moment.

Pull it aside and make sure her handbag is under it. I put my jacket on top. If anyone comes in I'll pretend I'm looking for something in my own jacket pocket.

I pull on the zip and slip my hand inside.

Rummage.

Times passes.

Her bag is full of junk. Slowing me down. Taking longer than my practice runs.

Can't risk lifting the bag off the hook to peer inside – that would look too suspicious – so I'm searching with fingertips, waiting to come across an open safety pin.

Where are the keys? Where are the keys?

Touch metal. Lipstick.

Noise from the stairwell.

Shit.

Touch metal. Compact.

Door at the top of the stairs being pulled open.

I'm going to get caught.

Touch metal. Keys.

I pull them out and shove them in my trouser pocket.

I fucking love this shit.

Heart pounds. Prickly heat across my back.

Just in time.

John III comes in and says, *Hi, man, how's it going?*

I return the greeting which he takes as a cue for getting sympathy for being dumped by Siobhan. Seems like he thought the blow job he got on the bowling night was a prelude to romance.

I nod as if I care and finger the keys in my pocket.

Women, says John III, *fucking mystery.*

We part company.

I stop on the stairs and start to breathe again.

Adrenaline bitterness fading from the back of my throat.

Down to the shop floor for the waiting game.

My lunch is at two but Marion goes at one. I spend the hour expecting to hear that Marion's keys have been stolen and we're all going to be searched.

Marion returns from lunch all smiles and I go for mine. I'm sure she watches me all the way to the stairs.

I wait until I am well away from the store before taking the keys from my pocket. Warm metal. Worn wooden crocodile key ring. Fingertips exploring the textures. Touching what Marion touches.

Two Yales and a mortise key, other smaller ones that look like they're for a piggy bank or record box.

I take the two front and single inner door keys off the ring and put them on a plain one, making sure I know the exact order to put them back. I take them to the key cutters and ask if I can collect them within the hour. No questions, no suspicions. Just a guy getting an extra set for his girlfriend.

I need to kill some time.

I think about walking up to Sarah's office. What would I do if I saw her or if she saw me? I have been tempted now and again despite what she did. I promised myself I would be careful – no more mistakes. I feel sad for the photographs that I've missed over the last few months but those feelings give way to anger. She forced me to change. She destroyed what I had. I'll never forget that.

I calm myself by walking around shops and, before the end of lunch, I have a duplicate set of Marion's keys.

Getting the keys back in her bag is going to be the trickiest part. The staffroom will be busy with the late shift crossing over the early shift. If I think it is too dangerous to try, I'll 'find' them on the floor and pass them on to the duty manager. She'll ask around and put up a notice. The croc key ring will make identification easy.

When I get to the staffroom, it is busy but no one's near the coat racks. I go to where Marion's coat and bag are and hang my jacket beside them. While I make a pretence of doing something with my wallet, I unzip her bag and drop the keys in.

I'm almost disappointed it was that simple. If stealing keys is this easy, just think of all the other workmates' flats I can access.

Back to the shop floor with the duplicate set warming nicely in my pocket. Anonymous access to her life. I can choose when I want to go in. I can choose what I want to explore. What power.

I get a buzz from the thought all afternoon.

The next stage needs even more careful planning. I think I'll have a look around first. I'll need to become familiar with her habits. That means realistically it'll be three or four weeks before I can go to the next level. But that is not a problem.

I am a patient man.

Calm.

Methodical.

This time, there will be no silly mistakes – everything is going to be perfect. Just the thought of it makes me tremble.

To think that I was so contented with photographs.

THE THRILL OF BEING CLOSE

I spend as much time as possible watching Marion's flat.

Watching someone this close feels odd. There are so many more possible problems than before – not least being seen yourself and not just by the person you are watching.

Give me the anonymity offered by a telescope or telephoto lens. You have your distance – you have your safety zone. Separated from your subject by a lot of space – that's comforting. But not any more. This is part of the change.

There is a thrill being close. You've felt it yourself. Remember when you used to play hide and seek? You're in the best hiding place ever and the hunter is very near. You are holding your breath and the butterflies are dancing in your stomach. You know that, any second, you could be found but that you might be OK. You fight back the urge to squeal with excitement. That is the thrill. Or when you were hiding in the dark waiting for a sibling to pass so you could jump out and shout an almighty *Boo!* The thrill of being discovered – the thrill of being close – the thrill of being hidden.

So I am on the streets. Getting down and dirty. Where mistakes can be made. Where police can be called and questions can be asked. Where I can be seen.

Because of work, I only watch Marion at certain times – mostly evenings and the odd early morning. It is such a help that I know when she works and when her shifts end. I've started paying closer attention to her conversations at work. Plans to go out for an evening, to see a movie, to meet a friend – it is all ammunition.

I shouldn't get too comfortable. I won't always have insider's knowledge so I shouldn't rely on it too much. But, for now, I am content to cheat just a little.

Top tips for watching people

You need different disguises. I realise that is something of a comedy word. You are chuckling at me now – an image of me, with a false beard and long raincoat, furtively peering from behind a wall – but I am being serious. Getting the information that I absolutely need requires me to watch Marion's flat and that means being in her street and that means risking being seen.

You have to accept that you are going to be seen at some point – more dangerous for me as Marion would recognise me. The real trick is to make sure that, when you are seen, you are remembered for something insignificant, something that can be easily changed. Clothes are obviously the easiest things to do this with. Wear a hat, wear a brightly coloured shirt – anything that distracts the eye from your face. Wigs are quite good too. I don't mean the one for £3.99 in the joke shop – I mean a proper wig. They are expensive but useful now and again. They can change the whole shape of your head, especially if you are in silhouette.

I am not above the false beard. Laughing again? You need to shop at theatrical suppliers, though. You need them to look convincing – not like Doctor Fu Manchu or Santa. Again, it distracts the eye from the features you are stuck with.

You are beginning to see that successfully watching someone up close is an art in itself. I am good at it but I am no expert. It is time consuming and difficult. And you thought that watching people was all about standing on a box in an alley trying to get a glimpse of some tits.

The key is being subtle in your disguise – no false noses and humps! Cause diversions, confound the eye, obfuscate.

I have a collection of glasses bought from various charity shops – the glasses of the dead, somebody called them, but I can't remember who. Glasses are great distracters. All people see is some specky bloke in a woollen hat. Pop round the corner and take them off and you are a completely different person. Perfect. But remember to be careful with your steps when you are wearing specs that look like the bottom of a bottle.

You might think that coloured contact lenses would be a good option too. That might be taking things a bit far – you really don't want to get nose to nose with people. Though I suppose, if things did go wrong, they'd help make it a bit more difficult to pick you out at a police line-up.

Be seen – but don't be recognised.

Another good idea is to alternate between the open air and a car. Clearly, if you are hanging around a street corner day after day, you are going to arouse suspicion. Sitting in a car listening to the radio is less obvious. You could be there for any reason at all. Make sure you rehearse a plausible one if you are challenged.

Remember, you can't go and sit in the same spot every day or, again, suspicion. Park further up the road. Park in the next street. The best trick is to drive by your subject's house now and again. Mix up the times you drive by – ten minutes later, five minutes after that, wait another twenty-five or so. You probably won't miss too much – just make sure you keep a note of what you see when you drive past. Over a few days, you will have a better picture of your subject's habits – home from work, out for the evening, bedtime.

You can hire cars quite cheaply for a few hours these days. Do that to stay anonymous. People wouldn't glance twice if you were in a different car each day. People are used to seeing different cars parked in their street. That is what streets are – a jumble of different colours and makes of cars. But cars carry risks with them to. Licence plates. You can be sure that the curtain twitchers are writing down the numbers of any car that doesn't seem to belong and once they have a note of that number they are on the first step of the trail that'll lead right to your door.

For on-foot watching, you can go to extremes and borrow a dog. Put on your disguise and then walk the dog by the house you are observing at any time you want. No one will question someone walking their pooch and the beauty of it is you can make it a regular thing.

I hate dogs.

Or you can pretend you are jogging. Add some theatrics and stop close to the house as if that is as far as you want to run or stop to tie a lace. Keeps you fit too. Again you can do this regularly and people will stop paying attention.

Clearly the important rule is to blend in. Once you do people will ignore you – they've got far better things to do.

However, remember that you could get carried away by it all – all the drama and excitement. It would be easy to become distracted from the job at hand – the dressing-up and being a super-cool master of disguise become their own thrill. A word of warning again. It is expensive and time consuming and you don't want, when that knock comes at your door, to be found with a closet full of costumes. What would they think?

You can see that you need imagination to do this watching business. But, if you are some loner trying to get your jollies by stalking some poor person, get straight to the doctor. You need help. This is an art and it is only for artists. Not crackpot stalker loons.

On the streets. In the fray. Watching Marion. Planning for the best moment and building my courage.

I decide when best to get into Marion's flat. I am against doing it at night – there would be too many factors working against me. She would have to be out for the evening and that has the risk of her changing her plans and coming home early, perhaps with company. Bad idea. If she had left her lights off, then I would be stumbling about with a torch – a bit of a giveaway. There are flats around hers that would have people in them, settling down for the night. People naturally become more wary at night. Streets full of twitching curtains – nosy neighbours checking up on their fellows.

So that means it has to be daytime. Fewer people in the flats around hers to notice me and I could have any number of legitimate reasons for going into her building. I won't be mucking about waiting for the security door to open either, so less chance of running into someone.

Daytime it is then. I'll either have to call in sick or wait for a day when I am off. Best if it is the latter. Don't want to use my sick days for something like this – you never know when you are going to need one for something unexpected.

Delaying entry for a few days until our rotas are just right lets me get in some more watching. But I don't mind telling you that I am getting a bit jumpy.

If I was caught, I don't know if any amount of explaining would get me off the hook. No. Need to keep focused on the job in hand. Can't give in to doubts and fears. So stay focused, stay frosty.

Marion is a creature of habit. The main habit of the moment is staying home. She seems to have at least a couple of close friends and she is quite popular at work so being a stay-at-home doesn't seem to fit. No, the answer lies in the fact that there is no evidence of a current boyfriend. From past experience I know that it probably won't be long before she has a new beau. The list of her boyfriends is legendary at work but I don't believe for sluttish reasons. She just can't keep them. She could write a book about getting someone to go out with you but she'd need help with the chapters on making him stay.

There is no logic in the world. It would seem strange to some that dizzy, plain Marion could attract such a long list of blokes. Perhaps it is because some men like someone they can look after and Marion can have the appearance of an injured doe on occasion. But the way of the world is that, once these men are attracted, they want to switch roles and become the ones looked after – perhaps that's just not Marion's style at all.

Shame really – that she doesn't have a current boyfriend, I mean. That would be good. Listening in on people's lives is only interesting if they have something to say and so few of us have anything interesting to say when we are by ourselves. Yes, I hope she gets a new boyfriend soon for a whole range of reasons.

However, for the moment, she is on her own and that is why she spends so much time at home. Brooding. You would think that having been through this so many times would make her immune to the break-up blues but I suppose that she probably thinks that every one of them is *the* one and so every broken relationship troubles her heart.

Marion gets ready for bed between ten and eleven and her light goes out not long after. At least that is what it looks like. If I had a little more time I could form the perfect picture of her habits but I am not too concerned with her precise movements in the evenings just now. I can explore them from the comfort of my own flat later.

Night watching can be as boring as day watching. If you are sitting in a car you are not going to see much. Most people don't look out their windows often so you'll be staring at curtains for most of the time. To qualify this, though, I have to say that just about every street has its nosy neighbour. I can almost guarantee there will be one curtain twitcher in your street. They are easy to spot because they are so bad at doing it discreetly. They work under the assumption that, if they think you can't see them, then you actually can't see them. They are wrong – a constantly moving curtain is a dead giveaway.

Nosy neighbours are a watcher's greatest enemy because the mindset of such a person is to be suspicious, to complain, to call the police, to keep tabs on everyone. Once you have seen one of these people looking out of the gloom of their sitting room, you know that you will have to take extra precautions. They are just itching to get on that phone and tell the police that there is some miscreant lurking out in the dark. I don't want to stereotype here but it tends to be older people that do it. People that have given up doing anything in their own lives and feel that they have to interfere in other people's. It is sad really – they must be quite lonely. I am pretty sure that some of the old blokes that curtain-twitch are just out for a glimpse of a pretty girl – or any girl. It would make their day to see a bit of flesh. Might even make them stop scowling for a few minutes.

I've spent ages deciding exactly what equipment I should take on my first visit and had to work hard to ensure my wish list got cut down to a manageable size. Yes, it would look strange if I arrived at her door with a suitcase. I think I have all the essentials but I know that this will probably be the first of many visits so no need to cram everything in this time. This is more of a recce.

All set. Next week the rota has me off and Marion on.

Just have to wait now.

I'm glad I have a bit of grace before the deed.

I've got plans for the weekend.

OUTDOOR MAN

I stretch back on the tartan rug and feel the sun warming my face. Sky is cerulean. Cotton wool clouds in the distance – calendar-photo perfect.

I savour the moments as I wait for Will and Laura.

Just about got my breath back after my jog uphill with a full rucksack. I had to take a shortcut across fields, making sure I avoided the cow shit, so I would arrive with plenty of time to spare to set everything up. I've become a bit of an outdoor man over the last few weekends – all in pursuit of 'Project Will and Laura'.

I've been taking things slowly. Slow and subtle – my new motto. Both 'Project Will and Laura' and 'Project Marion' use my new technique. Plan, plan and plan some more. Nothing should be rushed – everything has its own pace. You just have to find the right one and stick to it. You have to use your mind. You have to use your cunning.

Will and Laura spend most weekends doing something active. Their favourite pastime is a few hours of brisk walking in the countryside on a Sunday afternoon. There are plenty of good walks within a half-hour of the city. They have a book that lists them all. I've watched them looking at it, sharing their planning of routes.

I've got my own copy. After following them a couple of times and familiarising myself with their favourites walks, I could quickly work out which one they were heading to. With a bit of creative improvisation, I was able to make sure I passed them walking from the opposite direction, greeting them with a hearty *Hello!* before marching off on my merry way.

The object is to get them familiar with me. Start off with saying hello. Hellos become smiles and admiring the weather and scenery. Strangers become smilers become acquaintances become friends. So very simple.

A couple of weeks ago, we reached the acquaintance stage, pausing for a few minutes to chat. For most people this is often as far as it gets.

I met them ten days ago in the supermarket – not such a strange thing as we are neighbours. Of course, to them, I won't be living in the tower block – the rented flat will be my home. But we are not quite there yet.

I think you must be stalking me, I said as I bumped into them in the dairy aisle. We chatted about nothing for a while and then parted. Will threw a *See you again soon!* over his shoulder and we all laughed.

Held off meeting them last weekend. I watched them set off. I wanted to follow but knew that, to do this properly, I shouldn't meet them walking every week. I have to meet them out of context more. That is such an important thing to do. Makes me more memorable.

Will is the contact point. He is the one I would have to work on, create a bond with. Can't be Laura. Laura is the point of the whole exercise and that has to be hidden.

Last week I ran into Will in the changing room at the sports centre across the park. He was playing squash with a colleague from work. I had just finished a swim. *Do you live round here?* I asked innocently and he said that he did. *Do you?* I told him a friend has a flat on the other side of the park and I was meeting him later and I felt like burning some calories beforehand. He said, *We must play squash sometime.* I smiled and thought, *Oh, fuck, it'll kill me!* and nodded enthusiastically. *That would be great.* We introduced ourselves, we shook hands, we showered side by side.

All these preparations leading to today. Now we move from acquaintances to friends – if it all goes according to plan.

I'm feeling kind of nervous.

I know they'll be coming up the trail in the next few minutes. Followed them part of the way here and then legged it over the field to get here before them.

There are other people about because it is such a nice day so I've set up a little way from the track. Rucksack bursting with all the goodies I would need to tempt them. I know what their favourites nibbles are. I've been watching them long enough to find out.

They come into view and I give them an enthusiastic wave. They wave back and I jump to my feet.

I was hoping I'd meet you, I gush. *I was stood up for lunch al fresco at the last moment and I sure as hell wasn't going to let that ruin my day. I was hoping I would meet some nice people to share my glorious repast with and you are the perfect candidates.*

Just listen to my patter.

Will and Laura make polite noises that they couldn't possibly impose but I shush them effectively with I *positively insist.* Don't know where the slightly camp lilt to my voice comes from. Have to run with it now. I can soften it later on – maybe only use it when I'm being dramatic.

I force a couple of glasses into their hands a pour a little fruit smoothie into each one. *Fruit smoothies, I'm afraid*, I say. *Driving today.*

They can't refuse.

Please sit at the dining table, I say, expansively gesturing over to the rug. I think I was born to play this character.

They sit.

I've got you hook, line and sinker. No chance you'll get thrown back.

I have a feast with me. Three kinds of cheese, a selection of fruit, French bread, sun-dried tomatoes, black olives, pumpkin seed salad with an olive oil and balsamic vinaigrette, fresh pasta salad with sunflower seeds and raw cashew nuts.

We eat and we drink and we chat.

I tell them I'm reading a wonderful book on cosmology by Greene. I get carried away and tell them I've just finished a great biography of JFK. Will immediately launches into a discussion of the book and the fall of Camelot. Lucky I read it just in case I got a chance to bring it up.

It surprises all of us that we have such similar tastes.

They ask me over to supper next week to thank me. *The least we can do after this stunning picnic.*

This is so easy.

Full interaction. I can't believe the confidence I've found over the last few weeks. I wouldn't have thought I could relate to my subjects in such a way – that I could create this whole scenario and reap the rewards.

Engineered by me.

All of it.

Master craftsman.

I bask in the glory of my victory.

Acquaintances to friends.

Soon we'll be firm friends.

Soon we'll be inseparable.

This is better than it could ever have been with Sarah and her lot. They weren't the right ones. But Will and Laura. They are perfect. Exactly what I've been looking for.

The sun catches Laura and I glimpse Hélène sitting beside me.

JUDAS HOLE

All my planning and the day finally is here.

Alarm is set to go at six and I spend an hour just watching it tick-tick round waiting for the buzzer to go off. You know how much I hate this time of the morning. When you are so groggy that you can't do the sensible thing and just get up. No, you just lie in a stupor, trying to will yourself to move. It is always at times like this your little concerns become fears. Anxiety grabs you by the stomach and squeezes until your worries are magnified beyond all proportion.

Six, the alarm rings and I'm finally moving. No extra fifteen minutes in bed today – I'm heading straight for the bathroom. I have a cool shower for ten minutes to shock myself alive.

The idea of breakfast makes me feel queasy so I plan to take a couple of bars of chocolate just in case I need a sugar rush during the morning.

I spend a little time looking in my bag to make sure I have everything I need. I spent most of last night checking it was all right but somehow I seem to doubt it now and spread everything out and recheck it against my list. Present and correct. Neatly repack it into the bag making sure that the things that I'll need first are right at the top.

I still have some time to kill. She won't be leaving for work until about eight-thirty and I don't plan to be at her house until about ten past eight. That leaves me almost an hour to waste. There is no point in going too early. Me sitting in my car near the house for an hour or more would just look suspicious.

I can't settle to anything. Early morning television irritates me and what seems like half an hour of watching is only five minutes. I wonder if I should develop some photographs – the new ones of Will and Laura. That always makes me feel better. I don't think I have enough time and I hate to rush it.

I look through some photo albums but that is not much fun either. I think about digging out some of *her* photographs, just for a quick look. But I don't feel like going to that place today. No, find something else instead.

Time is dragging. I just want to be in the thick of things, letting my instinct and my planning take over. I hate this endless rumination. Sometimes I feel that I think too much, that I would give anything to have a few moments when my brain just stops. Enter into the bliss of thoughtlessness. Sounds like heaven.

I've had enough.

I decide to leave.

It is about fifteen minutes before I need to but I'll drive around for a while, tracing the route that she'll take to the bus, just on the chance she leaves early for once.

I am doing no good pacing about my flat – action will steady my nerves.

I know she'll still be in bed just now. Probably having put her alarm to snooze and then snooze again, under the duvet, in the warmth. I imagine snuggling up close.

I put the duplicate set of her keys in the zipper pocket of my jacket.

Panic.

I should have checked if the keys worked. But I decided that was too risky. It would be infuriating if I copied the wrong ones.

Tell yourself that they are the right keys and stop looking for things that could go wrong. But such an obvious thing – what other important details have I forgotten or simply not thought about?

Stop it.

I have planned everything. I have imagined, in obsessive detail, all the things that could go wrong. Don't forget I'm pretty good at thinking on my feet. I'll cope with any mishaps.

Just get on with it.

Traffic is building up when I leave but I have anticipated this. It takes around the time that I thought it would to get near her flat, although leaving early has put me ahead of schedule.

I drive around the streets surrounding her building. I have spent days debating where would be the best place to watch her leave from. Should I park close enough to see her leave? Should I park near the bus stop to make sure that I see her get on? The best compromise is to park in a side street just off the route she takes. Less risk of her seeing me and I can follow her to the bus stop, even follow the bus for a bit if I'm feeling really jumpy. Then I'll drive past her flat to make sure the coast is clear before parking a couple of streets away. Prefect. Precise planning.

I settle in to watch and realise that I am eating one of the chocolate bars.

I look from the car clock to the bottom of the street where she'll pass. She should be here by now. Running late again. What if she is not feeling well today? What if she has just called in sick and has crawled under the duvet again? How long should I wait?

Get out of bed, get dressed, get out the door.

Look at the clock.

Look at the street.

Should I drive to the flat and see if her curtains are closed? Should I ring the door bell or call her just in case she's decided to have *just five more minutes*?

I see her.

She is wearing the same old raincoat over her uniform with the same old brown handbag.

I don't rush to the main door once she has turned the corner.

Have you ever noticed that, in every thriller, a person leaves their house and our hero sneaks in? Suddenly we cut to a shot of the home-owner – forgotten important papers, forgotten to feed the cat, forgotten their umbrella. They turn back to their house, our hero oblivious. The person opens the door and walks into the room we saw our hero in just a moment ago. He is nowhere to be seen – hiding in a closet or jumped over the back wall just in time.

Nonsense of course but that doesn't stop me driving to the bus stop to make sure she gets on.

I see her standing in the queue as I drive by. To her, I am just another car commuter – not worth a second glance. I park a little bit further up the road and watch her in the rear-view mirror. I am not there for long when the bus arrives and she gets on. As it passes me, I wonder if I should follow it to the city centre to make sure she arrives at work. That would be overkill. She's on the bus – she's not going to be back any time soon. I won't be disturbed.

I park. I take a deep breath. Steady my resolve. Iron in the soul.

My hands are shaking.

Grab the steering wheel tightly as I try to regain my composure. Nice long, deep breaths. Keep them slow and steady so I don't get too light-headed.

Calm.

Serene.

Waterfalls. Green fields. Deep breath. Sun on a sandy beach. Blue sky. White fluffy clouds. Hélène and muslin.

Moments pass.

Just a bit longer until I am sure I'm calm – then I'll go.

I begin to feel a bit better despite the aching queasiness in my stomach but I've still got a long way to go until I reach a comfortable state. I'm kidding myself – I don't think that I'll ever feel ready. Only one thing for it – just do it now. Action instead of thought. I'll have a few minutes' walk until I get to her street to steady myself. That'll be enough.

I grab my rucksack and lock the car. Now or never. Now or in a few days, a few weeks. No – it has to be now. I can't delay much longer. I have my timetable.

I spend a long time looking up and down the street. I hope that no one is paying much attention to me because I'm red faced and sweating and fidgeting. *Suspicious.* I must look like every thief and mugger and stalker that has ever lived. Standing, as shiftily as I am, eyeing the street, the houses, the passing cars, miscreant written all over me. There must be a dozen phone calls to the police happening right now. The twitchers doing their God-given duty. I know I have to move now or else I'll get stuck here. I feel quite giddy. Heart racing. Churning stomach.

I know what I am doing and I know why I am doing it so why do I feel like this? Just stop this pointless self-analysis before it starts to take hold.

I cross the road quickly and with as much confidence as I can fake – as much confidence as a bright-red, sweaty, shifty-looking house-breaker can assume.

The key is in the security door and I am inside the building.

Coolness, semi-darkness.

I let out a huge sigh and then hold my breath, listening. There is music coming from one of the flats in the basement and I can hear a phone conversation from one of the doors ahead but it sounds like there is no one in the hallway. I suddenly become aware that I am standing by the main door. Why not stick a sign to my chest saying 'up to no good'? I quickly and quietly move towards the stairs. I've put on trainers to make sure I make as little noise as possible. Risk of footprints but I'll bin the trainers later.

Her flat is on the top floor. Black storm doors, chipped paint, red showing underneath. Brass fittings. Plastic nameplate.

My hand is shaking badly as I try to put the key into the lock. Sweat pouring down my back. Heart kicks – so hard I can feel it banging my chest. Difficult to swallow.

What am I doing here? I should go back to what I know, what is safe.

Try to focus again but it is getting more difficult. Control. Control.

Oh, God, what if the door behind me opens? I turn to it. There is a peephole in the middle, three quarters of the way up. Light shines through it. No nosy neighbour watching from their hallway.

The key slides in and I turn it. Once. Twice. Double mortise lock, good security. Necessary for insurance. Just the Yale left. In some ways, I am surprised that she only has two locks. I have three on my door. I even got a new door like this one – heavy, solid.

I hear some noises from downstairs. All I need is someone to wander up to borrow some sugar. If I am seen, I am sunk. Whatever made me think that this would be a good idea?

Time for speed.

I slide the Yale into the lock and turn. I'll be inside in just a moment. Nobody will have seen me – I'll be safe. It doesn't turn. Insides spasm, prickly heat down my back. I begin to panic. I have to decide whether to stay here or make my getaway. I take the key out a look at it. It is definitely the one I got cut. It is definitely Marion's key. Those bastards at the shop. I should have known not to trust a shop that does shoe repairs as well as key cutting.

One more try and then run for it. No – running would attract attention. I had worked out a whole set of excuses if I was discovered. All of them seemed perfect when I was in the comfort of my flat. I can't remember a single one now. Hopefully blind instinct will take over. I'm a deliveryman. Special mail. I'm here to read the meter. Fuck I'd be spotted as a fraud instantly.

Key in the lock again. Turning. No, still sticking. Can't try again – I'll be caught. Breaking and entering. Five years. Search warrant for my home. Now that would be something. The police would think I was a pervert. Sexual deviant, fifteen years. Inmates would see me as a sicko. Beaten, raped in the showers.

I pull the key out a little and wiggle it. It catches. It turns easily. Yale keys – always trouble.

I open the door and then I'm in. Gently close it behind me. I look out the peephole. Noises from downstairs muffled. No one appears. Door opposite stays closed. Light still shining through the peephole in it.

No one knows I'm here.

Secret.

Safe.

Stupid to be so worried. What was the big deal? But I'm still shaking. I'm still sweating. What a rush.

I didn't put on any deodorant this morning, didn't want to risk leaving an unfamiliar scent in the house. But I didn't think I'd be sweating this much. Maybe I made a mistake. Stale sweat aroma when she comes home, another give-away. Hopefully it'll be gone by tonight. Fingers crossed.

I turn to face the inner door. Frosted glass panel taking up more than half of it. Nice geometric design. Another Yale. Turns easily first time.

I'm inside. I am actually inside her flat. Plans reaching fruition. I like this – yes, this feels right.

This is definitely Marion's flat. It is a glorious clash of styles and colours – nothing seems to match very well. An interior designer would have a fit. I like it.

I go into my bag and start to take out my tools. First thing – latex gloves. I really hate these things. They smell disgusting and I don't like the way your hands feel when you take them off – too slick, ingrained talcum powder – but they are necessary. Can't leave any fingerprints. I have some moist wipes and hand cream for when I take them off.

Next thing out of the bag is masking tape. I take a piece, open the inner door and stick it over the storm-door peephole. I know that it will leave a residue – must make sure I wipe it away. I'll be using a flash in the hall and I don't want a passing neighbour to see it.

I take out a balaclava and put in my pocket. If she comes home early I can slip it on and pretend I am a burglar, rush past her and out the door. Every eventuality covered, I hope.

I have pen, pencil and a notepad that I put in my top pocket and my handy-dandy little measuring gizmo. These items are to help me map the flat as accurately as possible. It is important to have a clear image of the whole flat. Going down this path means that detail is everything, every scrap of information is important. I can be no longer content with little hints and clues that I use a leap of imagination to expand.

Last out – my Polaroid camera. It is loaded and I've brought several spare packs of film with me. Polaroids are an expensive way to take snaps and the quality is not so great. But I need the instant reference that they can give me while I'm here and I can't be bothered squinting over a digital camera screen.

Digital snaps for next time.

I put the camera strap around my neck and then unclip the lens cover.

My previous excited panic is replaced by a better sensation – that deep expectant thrill in the bottom of your stomach that rises to fill you completely when you know you are in for a treat.

The hall isn't too long and there are four doors off it. One of them is going to be a cupboard. That leaves living room, bedroom and bathroom. I know in these flats the kitchen is off the lounge.

First photograph before I go exploring.

Flash

Photograph one. Frozen moment.

I take the photograph from the front of the camera and write on it: Hallway, from door. She has an interesting mix of pictures in the hallway. Prints of cats and I am sure that is a Monet print, something with lilies in water. I am excited by what I will find behind the first door. It is a cupboard just as I thought. There are a couple of shoeboxes in the bottom that I am keen to examine. I hoping they hold photographs, but I hold off this pleasure because the rooms are today's focus.

I take a photograph.

Flash

Photograph two. Hall cupboard.

Raincoat hanging on door, vacuum cleaner, ladder, boxes, extension cable, shoeboxes, paint tins on the floor with drips down the sides, blue, white, yellow.

The next door. It is open a little and I can tell instantly it is the bathroom. The light I can see is the unique bathroom kind – frosted glass windows and the cold shine you get from off tiled surfaces. It is quite a nice bathroom. Full of knick-knacks absent from mine. My bathroom is quite functional, there for a purpose – well, two if you count its use as a darkroom. That's why I have no clutter. But this bathroom has jars with coloured sand and tiny scented pillows, many bottles of shampoo and conditioner and foot lotion and exfoliating creams. Female bathrooms – all pastels and light, interesting smells and textures, bottles of exotic face scrubs and foot pamper creams. Male bathrooms – all dingy with clogged sink, scum ring round the bath, clutter of razors, shaving foam, little bits of beard hair, single bar of soap with the ever-present pubic hair.

Flash
Photograph three. Bathroom from door.

The bath has one of those solid glass screens on it for the shower. The suite is white, all shining clean. She seems good on housework. Mirrored cupboard above the sink.

I open the door and take a picture.

Flash
Photograph four. Bathroom cupboard.

Dental floss, painkillers, cotton buds, pack of condoms opened, pack of condoms still in cellophane, toothpaste, plasters – the usual stuff.

Yes, all in all, a pleasant bathroom. Image of her in the bath enters my mind – candlelight, bubbles, a glass of wine, a little treat at the end of the day.

Time to move on.

The bedroom is next.

I pause at the door wondering if I should save it for last. My excitement gets the better of me. Besides, it means I can come back for a second rummage later. Twice the fun.

If you want to find out what a person is really like, the bedroom is the place to explore. You could argue that the lounge would be the better for gathering intelligence. There are so many hints and clues that can be found in there. People usually have bookcases in their living rooms so you can see what their interests are. The same goes for their DVD and CD collections and there are bound to be some magazines lying about. Yes, you can definitely find out much in that one room.

But people tend to have eclectic tastes which confuses things. Anyway, what deep personal knowledge can you gain from seeing that they have a copy of the latest Ian McEwan next to a Rosamund Pilcher on the shelf? Only that the person has diverse reading habits. Shirley Bassey and Coldplay side by side. What hidden truths do they reveal? The truth is a lot of people have the same books or CDs or DVDs in their collection. Nothing more profound revealed by that than these people like to read, watch and listen to bestsellers.

You also have to be careful with your assumptions. There will be red herrings dotted about the place.

Lounges are places to entertain so you fill it with things that you want people to notice – the books that make you look intellectual, the music that tells people you are sophisticated, the European cinema that makes you cosmopolitan. Posturing artifice designed to create the idea of the person that you'd like others to see.

The bedroom is the place where the public face falls away – the one room that people keep for themselves. The only entertaining that goes on in here is the intimate kind. Nothing placed in here to fool people into thinking what a great person you are, what a rounded individual – only personal items that reveal who you really are.

Your bedroom is your haven, your escape from the world. No matter what sort of a day you've had, curl up in here and you'll feel protected. Sanctuary. Hidden. Safe and still.

I can't wait to explore.

I look around the door and raise the Polaroid.

Flash
Photograph five. Curtains open.

Fabric blinds pulled down. I know she always keeps the blinds down to prevent anyone watching from the back lane. The bedroom is a clutter – piles of clothes lying around, dressing table strewn with beauty products. It is quite a surprise after her tidy bathroom. See what I mean about showing the inner person? Even more proof that she doesn't have a current boyfriend. Mess not being too impressive for an evening of romance.

I must admit that I was expecting something quite grand in her bedroom – four-poster bed, lots of lace, pink cushions. What a romantic I am.

The room is functional. Built-in wardrobe, dresser with mirror, a chest of drawers on both sides of the bed, ottoman at the bottom, clothes-covered chair in the corner. Big cushions on the wall instead of a headboard. White bed linen. All quite commonplace, quite ordinary. I am a little disappointed. This room has occupied my thoughts for a long time. Maybe that is the problem – it could never live up to my expectations. Never mind. There'll be hidden treasures in here I'm sure.

Explore the chests of drawers first. Camera to the ready. First thing to do is note how far each drawer is open. It is important to make sure I leave everything as I find it. I am pretty sure that Marion is not the sort of person to take much notice of tiny variations, but it is necessary for me to observe all the rules. Some people do paranoid things like putting slips of paper in doors to find out if someone has opened them or hairs stuck across drawers. No need to do that if you live alone – no one is going to be snooping around your drawers. But, if you live with flatmates, take as many precautions as you can – they won't be able to stop themselves rummaging the moment you go out.

I gently ease open the top drawer of the right-hand side chest of drawers.

Flash

Photograph six. Top drawer.

Underwear. Panties. Two piles. Left hand side, big safe secure, everyday ones. Reassuringly robust. Right hand side (smaller pile) delicate, lacy, skimpy knickers and thongs. Sunday best, dressing-up underwear.

Flash

Photograph seven. Middle drawer.

Bras, stockings, tights, socks. Same as drawer above with the bras, several everyday ones, some sexier ones and tucked in the back a couple of Wonderbras. Oh, a couple of teddies too – wonderful.

Flash

Photograph eight. Bottom drawer.

Mainly nightshirts and pairs of pyjamas. On impulse I take off a latex glove and use a moist wipe to take the talc away. I wait a moment until my hand dries and then touch the top set of pyjamas. Brushed cotton, soft. Must use a good conditioner. Must feel nice next to her skin.

I put on a new glove and walk around the bed to the other set of drawers.

Flash

Photograph nine. Eclectic drawer.

Cotton wool balls, face cleanser, moisturisers, anti-wrinkle cream. Drawer for 'last-thing-at-night' rituals. Then couple of condoms. Plain, not ribbed, not flavoured. This is becoming an interesting drawer. Ubiquitous copy of *Women on Top* and what is that tucked behind the box of balm-infused tissues? Vibrator. Pink. Fun. Girls and their toys. Well, what else would you keep alongside a book of sex fantasies? Have a read to turn herself on and then buzz-buzz. I almost expect to find a bonk-buster next – all innocent milkmaids with heaving bosoms and handsome scoundrels with tumescent members. Funny that a woman has a book like that to stir her passions and a man would use a glossy lad mag with pics. Says something about imagination. Something under the tissues. Could it be? Special prize. Looks like a diary. I want to snatch it up and read every word. Next time. Stay focused. Really need my digital camera for that. Maybe laptop and scanner would be best. Might have to have a quick leaf through it before I go today. Tease myself with some of the exciting things I'm going to find out over the coming weeks of watching. I'm so happy.

Flash, flash

I feel so comfortable in Marion's flat – a nice sense of belonging that usually only comes from looking through windows. I could really feel at home here. Integrate perfectly.

Maybe I should make myself a cup of tea, a bit of lunch, settle down in front of the box or read one of her books, listen to a CD, find her photo albums, sit back and wait for her.

Home, dear? Had a good day at work? I've run you a bath and dinner is on. Later, I'll give you a foot massage while you watch the telly.

If she walked through the door now, would she be happy to see me? Would she smile and let the troubles of her day fall away? Would she be content that she had, at last, found someone to spend her life with, someone to start a family with?

Of course not. She'd take one startled look and run screaming down the stairs.

Don't get caught in the daydreams. Just watching and listening for now. That is what I am here for. That is the plan. Have to stick to the plan. No time for fantasy, that way will lead to troubles. I here to find the best places for my equipment. Next visit I'll place it. Then wait, watch, learn.

I'll know everything about her. Every intimate detail. Every thought. Every truth.

Then it will be easy.

Remember Marion is an object at the moment – not a subject. Everything I know about her just now is meaningless. I'll only understand with information, direct observation. What I have now is a series of snapshots, as cold and unyielding as any photograph. I'm transcending them. Moving beyond to something purer, something glorious, something intimate.

Savour the bedroom for another moment. Suck in the ambience. It is beginning to grow on me. Nice cornice in this room too. Old. Ornate. Full of intricate design. Lots of gaps and shadows to hide tiny lenses.

I go back into the hall and check the internal hatch to the loft. It is near the front door. There is a bigger hatch out in the landing but it's padlocked. There is probably a key for it in the drawer near the door but the hatch in the flat is going to be best for what I need. No chance of discovery.

Lounge next. Thrill of a new room rushes though me. Trepidation too.

The door is ajar and I can see sunlight. This will be the most danger-ous room of all. Bay window – curtains fully open – no nets, no blinds to hide behind. Flats across the road look right in. No privacy. Too many chances to be seen.

Need to get in and close those curtains. Either that or forget about this room completely and there is no chance of that. This is one of the important rooms. Need to have eyes and ears in there.

When I go into that room, I'm exposed to prying eyes. Some neighbour across the street might take a nosy look out their window and catch sight of me all latex gloves, dark clothes, creeping slowly to the window as if going slow would stop me from being seen. I'd look every inch the thief, every inch the panty sniffer as I reached the window and pulled the curtains closed.

Neighbour's fingers shaking as they punch the number. *Police? Strange man. Burglar. In the flat across the street. Come quick. You can catch him. Take him to the station. Strip search. Put him on trial. Expose him to the public. Prison sentence. Make him a fat boy's bitch. Shame. Guilt. Found hanged in cell.*

I could crawl along the floor and pull the curtains closed but that would probably have itchy-fingered neighbours again reaching for phones.

Only one real option. Only one that can work. Make it look like I belong here, a part of Marion's life. Wander to the window with a mug of tea. Take a sip. Now I'm the new boyfriend left in the flat by himself. Would hardly get a second glance. Anyone that sees me will know I've seen them and will be too embarrassed to stand and stare or dart behind the curtains for a sneaky peek. Best if it looks like the new boyfriend just got out of bed. Here he comes for a couple of hours of daytime television – natural for him drawing the curtains to keep reflection from the screen.

I'm prepared for being him. I open the inside pocket of the bag and take out a mug. I place it on the floor. I've practised miming drinking from an empty cup.

Time to get changed.

Shoes first. Velcro tabs for easy removal. Jacket on top of my bag. Sweatshirt follows. Trousers, elastic waist so that I can take them off quickly. I'm wearing baggy blue boxer shorts. Not the sort I would wear myself but exactly the ones Marion's new boyfriend would wear. I'm debating about my vest top and socks. If I wander to the window just wearing my boxers it would look more like I had just got up but an almost-naked torso might attract eyes so it may be best to keep the top on. Socks are different. My feet won't be seen but I feel it would help me get into character.

I can see the lounge carpet through the crack in the door. Hardly any shag. I won't leave footprints.

Decisions. Decisions.

I go with bare feet for this one. This is what the boyfriend would do if it was him and I want this character to feel like he belongs here. I'll just have to remember where I walk and take the DustBuster across the floor once I'm done. Best not to leave any skin cells with DNA clues.

Take the black wig from my bag – scruffy, collar-length hair. I put it on and muss it up to give me that just-got-up look. From a distance, you can't tell it's a wig.

Mug in hand.

Deep breath.

Step towards the door.

Stop.

Still got latex gloves on.

Back to bag and take them off. Moist wipes to take away any trace of talc. I put a new pair into the mug.

Back to the door.

Heart. Pound. Pound. Pound.

Push the door open using my nails.

Full commitment. Be him. Be him. Be him.

Walk in.

Sofa. Chairs. TV. Bookcase. CD player. Coffee table. PC on desk behind the door. Door leading off to kitchen.

Bowl and mug from breakfast on table, magazine open at a fad diet page.

Curtains open. Clear view of the windows across the street.

I don't spend too much time on the room. I'm supposed to look comfortable here. I'm supposed to look as if I am with familiar with it.

I can make it to the window with only a slight detour round the coffee table.

Rub my toes against the carpet as I walk. Marion does this. Marion has walked barefoot where I walk. I can feel her through each step.

I stop at the window and look out into the street. Lift the mug and pretend to take a swig of coffee. I've decided that he doesn't drink tea. He is a coffee man. Milk. Two sugars.

No sign of anyone at the windows across the street. People either at work or still in bed or making breakfast or on the school run.

Look at the bay windows on either side of Marion's.

No signs of life.

Couple of people in the street. They don't look up.

A car passes.

Fake a yawn. Scratch my balls. Can't ever remember clawing at myself in this way but it is something he'd do. I've seen people do it in movies to add an extra dimension to their characters.

Second sip.

Getting into the part.

I like being the new bloke in her life.

Woke up with her this morning. Spooning before she got up for a shower. I stayed in bed – post-coital dozing. Still there after she left. Trip to have a piss. Then through here to look out on the day. Coffee in hand. She brought me it before she left. Cold now. I still drink it though.

People seeing me at the window would accept who I am. They'd see the long hair, the T-shirt and boxer shorts and know I am the latest.

They see Ralph. Not used that name before. Ralph is twenty-eight but looks like he could be anywhere from mid twenties to early thirties. He's between jobs. He's taking it easy for a couple of months. He met Marion a few days ago. Nightclub. Danced together. Snogged for a while. Back to his for sex. Both thought it was probably a one-night stand but the next morning he didn't say, *I'm expecting people round*. She didn't say, *I need to get home for the boiler man*. They looked at each other in the morning light and didn't panic at what they saw. They moved close to each other. Lovemaking instead of sex.

They don't know if it is a relationship yet. They are just seeing what happens.

With Marion's track record, it might not be for long.

I reach over to pull the curtains closed. No gloves. Pay attention to where I touch. Pull one side to the middle, take a step, reach out for the other. Room is dark. Curtains nice and thick. Flash will be hidden.

I take the latex gloves from their hiding place in my mug and put them on. Retrace my steps back to the hall. I decide that I'll stay dressed as the character for the moment – I'd only have to get changed again once I've finished so that I can open the curtains again. Don't need the mug though.

I take a pair of little rubber socks – the kind you can buy at swimming pools to protect your feet from infections. I slip them on. Using them mainly because I have them – could just as easily put my socks and shoes back on. They feel odd against my skin.

I check the computer first when I go back into the lounge. Don't think she uses it much. Layer of dust on the keyboard and the thing looks fairly old anyway. It is little more than a word processor. Doesn't even have a modem so my little plug that records keystrokes is useless. Shame. If she used the internet, I could have found out her credit card numbers, security digits, passwords. Never mind. I'll get to use it soon.

Bookcase next.

Flash

Range of paperbacks and hardbacks – cookery books, travel books, fiction. Nice selection of Anne Hooper and Tracey Cox titles. Couple of illustrated *Kama Sutra* manuals too. Don't know if she bought them or they were presents. Interesting that they are on display through here and not hidden away in her bedroom.

She has a book of Weston nudes. She hadn't heard of his work when I told her about him when we were bowling. Must be a recent addition. I'm glad my passion for the subject captured her imagination. Maybe it is good to be the more interesting me when I'm out with my colleagues. Just think what wonderful knowledge I could share with the world.

I take a series of snaps of her bookcases and CD racks. I'll go through them in detail later.

Kitchen last.

Flash

Vinyl floor covering, wood effect. Nice kitchen units. The usual kitchen kit.

I open a cupboard and see her mugs. I take off my glove and touch one. Marion uses this mug. Marion holds it and drinks from it. I lift it to my lips. This is what Marion does.

I wipe it before returning it.

Back through to the lounge. Notebook out.

Back through the rest of the flat. Measurements and plans.

DustBuster removes any trace of me. I don't go barefoot to open the curtains this time. Stop and look out again. Windows clear, dog walker in the street, doesn't clean up the mess.

I remove all evidence of my visit. Check each room against the Polaroids as I go.

I get an urge to strip off and lie on her bed – but I'm strong.

Last look when I'm in the hall.

Photos taken, plans forming.

Remove tape from peephole, check for any stickiness, have a look out.

Clear.

Walk to my car without incident. Drive until I am a mile away and then stop.

Ten minutes before I stop shaking.

A SWEET GIRL TUCKED AWAY

Will tops up my wine glass.

It feels good being in their flat but slightly unreal. Like thinking you know something well and then discovering that you've not got it quite right.

Tonight I'm here for the promised meal as a thank you for the picnic.

I've put them to a little trouble because this version of me is vegetarian. Laura rose to the occasion admirably and made a delicious avocado salad with cheese tarts. I was expecting some limp lettuce. Think I'll have to fry some rashers when I get home.

Conversation has been scintillating. I've been on top form, slipping easily into chitchat. I've got quite a talent for this sort of creative improvisation. I've led the conversation for most of the night – been showing off a bit. I don't normally get the chance to appear interesting. Every word is normally controlled tightly so that I don't give anything away. I need them to be interested in me but I'll have to make sure I don't come across like a know-it-all bore.

Laura joins us. I had tried to insist that I would help with the washing up but she wouldn't let me. Shame. It would have been good to spend the time alone with her.

So, anyone special in your life? Laura's question is expected but I haven't prepared anything. Couldn't settle on a story. *Single. Why? Just come out of a long relationship. What happened?* Should have made some notes on this – something to fall back on if I dried.

Any sweet girl tucked away somewhere?

I could say, *Well, there is one woman in my life but she's been dead for a hundred years.* Or I could say, *I did have a relationship with a 'sweet girl' that didn't really know I existed until she caught me snooping on her.* Or, *I'm currently spying on a work colleague using secret cameras and, with any luck, I'll be doing the same to you before long.*

I don't think about what I'm saying until the words come out of my mouth. *No sweet girl – I'm gay.* What? I try to cover up my own surprise.

And, before you ask, no sweet boy either.

They laugh. I laugh too. A giddy 'I don't know what I'm doing' sort of laugh.

Gay? What am I thinking?

Will and Laura smile at each other.

I told you, says Will. He turns to me, *She didn't believe me.*

Laura starts to protest.

At first you didn't, says Will.

What the hell? Do I look gay? Do I act gay?

Then I realise that I have been acting quite camp. Not in an over-the-top 'screaming-queen' way but subtly sending out the signals.

It makes sense now why I slipped effortlessly into that persona. If they think I'm gay, then I'm not a threat.

Will would be only too happy to let me see Laura without being a chaperone. He wouldn't get jealous of some poof being with his wife.

God, I'm so good at this – I am a natural. Even when I'm not consciously thinking of strategies I'm making plans within plans. You genius, you.

Yes, this version of me is gay.

Gay stops questions and suspicions.

Gay gets me closer to Laura.

We finish our wine and move to the sofa. Will goes to make coffee.

Laura asks, *How long have you been out?*

About ten years.

Did you always know that you were gay? You don't have to answer, I'm just being nosy.

You're not. I think for a moment. Try to remember a plotline from a film or a soap. For some reason, all I can think about is peppermint foot lotion being used as massage oil. Oh, what the hell, let's have some fun.

Well, I suppose I've always felt a bit different – deep down inside. I just didn't know what it meant.

Have you ever been with a girl?

I've had a couple of girlfriends. You know the thing – kissing after the school bell, touching budding breasts through school shirts and V-neck sweaters when teacher wasn't looking. It was all a bit of fun. Nothing really serious. Until my first sexual experience. It was with a girl. Just after we got under the sheets and got down to touching, I had a sudden urge to get a glass of water. I think I was just putting it off. Took me about ten minutes to get my drink and I was hoping she would have nodded off by the time I got back. She was waiting. We started again, kissing and petting, and, oh, my God, she put my hand on her fanny. I almost died of fright. No offence, Laura, but girls' bits are just plain weird – all those flaps and nooks and crannies. I think we both got a shock when I found her mutton button. When it was all over, I thought that was nothing special – a lot of fuss over nothing.

First time with a boy. Hallelujah! Hallelujah! Angels sang, the earth moved. Soggy and sticky in all the right places. I felt like I'd come home.

Yeooow, way too much information, says Laura.

Will comes back with the coffee. He gives Laura a kiss on the head as she takes a cup. Can't help but get an image of them on the floor on the painting sheets and have to concentrate hard on naming the stars in Orion. The belt – Alnitak, Alnilam, Mintaka. The top – Bellatrix, Betelgeuse, Meissa . . .

Will asks what we are talking about, then regrets doing so when Laura starts to tell him.

Will asks about work.

I've already found out that Will works for a drug company and Laura works as a speech therapist. Knew that a few weeks ago.

I say I'm doing some boring job to finance my real work as a photographer. I tell them I'm planning an exhibition soon and they should both come.

We chat for another hour.

We're firm friends by the time I leave. All the preparations, all the rehearsals, all the accidental meetings have paid off – engineered with great skill. Exactly where I want to be.

The gay stuff was a touch of genius. Once I made it clear that I don't talk about it much, they are touched by how open I am with them. They feel privileged.

Laura kisses me goodbye. Will shakes my hand. Will says that he's got a friend that he'd love me to meet. Mr Matchmaker.

When I get back to my flat I go to the window and look at Will and Laura's. Curtains closed. Light on in the bedroom.

Just give me a few weeks and that won't be a problem.

We've arranged that they'll come round to my flat in a couple of weeks – the rented one, naturally. I already know they are going walking in the Lake District next month so I'll start to work on suggesting that I cat-sit for them. *I'm here all the time – a friend lives in the tower block across the road. Oh, you can't see it from here. And I'm always at the sports centre on the other side of the park. Would be easy to make sure everything was all right when I pass – water the plants, collect the post, feed the pussy.*

It'll be nice to have them round at the rented flat. First time I'll have entertained there. I'll take their coats and put them in my bedroom, have some photography stuff in the hall so they can't hang them there. Make an excuse during the evening to go into my room and take a putty cast of their door keys.

New skill.

I'm able to take the impression and make a useable key. Straight forward enough, if a little fussy.

Either way I'll have access.

INTERSECTION OF GAZES

The next time my rota and Marion's crossed was a Sunday. Didn't want to risk being in her flat with lots of people home from work so had to wait for the next opportunity.

Almost two weeks later and I'm off on a day that she is working. Same routine as before – watch her leave her flat and make sure she gets on the bus.

Not feeling the same agitation as before. I'm still nervous but this time it is all thrills. I breeze into the building after checking the street. Straight to her front door. If I meet anyone, I'll smile and say hi. They wouldn't recognise me if they saw me again.

I've filed down the keys so the top one slides in and turns easily.

Through the door, close it. Check the peephole.

Latex gloves on.

Unlock inner door.

I've spent the last weeks studying my photographs and detailed plans. I know exactly what I am going to do. I know exactly where everything I need is.

Marion keeps ladders in the hall cupboard so that is first on the list. I take a photograph so I can return things to their correct home.

Ladder to the bedroom.

I need to drill three holes in this room for full coverage. One hole will take the colour camera, the next, the night vision camera. It only needs the smallest amount of light to work. I've tried it out and the picture is good. It is like watching in black and white but with a green filter over the screen. Last hole for the microphone.

I've identified the bits of cornice that provide the maximum amount of cover. The job will be so much easier because I have access to the loft. Most of the mechanism will be hidden where it could never be seen. I've got a couple of smaller cameras for times when I don't have the luxuries I have here. The cost though is a drop in quality.

I make quick work in the bedroom with a cordless drill and a Dust-Buster to catch any debris. I stick a tube through each hole lined up roughly in the position the cameras should be in.

I'll vacuum the floor once I've finished in the loft.

Lounge next.

Camera in this room is going to be in the cornice above the window. It is the most obvious place to put it. Only one for this room. Colour, with a fisheye lens that will give a more panoramic view of the room. There will be some distortion of the image but my tests showed that they won't be too bad. Got to make do with the tools I have. To get what I really want, I'd need full-size video cameras dotted around every room. Bit of a giveaway – I'll stick to the concealed ones.

Second hole for the microphone.

Entering the lounge almost the same as last time. Slacker boyfriend wants to watch some movie in the dark while his girl is out earning money.

Got a twist to it today. Boxer shorts, no T-shirt and with a cereal bowl. Malcolm's fitness tips paying off, not quite a six-pack but trim and tidy.

Strip down to my shorts in the hall. Take a deep breath and then saunter into the lounge. Looks almost exactly the same as before. Couple of different magazines on the table, early Louis de Bernières novel on the sofa, kitten bookmark sticking out.

Over to the window with my bowl. Enough of a swagger to make me look as if I belong here. I take a spoonful and munch nonchalantly as I check the street and windows opposite. I've got some raisins in the bowl so that I don't have to mime eating. It looked a bit hammy when I was practising.

I love this.

Someone in the flat opposite – not looking out their window. Passerby in the street – glances up. Quickly looks away and then steals a quick look at the semi-naked figure eating cereal at a window.

I've been seen. Now I belong.

Everything clear so I pull the curtains closed and go back to work.

I dress quickly and bring the ladders through. Only takes a moment to drill the hole.

Hall next.

Plastic sheet under the ladder just in case I dislodge any dust when I open the hatch to the loft. I've got replacement gloves for coming back into the flat because it is going to be filthy up there. Big clear-plastic bag at the foot of the ladders to throw grubby clothes in once I'm done.

The hatch has a couple of tiny bolts on either side – not nearly secure enough for my liking – but I have to work at them to get them moving. Hatch is hinged.

Got a torch headband and one attached to my wrist – hands free for working. I put my head through the hatch and listen for a while. Faint noises from flat further along. Safe to go up. Just a workman, after all, doing some stuff for Marion.

The loft runs the entire length of the top-floor flats, I could get into any one them, especially if their hatches are as poorly secured as Marion's.

The air is hot and dusty up here. Got to be careful. Take things slowly. Have to step on the crossbeams and not between them. Don't want a foot to go through the ceiling. Might be difficult to explain that one away.

I can see the bits of tubing from the bedroom – used clear ones so that I would see the light from below. Carefully work my way over and settle down by the first one. Take the rucksack from my back and open a pocket.

It takes me about an hour and ten minutes to set all three cameras, two microphones and the signal boosters. The rented flat is fifty-eight metres away. Should get a perfect signal. I've played around with the frequencies to make sure that they are not picked up by anyone else.

Power source takes a bit longer but I've made myself an expert at simple electrical jobs. Well, I can splice a wire without electrocuting myself. I could use battery packs but I'd have to replace them and what would happen if I didn't have access for a few days? Don't want the picture to cut out at a crucial moment.

I hide as much of the equipment as I can under loft insulation. Only someone that knew what to look for would find it.

I spend time adjusting the angle of the three cameras to make sure I get a perfect view. I've got a dinky little handheld screen to help me.

Last camera to be installed up here points at the hatch – a safety precaution. If anyone comes into the loft, I'll know to switch off my equipment so the signals can't be traced.

Everything is as sterile as I could make it. No DNA, no fingerprints, no fibres. Serial numbers of all the equipment destroyed. I've been thorough.

I've left some footprints in the dust up here but my trainers, along with all the clothes I'm wearing today, will be burned. I'm going for a swim after this so I can shower off any dust or fibres – don't want incriminating evidence from here winding up in my flat.

I head back to the hatch feeling like Charles Boyer in *Gaslight*.

You know it would be fairly easy to drill a hole into someone else's flat. I'd have to be very careful not to make too much mess. Sounds interesting – but not for now.

I stand on the top step of the ladders and remove my filthy gloves. Fresh pair in my pocket. Swap old for new.

When I reach the bottom step I switch off my torches and remove them. A quick scan of my clothes reveals I'm as grubby as I thought I would be. Strip and put clothes in the plastic bag. Towel to wipe away the sweat. Moist wipes to remove any grime from my face.

Everything in the bag.

Go to the lounge before I dress.

Camera is invisible. I vacuum below it just in case I've dislodged any dirt.

I open the lounge curtains again and look out. I want someone to see me again. I want to be watched.

Bedroom.

Can't see the lenses.

Open a drawer. Digital camera snaps as I flick through her diary.

Vacuum in here too.

When I get to the front door, everything is exactly as it was when I came in.

I take my checklist from my bag and run through it. Everything in order.

Peephole. Clear.

Leave the flat. Lock the doors. Leave the building.

Some people about but they're not paying attention. I go to the bus stop and take the next one that comes – get off after a couple of stops. Once I'm sure no one is following me, I quickly remove my wig and glasses and turn my coat inside out.

I'm a new person.

Takes more than twenty minutes to walk to the rental car. Drive to the sports centre near home. Swim. Shower. Evidence glugging down the plughole. Fresh clothes from a sealed plastic bag. Stuff I've been wearing is now safely in the boot ready for burning tonight.

An hour later I'm back at the rented flat.

I nervously switch on the three monitors to check they are receiving images from the cameras. Each one perfect. Well, the night vision one has flared out but that is because it is daylight.

Check the audio but I hear only a slight hiss.

I call Marion's number making sure I suppress my own. I hear her phone ringing through the speakers.

Everything perfect.

Everything ready.

Now all I need is Marion.

THE WATCHING ROOM

Sitting in the room with the monitors.

Think I should give it a special name.

The Surveillance Centre.

The Watching Room.

I have a clock beside me and I'm counting off seconds again.

I've been in a state of heightened agitation all afternoon waiting for the next few minutes.

Marion is due back from work very soon. Exact timing isn't possible – no way to predict if she'll go shopping on the way home or how long the bus will take.

I've got everything crossed hoping that there won't be an impromptu drink tonight. Any moment now and I'll hear her go into the flat. Then I'll see her.

See her – really see her.

I should have put a camera in the hall. Then I could watch from the moment she enters, experience her 'home-from-work' routine from the beginning.

Getting carried away. Got to be sensible about this. Can't have a camera in every room – just not practical. Besides, what would I see from the hall apart from her hanging away her coat, dumping her bag and the odd glimpse of her walking from one room to another?

Three cameras are fine for the time being. If I really feel I'm missing out on something great, I can always have a rethink.

Bathroom would still be an interesting place to put one. Does carry an enormous perv debt with it though. Why else would you want to watch someone on the toilet or taking a shower?

Tick-tock. Tick-tock.

Minutes stretch the way they do when you are desperate for something to happen. Sickening that they shorten to almost nothing when you get into the moment. Perceptions being tricked.

Noises from the speakers. Muffled. Should have at least put one of them in the hall.

Door slams shut.

Screens blank.

Wait.

Wait.

Marion walks into the lounge. Coat and shoes left in the hall. She is carrying a couple of plastic bags that she takes into the kitchen. A few minutes later, she leaves the kitchen and walks through the lounge. Not a hint that she notices anything out of place.

Bedroom.

Takes off her skirt and hangs it in the cupboard, shirt thrown into laundry basket.

Legs.

She hums a tune that I don't recognise. Sound is tinny from the microphones.

Takes off her bra and puts it in the laundry basket. She rubs her chest for a moment, freeing breasts held tight in place all day.

I haven't seen her topless before.

Large areolas.

Back.

Tummy.

She looks nice.

She pulls on a baggy shirt and trousers and leaves the room again.

Passes through the lounge into the kitchen again.

She comes back and sits down with a mug of something. No way to tell what it is. She has tea, coffee, fruit teas and hot chocolate in her cupboard.

She sits and sips.

Dinner on her lap, watching TV – looks like chicken, potatoes and peas. She has no dessert.

She watches TV until ten twenty-nine, then goes for a shower. I know because she has a towel around her when she appears on the bedroom screen sixteen minutes later.

I see her naked for the first time.

Wisp of dark hair.

Curves.

She is actually quite pretty – not glamour-model or actress pretty but ordinary pretty. She often says at work that she looks plain.

Each of the cameras has a video recorder attached so I don't miss anything.

She rubs moisturising lotion into her skin.

She dresses in baggy pyjamas.

She collects the book she's reading from the lounge and switches off the light. The screen goes blank.

Bedroom screen. She pulls back her duvet and gets into bed. She smiles as she pulls it up to her chin.

She reads for eighteen minutes and then turns out the light.

Screen goes blank.

Flare from the night vision camera disappears. Picture forms.

I watch as she falls asleep.

I watch as she sleeps.

Watch for days and nights. Every opportunity. What I can't view in real time I catch on playback.

Bedroom.

It is late.

Marion backs into the room.

She's kissing a man with sandy coloured hair.

Marion bumps against the bottom of the bed.

They sit.

They kiss. Hands on each other.

Kissing.

She pushes him so he's lying on the bed.

She unbuttons his shirt.

He helps, then throws it on the floor.

She unfastens his belt.

She unfastens his button.

She pulls down his zip.

He watches.

She pulls at his jeans.
He helps.
She takes them.
One sock left on, the other caught in the trouser leg.
She pulls it off and throws it to the floor.
She drops her skirt, steps out of it.
She kneels on the bottom of the bed.
She takes off her top.
He moves up and kisses her chest.
She pushes him back and does the same.
She moves down.
She pulls down his pants.
She kisses his erection.
He says, *Oh, yes.*
I hit the sound button so I don't have to listen to him.

She moves across the bed and opens a drawer.
Throws a wrapper on the floor.
She puts the condom on him and rolls it down.
He watches.
He pulls off her knickers and moves her so she straddles him.
His head between her legs, kissing.
He brings a hand between her legs.
Her eyes are closed.
Her head falling slowly to one side.
Her mouth opens.
Her tongue plays on her bottom lips.
She brings her hand to her breast and squeezes.
They stay like this for a while.
She moves her hand back and pulls on his penis.
He is working harder.
She starts to move her hips rhythmically again his mouth.
She lifts herself away from him and sits against his chest.
She slides herself down and guides him in.

An hour later.
He leaves the bedroom.
She waits a moment and follows. Still naked.
He comes back.
Then she comes back.
She turns out the light.
They sleep.

RAIN

I am standing in an alley in the rain. Watching.

I have been here for more than an hour. I am soaked to the skin.

Cold.

Waiting.

A taxi pulls up across the street. I see money exchanging hands through steamed up windows. Sound of a door opening then slamming. The taxi pulls away.

Dave stands looking at the sky as if he's not really sure what rain is. He shakes his head and drunkenly shuffles between parked cars to the pavement.

I followed him from here a couple of hours ago. He went to a pub. He's not with any of the gang. I didn't go in – just watched. When I got bored, I came back to his flat.

Lights still on in a front room – Chris watching late night television by herself. Nice that she lets Dave out for a few pints with the boys. Does she mind if he flirts with other girls? Does she mind if he takes one into a toilet cubicle? Does she mind if his sex-stained hands drunkenly paw at her when he comes home?

Living room light goes off. Bedtime. She's getting ready for bed. Nightshirt? Pyjamas? Nude? *Don't wait up, my love.* But he will wake her when he gets back. He'll sway through the door, trying to be so very quiet but making more noise by doing so, fall on to the bed, kick off his shoes and throw his shirt and trousers on to a chair. Under the covers, reeking of smoke and booze, he'll give her a hug, try to get passionate, but she'll not be interested.

Not tonight.

It's going to be different tonight.

Enough time passed since my face on the road.

Enough time passed so I am a dim memory.

Kept my head down.

Kept out of their way.

He stops on the step leading up to the main door. He's searching for his keys. Wet shirt clings to his perfect body.

Mr Fitness.

Mr I'll thump you into next week.

Mr Bully Boy.

Mr Pick On Someone Your Own Size.

Pull my hood tighter. Dressed like a yob. People will think I'm some drug-crazed teenager after a mobile phone or a few notes if I'm seen.

He is at the door inspecting the lock, wondering why he can't seem to make the key fit in the hole.

He isn't aware of me moving behind him. He doesn't hear me take the metal bar from under my tracksuit jacket. Oblivious until he feels it strike the back of his head.

Cracking sound.

Blood on my face. Wet. Warm. Salt and copper.

He's on his knees groaning. I step to one side. Better angle.

Arm goes down.

Fever of rage.

This is for punching me.

This is for hurting me.

This is for forcing me to change my life.

Crack.

Moans of pain.

This is for my humiliation.

This is for my shame.

Lean in and drive the metal bar against his face.

Nose bursts, teeth break, lips split.

Again.

Face a bloody mess. He's not moving now. The gurgling and bubbling from his mouth stops.

Upstairs Chris still curled up in bed. Dreaming violence.

Blood on my clothes.

Blood on my face.

The position of the blood splatters on the wall suggests he was struck violently from behind and then repeatedly in the face, as he lay against the door.

My body shakes with the power I've released.

I am victorious.

I am a warrior.

I am a myrmidon.

You shouldn't have underestimated me.

Matt next. Craig next. Sarah next.

I take his keys.

Go up to the flat.

Spend some time with Chris.

She thinks it's him as I slip between the sheets. She yields to my touch. She sees it is me. She smiles – prefers it is me.

I shake a big fat raindrop from my nose and watch as he staggers against the open door. He closes it behind him with a bang.

I wait for the light to go on in the bedroom.

Same time next week.

I walk to my car.

One of these days, you bastard. One of these days I'll make you pay.

Marion on the lounge screen.

She is sitting, curled up on the chair in her pyjamas.

She has a bowl of popcorn beside her.

She is watching a movie.

Sound on the monitor is down so it doesn't distract me.

Watching Marion.

Box of tissues beside the bowl.

Must be a weepie.

She eats some popcorn without looking at it.

She dabs her eyes.

She rubs her toes.

She leaves the room for a toilet break.

She settles back into position.

STARGAZING

It is cold on the roof – the sky almost completely clear of clouds. If you stand back from the edge, the glow from the street lights almost disappears and the sky fills with stars.

When I was a child, I used to think that stars actually twinkled, that they pulsed with light. It seems much more romantic explanation than the distortion of light through layers of atmosphere.

I'm not here just to look at the sky.

I take the telescope closer to the edge and set it down.

The city opens before me – the veil drops, secrets are exposed.

I look.

This city is mine. I see everything. I see everyone – my gaze piercing stone and fabric and flesh. You can't hide from me. No soul can hope for safety in the shadows.

Zeus on Mount Olympus, watching mortals going about their small lives. Insignificant beside the universe around them. But still glorious.

I dissect lives. The telescope is my microscope. Revealing detail. Revealing the story of mankind.

I fill my lungs with the cold air. Night swells in me until I feel bloated with the possibilities before me. Each sweep of my gaze tells a different story – part of the hidden pattern. Every window a portal to a life. Each gap in the curtains offers a glimpse of something unique.

I feel privileged. I feel fatherly. I feel empathy.

From the man laughing at the box, from the lonely crying for friendship, from the lovers exploring flesh, I am with them. I am part of them.

Window to window. Life to life. Experience to experience.

I'm searching.

Looking for clues, for signs.

A couple argue. Woman stands by her curtains looking into the night. A man sleeps – a woman rests against him. Friends talk outside a pub. Diners in a restaurant. Man jumps from a diving board, another takes his place. Couple walk hand in hand. Children drink by street corners. A man sits writing. Woman throws up in the street – a friend holds on to her. A man pulls curtains closed. Rooms illuminated – television blue. Crowds leave a concert. A woman drinks in her hotel room. Sleepers. Drinkers. Eaters. Lovers. Fighters. Talkers. Criers. Darkrooms. Empty rooms.

My head vibrates with experience overloads.

I need to take a break for a moment.

I take the telescope back to the deckchair positioned a few metres from the edge. I'll watch some stars for a while.

I put the tripod next to my camera. Telephoto lens, very fast film – perfect for grainy night shots with no flash. When I go back to the edge, I'll take some photographs.

I pick a star and look at it. Chosen at random. I don't know what constellation it is in or what it is called.

No one else in the world is looking at this star as this moment. I'm watching something unique. The light that has travelled for millions of years. It hits my telescope lens and is mirrored on to the back of my eye. Now the moment has gone forever.

That star might not be there any more. It could have faded and died hundreds of years ago only this echo of its existence travelling through space, through time, at the speed of light.

Everything we experience has happened in the past. In a sense we live in the past. When we look at something we see reflected light. It travels to our eyes. The information is transferred electrochemically to our brains, we have an experience. It might take a fraction of a second but what we experience now is actually something from the past. It doesn't affect us because the time difference is too small to be perceived.

I turn the telescope to the moon. It is crescent. Surface details are clear. It shines brightly. Albedo is about zero point one two. That means the moon reflects, on average, about twelve per cent of the light that strikes it from the sun.

Fruits of my research.

I am not alone.

I sense the presence before I hear it. Footfall on the gravel of the roof. I turn my head sharply from the eyepiece to see who is there. Body instinctively ready for something dangerous happening. I'm on a roof after all. It would be easy to have an accident.

The caretaker approaches me.

Panic diminishes but I stay on guard. Don't trust this man.

It is unusual for him to be on the roof. He hasn't joined me for a very long time.

I'm glad I had left the edge when he came up. That would be difficult to explain.

I haven't seen you up here for a while, I say. Make some polite conversation – he might just be checking up.

I'm a busy bee, he says. *You're still stargazing, I see.*

As often as I can. Haven't had much time recently myself.

Yes.

I don't like the way he said that. I don't like the way he is looking at me. I try to cover my uncomfortable feeling by talking about some of the things I've seen. I embellish a little, knowing his ignorance means he can't contradict me. I hope I'll bore him enough that he'll go away.

He doesn't seem to be even feigning interest.

He walks closer to the edge of the building. *What a view,* he says.

I am quiet.

He turns. *Great view, don't you think?*

I nod.

He makes a bad pantomime of noticing my camera on its tripod. *Big lens. Taking photographs of the stars?*

Of the moon actually. Greater detail with that lens.

He is looking at me in the oddest way. I start to feel uneasy. Something bad is going to happen. I need to distract him. Take his mind from the camera. Think of something, think of something. Got it. Ask about his rental business – he won't be able to resist telling me about his latest additions, giving me explicit detail.

You come up here a lot don't you?

Beaten to changing the subject – need to be quicker. *Not much recently.* Try changing the subject again. *How . . .*

He interrupts, *You come up when it's cloudy too. I noticed.*

I say nothing. What does that mean? There is innuendo in his tone.

He stares at me – as if he is sizing me up. He has that annoying half smile on his face, like he's read my secret diary or rifled through my underwear and wants me to know.

Do you want to have a look at Mars? I move to the tripod.

He doesn't respond immediately – just watches. Then says, *I'd prefer to look at something else.*

What? Fuck. Is this some sort of sleazy pick-up? I still want access to the roof but no way can he believe I'll let him touch me to keep the key. He can threaten to take the key from me but he's got no hold over me. I have a copy. I'll just need to be careful coming up here. He is not going to limit my watching – not with darkness coming earlier in a few months.

He turns back to the edge. *What I want to see is what you see. Down there.*

Oh, no. *Down there?* I force the innocent question out.

You know what I'm talking about. You and your camera. You're not taking pictures of the moon. Not on cloudy nights. Not when there are more interesting things to point it at.

Spasm of fear. Don't let him see that I'm panicking. Don't give any sign that I know what he talking about. I try to look as if I don't understand.

Nothing to say? Don't be worried. I'm not going to call the police and tell them I've caught a peeping Tom. He pauses for effect. *Not yet.*

It is working – I'm trembling.

I've got a business proposal for you.

Don't think I can speak.

You must have lots of lovely photos by now. Lots of photos of girls – tits and fannies out. Lots of photos of fucking. People would pay to see that sort of candid stuff. You got any of that? We could make a fortune if we could video some of that.

Blood pounds. Fight or flight.

Pornos are good – don't get me wrong – but punters want something new, different sort of spice. Real candid-camera fucking. What do you think? Can you supply?

My mind is numb.

Found out. Found out by this little maggot. I feel the urge to run at him and push him over the edge. Get rid of the problem before it starts.

I can only stare.

Have a think about it he says as he walks back to the door. *Don't take too long though. I've got such a problem with my waggling tongue.* He turns and walks towards the roof door. *The girls fucking love it though.*

Left alone.

What should I do?

Maybe I should throw myself off instead.

WATCHING AND WAITING

Everything was going so well. Watching Marion is a treat. Moving closer to Will and Laura, building friendships, becoming trustworthy. Then he has to come along and spoil it all. Threats and promises and ultimatums. Well, I won't let him take what I've got. I've come too far to let such a little man destroy my dreams.

Need to find a solution.

Got to follow him for a few days.

Got to find something I can use. Some sort of leverage. The taped photos in his flat suggest there is something bubbling under the surface – some weakness I can exploit.

Not sure if it'll be enough.

Plan for the worst.

I've started moving my files and photo albums to the rented flat. Out of harm's way. Can't risk a knock at the door from whomever he decides to tell. Can't let anyone see my photographs and files. No way to explain them away.

I've made sure he's not been about when I've taken the boxes to my car. If he was to find out what I'm doing, he would rat me out in an instant.

I've been avoiding him since the roof but I'll have to face him at some point. If I don't, he'll come and find me.

I thought it might be good to tell him the reality of watching people – that you actually see very little and almost none of the stuff he wants from me.

He wouldn't believe me.

I suppose I've got a few of the shots he's looking for in my albums. People in states of undress – fresh from the shower – the exhibitionists. I could hand them over. It wouldn't be enough.

I could give him the photographs of Will and Laura the day they were decorating. Or I could give him some of the Marion tapes – two blokes since I've been watching. They're exactly what he's looking for.

You can never satisfy a blackmailer. He'll just keep on asking for more and more until I'm no longer useful and then he'll call the police.

What could he tell them?

I'll soon have moved everything incriminating from the flat and it'll take a lot of digging to connect me with the rented one.

So what am I scared of? He can't prove anything.

But he must know that I'll figure that out. He's not clever enough to bluff me. He must have something, some kind of evidence.

What if he's been following me?

I've been so caught up with my own stuff that I've not been taking precautions. He might have been sniffing about.

What if he knows about the rented flat? What if he knows about watching Marion?

Getting too worked up about what-ifs.

He could know anything. Or everything. Or nothing.

The only way I'll be sure is if I follow him.

He's a real little Fagin – wheeling and dealing. Got his nice little rented porn business. He now uses a couple of the students from the ninth floor to help him out. They must be passing stuff out at uni or something. Probably pays them in freebies.

What do people most want? he asked me once. *Happiness? Peace? Love? Porn,* he said. *But do they want to go to a shop and look seedy? Do they want to give their credit card details to some mail order place? Can they even work the internet? No, they need me to help them out, keep them clean. Bert to the rescue.*

Whatever you need he'll pop round in a flash with a flesh flick or a skin mag in your moment of need. Door-to-door porno salesman. Now that is business culture in action. See an opportunity. Exploit a gap in the market.

He's got lots of clients in the tower blocks and I'm sure he goes further afield too.

He's not fussy who he sells to. Teenagers? Who cares as long as they've got the cash? Old blokes? Come back for more and more.

But this is the interesting bit. He goes to a rundown industrial every couple of days.

Next to a tile warehouse, there is a building with a silver roller shutter, security camera over the door.

He goes in. Comes out with boxes. Boxes of DVDs.

I'm interested enough to watch the place for a while after he leaves.

Over the course a few hours, there are comings and goings.

Van arrives. Loaded with boxes. It leaves.

Big breasted young women arrive, wearing tight tops and short skirts. Young men in muscle-hugging short-sleeved shirts. Middle-aged men in baggy leather jackets. Vans being loaded with boxes. Caretaker making a collection.

You know, I think this place is a blue-movie studio.

It all fits.

Has to be a porn studio.

Judging by the number of people going in, there must be a couple of sets working at once. I'm a bit surprised – would have thought, in the digital age, it would all be location work.

It all looks kind of dodgy, though. Porn has a legitimate face these days – not the reputation it once had – but this warehouse just doesn't shout *above board* to me. Doubly so if the caretaker is involved.

Could be organised crime. Bert in with the city's shady underworld?

It could be the break I'm looking for.

It makes me feel sick too. What have I got involved with? Has the caretaker mentioned me to members of the local mafia?

I can see this spiralling out of control.

Mob beatings and extortion and being found in a gutter with an ice pick through the back of my head.

Got to tread with even more care.

Got to think of some way out of this that will get me off the hook.

Don't want to solve the caretaker problem, only to have someone much bigger, much meaner, step into his shoes.

Got to keep focused on the task in hand. Follow him until I have something concrete.

I see him talk to a couple of prostitutes at the same place I went. They know him by name. They give him 'nice-to-see-you' smiles but you can tell their eyes are cold and hard as they talk to him. He's no friend at all.

There might be a drug angle too. Evidence is sketchy. Seen him giving something to a group of youths. Small bag. Can't be tapes or mags. They give him money. Just not sure enough to say that it is drugs. Could be anything.

Bits and pieces I've gathered over the last few days might be enough to scare him off. But just might be enough to get me a good kicking from his associates.

I could make an anonymous call to the police or send them some of my surveillance shots. Would they do anything? Is he too small-time to waste effort on? Or could he be a way to get to the bigger fish?

Photos of his activities could tip him off it was me. They might implicate me somehow. He would definitely hold a grudge. He'd be like a dog with a rabbit. He'd never let me go.

Can't let him spoil things for me – not when everything is going so well.

Need something foolproof. Something that doesn't lead to me.

Maybe there is some way I can exploit his underworld relationships.

Got to come up with a plan.

Hélène watched as he pulled on his trousers and waited for him to leave. He was hardly more than a boy but he was pretty and grateful. In the old days, she would have wondered for a moment if she should charge him but she knew that generosity would be replaced with realism and she would accept the coins gratefully.

As the door closed, she checked the bedside table almost expecting to see payment. Old habits, best forgotten.

Hélène found that many of her afternoons were now spent this way. Hélène no longer cared if the men she spent time with were discreet. Hélène cared nothing for her own reputation these days.

Henri had made money from his new photographs. The famous American Series. He used middlemen from the beginning to keep his identity hidden.

Hélène tired of the constant battle to preserve Henri's well-cultivated legitimacy. Hélène almost begrudged the fact that Henri was beginning to grow a reputation as an important artist.

Hélène had waited, night after night, for him to come to her room – she cried and prayed when he did not. Hélène knew that he would meet young things in salons and studios and knew that they would sit for him and then love him. She saw the adoration in their eyes and the appetite in his. Henri was discreet. Henri was careful. Henri did not want a scandal.

Hélène found lovers too. Hélène had many men friends. Hélène knew this was not revenge against Henri but a reaction to her fear.

Henri was talking about leaving America for a time. He lived for the hard-won respect he enjoyed as an artist there. But to have that adoration back home. Henri planned for them to return to Paris.

Hélène knew that she did not want to go there ever again. Hélène had almost forgotten that life and did not want to be reminded of it. Hélène believed that to go back there would be more than she could bear. Hélène knew that she would eventually meet someone who knew her from before and that all her affected airs and graces would crumble in an instant.

Hélène knew that she had to stop Henri, make it impossible for him to return. How to do that?

Hélène had given some of Henri's photographs to some of her gentlemen friends, keepsakes to remind them of the sweet hours in her arms. Hélène knew that these men would not keep these gifts secret.

Hélène waited for the scandal. Hélène hoped that it would not break them.

IN THE FLAT

I've been practising with the lock pick. Yale locks fitted to bits of wood help sharpen my skills. It is not just a case of sticking it in and wriggling it about for a moment and hearing the magical click. Fastest time so far is one minute forty-seven seconds. That is pretty fast.

I knew that I would find a use for the lock pick. The caretaker uses his mortise locks if he is going out for the day but, when he makes his rounds with his movies and magazines, he only uses the Yale.

I don't have much time left. In the next day or so, he is going to force me to be part of his scheme or he'll take action against me.

My observations over the last few days have let me work out his routine. He doesn't go out in the mornings if he can help it, so afternoons and evenings are for business. If he is on his rounds in the tower blocks, he is usually away for about thirty-five minutes. I plan to be in and out in fifteen and that includes the time it takes to open the door.

I'm not completely sure what I'm looking for. I'll know when and if I find it. Got an idea of what I need to discover. Got a plan of how to use it if I do.

I've got my gear together and I'm waiting for him to go out. I'm sitting in my car.

He always starts with the other block of flats. I think he's currently got nine clients in there but I've not been able to get close enough to confirm that. He comes out of my block and walks to its twin, bag of goodies in his hand – looks like he's carrying a tool bag but I know it is full of his filth.

I wait until I see him go through the main door and then I sprint to the foyer of my building. His flat is on the ground floor facing Mrs Collins'. She doesn't go out much these days – getting too old for that – but, just in case she gets a bit nosy, I tape her peephole.

I start on the door.

God, I'm getting bold these days – picking a lock during the day when I could be discovered at any moment. I've brought a balaclava but I decide against using it. Call me Raffles. Call me the Gentleman Scoundrel. Fighting crime with crime.

Personal best – one minute and twenty-six seconds. The lock clicks and I push the door open.

Back to the foyer for a last look – coast is still clear.

His flat stinks. The freak really needs to start washing more often or start wearing a deodorant. The place needs some nice scented candles and a through breeze.

I don't bother looking through the bookcases in the hall. What I'm looking for will be in the bedroom. This rooms stinks worse than the rest of the flat – bed unmade, clothes on the floor, remnants of food and boozy carry-outs. Pictures still on the walls by the bed – faces blanked out with tape and marker pens.

Widescreen TV on a chest of drawers opposite the bottom of the bed, video and DVD machines on top, pile of discs and tapes beside them.

Some unmarked boxes – they could be samples of the stuff he collects from the warehouse. I'm tempted to see exactly what they are getting up to in there but I can't afford to waste the time.

Look at my watch – three minutes and forty-eight seconds.

Where to start? Bedside cabinet. Bookcase stuffed with papers and books and magazines? Chest of drawers? Wardrobe?

Has to be the chest of drawers. Don't imagine it is just for clothes. Bottom drawer is the place to look first. He's going to be obvious and keep the juicy stuff in there. Latexed fingers wrap around the handles and I pull slowly taking care to see if I'm dislodging anything he's left to tell if someone has been snooping.

As predicted, smut – still images, more magazines, more tapes. Eclectic tastes. Fetish. Bondage. Masturbation. Group. Single. Couples. Forced. Lesbian. Animal. Hard. Soft. Lingerie. Posed and candid. Don't want to touch this stuff even through my gloves – as if the taint will seep into me and contaminate me, right to the bone. Long shower when I get back. Scrub away the filth.

I move the contents of the drawer around to see if what I need is buried underneath. Frown fixed on my face as I look at images I would prefer not to be in my head. *You are one sick puppy.* No sign of what I'm looking for – might not be here.

I check the other drawers. Mainly clothes.

Top drawer has some more face-taped photos. Quite extreme material but nothing you couldn't find on an early erotic French postcard. This drawer also has what I imagine are sex toys but some of them would not be out of place in an Inquisitor's knapsack. I wonder if he has cause to use them with anyone apart from himself.

Still not what I'm looking for.

I look around the room. Where would he keep it?

There is enough hardcore here to cause him problems if he is raided but he's made no effort to hide it well. The stuff I'm looking for will be somewhere else. Separate from the run-of-the-mill porn.

Second pass at the room.

Maybe he's making fewer deliveries today. Maybe he'll come walking in any moment and find me.

Fear, just like the old days.

I swallow the fear. I won't let it beat me. If it had any hold on me I wouldn't be standing in this room. I'm a changed man.

I've planned what I'd do if he came back early – pull on the balaclava and rush him. I've got surprise on my side. I've also got a friction-lock baton in my pocket. A flick of the wrist and it extends to become fifty centimetres of tempered alloy steel. Police use them around the world. Easy to carry, easy to conceal. Got a video of defence techniques with it. Crack his head. Solve my problems.

Under the mattress? Perhaps. Difficult for easy access and a bit obvious. Under the bed? Not sure I want to think about all the soiled tissues waiting under there. Might have to get down on my hands and knees and rummage in that sewer if I'm not lucky soon.

Turn back to the chest of drawers. Just might be. I pull the bottom drawers open again and feel the underside. Damn. Nothing taped to it.

I do the same with the other drawers. Nothing.

I pull the bottom drawer out and place it on a pile of clothes. Lean down to look, pen torch in my hand.

Heart jumps. This could be it. A part of me hopes that I haven't found it. A part of me hopes that I am wrong. But I need it to be what I think it is. It is the only ammunition I'll have against him.

I reach my arm into the space and pull out the first of four large brown envelopes. Through the paper, I can feel the thickness of bundled photographs. The envelope is one of those ones with metal tabs that keep it closed. One of the tabs has broken off. It is easy to slide the folded flap over the remaining one and open it.

Deep breath. I know what to expect. But I need to check that it is what I think it is.

Whole body tense. Take out a print.

Eyes closed. Don't want to see. Don't want to be right.

Got to look. Got to be sure. Just open your eyes for a moment.

Stomach lurches.

Turn the picture back over. Don't want to think about it.

I put the photo back into the envelope and take another from the middle of the pile. Peer through screwed up eyes as if will offer some protection from the image.

Fuck – even worse.

I take a ziplock plastic bag from my pocket and put the envelope inside and seal it. Put the bag into the large inner pocket of my jacket.

Put the drawer back.

Check the room for signs of my visit.

Pause at the front door to listen.

Door opens and gently closes behind me. Pull it until I hear the lock click.

Take the tape from Mrs Collins' peephole.

Foyer still clear.

No gossipmongers.

I run all the way to my flat and don't stop until I'm inside. Sit on the floor with my back against the door.

I'm shaking.

Outrage?

Disgust?

Soiled?

Don't know if it is directed at him or me.

Need to stay focused. Still got things to do.

Very risky taking the whole envelope – he will notice it is gone if he looks for it. He'll know someone has been in his flat. He'll know it was me.

Got to get his envelope ready. Put in the note. Put in the photos. Deliver it.

A couple of days ago, I made sure that I bumped into Creeping Jesus. I made a point of chatting to him for a moment. I patted him on the back when we parted. Tape on my hand. Got some fibres. Fibres transferred to the envelope that I've prepared. Sterile environment to do it. Don't want any trace of me on it just in case it falls into police hands.

I feel bad that I've had to use Creeping Jesus. Of course, any investigation would stop at him. It would be a wrong turn but it would keep the scent away from me.

Letter is printed. Bought the paper from a supermarket and dumped the sheets that I didn't use. Used an old printer that I've dumped too.

First photo is of the caretaker handing over a package to one of his clients – just the usual video stuff – but the letter strongly suggests that it is not just a mainstream porno flick.

Used the machine at work so that it looks like someone took the photo on a snappy camera and got it developed in a shop.

The photo is sterile. No trace of me.

Make sure I cropped the other man's face out of the photo. Don't want an innocent to suffer – just the caretaker.

Add the photographs I've just removed. Don't look at them as I put them in.

I'll have to wait until it gets dark before I deliver it. Got my fingers crossed the people at the warehouse have nothing to do with this sideline.

Followed one of the guys that swaggers about as if he is in charge. A family man – counting on him doing what needs to be done.

When I've finished preparing my package, I head to the car and drive to the old industrial estate. Wait and watch until the warehouse is empty. Wait another thirty minutes before I make a move.

Face hidden by a hood so the camera won't see it, I push the package through the gap in the shutter for post.

It is an outraged, threatening letter. It says, if they don't sort out Bert, the police will get a tip-off that they are involved in it too. They might be involved anyway but they won't want to risk such a weak link blabbing to the police if he is arrested.

Got another plan if they don't take the appropriate action but need to psyche myself up for it.

I drive out into the country and take the bag of clothes I wore and the gloves and burn them.

Back to the flat for a long hot shower.

I've got you, you fucker. You made a mistake when you threatened to blackmail me.

I'm counting on gut-instinct revulsion to the images I took from his flat. People could forgive the hardcore, the violence but not that.

You left me no choice.

You're going to burn. One way or another.

FEEDING THE CAT

It is a joy installing equipment at Will and Laura's. Using it as a way to distract myself from spending all my time ruminating on the problem.

Pussycat- and house-sitting means I'm legitimate. I can stay in their flat as long as I want without neighbours prying. The down side is having the cat here. I thought about putting it in a cattery for a few days – I almost did.

I've got my plan worked out well in advance. I know where to put things and how to conceal them.

It is completely different from the Marion experience. No handy loft to make my life easy but I always knew that working in the field would be different. This time it is camouflaging cameras in the cornice and running wires round the room, hiding them behind the mouldings. Not ideal – but needs must.

Range isn't a problem here – line of sight right to my window. Only street lights spewing EM radiation to distort the signal and that won't be too bad.

I have decided against the bathroom again. I really don't want to see Will reading while he's squatting. Some things are best left unseen, even if that means sacrificing completeness.

So – bedroom and living room for the cameras again. Got three left, two ordinary ones and a night vision. Once I take my equipment from Marion's I'll install one of that batch in Will and Laura's kitchen. They spend quite a lot of time in there and I'm desperate to see what goes on.

Could just get another camera and leave the one in Marion's but I'm not sure if I want to keep the rented flat going – becoming a drain on resources.

I'll decide later.

I stay overnight at Will and Laura's. Sleep in their bed. I leave the curtains open. I've set the video for the bedroom camera so it records me waking.

I'll install the lounge camera tomorrow and that still gives me a couple of days to test and conceal.

Will is a bit of a DIY man so there is always the chance that he could notice something. I'm counting on the fact that they have only recently decorated to keep my secret. Last time I was over, I probed a little by commenting on how much I liked the décor. Not a hint that they weren't satisfied with it.

I'm going to be pushed for time once Will and Laura get back from their hols.

Probably have to make myself a viewing timetable so that I don't miss anything between their flat and Marion's.

This is going to be a very different pleasure from Marion. Not only can I watch these rooms up close but I can also watch from my window. Complete coverage.

I feel a smug sense of satisfaction creeping over me. I've beaten your fucking curtains. There is no obstacle I can't overcome.

Bedroom.

Marion in bed.

Man with shaved head.

Sex.

It has been one sided.

He's been asking her to do things.

He hasn't returned the favour.

He finishes.

She expects it is her turn.

He reaches out and takes his underwear of the floor.

What are you doing?

He is silent.

He pulls on his trousers.

Are you going?

No response.

Hunting for socks.

What? You've got what you want and now you're leaving?

Finds sock, then the other.

Marion sits up in bed, duvet pulled up to cover her chest.

Well, say something.

He pulls on his shirt.

I think I can see him sneering, back to her.

Say something, you bastard.

Say something to her.

He is quiet.

Get out of my flat.

He looks at her.

What will he do?

I can't move. I'm not breathing. My heart is not beating.

If he does something I'll just have to watch. Impotent. He could do anything and I wouldn't be able to save her.

Nails dig into my palms.

Get out – you fucker.

He leaves the frame.

She throws a pillow at the bedroom door.

The front door slams.

I watch her crumple. I watch the tears.

Anger rising.

Why would he do that? How could he treat someone like that?

I want to comfort her. I want to go to her and hold her and rock her and tell her that it doesn't matter.

I grab my keys.

He's parked his car. No one but us in the street. Curtains all still. He hears me running behind him. He turns but I'm quicker. He doesn't have time to shout. My arms judder under the impact. He falls to the pavement. I raise the tyre iron and get ready to bring it down again. I stop myself. He's not moving. I lean closer. He is breathing. He begins to groan. Stay calm. I reach into his coat and pull out his phone and wallet. Make it look like a mugging. Drop them into a plastic bag. He moans while I'm rummaging. I scan the windows. Can't see anyone. Walk round the corner to my car. Drive away. Stop at river. Near the old boat yards. No one about. Make an emergency services call on the clone phone. Take his phone and wallet and the tyre iron from the bag and put them in a fresh one. Squeeze out the air as I tie a knot. Throw it in the river. I'll get rid of the clone phone somewhere else.

I take off the latex gloves as I get back in the car.

He wasn't aware of me following him. He won't recognise me. Face was covered. He didn't see my eyes. No one to witness.

Mugged. He'll just think he was unlucky. He won't connect it with Marion. What if he does? What would he do? She has no alibi. But I've got tapes. They show him leaving. They show her crying. They show her going for a shower to wash off his stink. They show her changing the bedclothes. They show her going to sleep.

I can prove it wasn't her.

I watch her on the screen as she sleeps. Green tint from night vision.

I don't know what to think.

Rage left me as I followed him home.

It is not my place to interfere. I'm watching Marion's life – I shouldn't influence what happens in it.

I was calm as I watched him park. I was calm as I ran up behind him. I was calm as I hit him.

I feel nothing for the man.

HAPPINESS

A weight has gone from my shoulders. The pressure gone from my head.

Bert the caretaker is dead. Talk of the tower block. Seems he was a victim of a hit-and-run. Someone also put a brick through his window, followed by a Molotov cocktail. Gutted his bedroom. Flats above had to be evacuated.

Gossips are saying that it is more than an accident. The story is that whoever knocked him down reversed just to make sure he wouldn't get up again. Police have been asking questions.

I wonder if there'll be a new caretaker? Wonder if I'll still be able to get on the roof?

I celebrate by cataloguing the tapes of Will and Laura. I keep the masters unedited but I've got into the habit of making copies and putting all the interesting stuff together. It reminds me of my window-watching days – hours and hours of watching for a few interesting seconds. Now I'm able to stick all those moments together.

Could stick all the footage of their lovemaking together and sell it as a lovers' guide – the wheelbarrow, the frog, the rider. They've been together for ages but it doesn't seem to have dampened their appetite.

Bert would have loved this stuff.

CONTACT PRINT

Three weeks since the caretaker problem went away and I'm still on a high.

Taking pleasure from watching again.

Marion pacing from room to room.

Leaves the bedroom.

Walks into the lounge.

Goes to the window.

Can't see her looking out.

Sits on chair.

Bites fingernail.

Gets up.

Goes into bedroom.

Lies on bed.

Feet working an agitated rhythm.

She reaches into a drawer. Takes out a small bottle. Paints her toenails.

While they dry, feet start to twitch again.

She keeps on checking her phone. She is waiting for a call.

Could be waiting for the man from last month. She wouldn't expect him to call – not after all this time.

She finally makes a decision and gets the phone from the lounge and takes it to the bedroom. She throws herself down on the bed and looks at the phone.

She starts to dial. Then stops.

She sighs.

She says, *Oh, fucking hell.*

She tosses the phone on to her pillow and lies back.

I was wrong – not waiting for a call, trying to make one.

Hands to her face.

Clenches her toes.

Turns on to her stomach.

She picks up the phone.

She looks at it.

She dials a number.

Noise from my hall.

She waits.

Noise from the hall. What is that?

She says, *Pick up – please pick up.*

Noise. Hall

Tapes are recording so I can afford to go and investigate. A bleeping noise. Walk towards the door. It is coming from my bag. My mobile phone. I look for it in my bag. I pull it out. Flip it open.

Hello.

Hello. Marion's voice.

Fuck.

I panic.

I head back to the screen room. I watch her. She says, *Hello, are you still there?* Voice comes from phone and speaker. I jump and turn the volume down.

Yes. Sorry. Still here. Who is this?

It's Marion – Marion from work.

What the hell is going on?

She says, *Euan gave me your number.* Bloody Euan always doing things I don't want him to. Knew I should have made up a number when he saw my phone. Couldn't do that. If he tried it and it didn't work, he would just have asked me again and I'd be forced to give it to him then – might even have looked like I was trying to keep it from him.

Just thought I'd call for a chat. I watch her on the screen. Covers the mouthpiece. Shakes her head, thinks she just said something stupid.

That's nice.

What are you up to today? Taking some pictures?

I'm – I'm looking at some pictures.

Good ones?

Emm, yes, good ones. Insightful.

Would you like to meet for a drink?

She takes me off guard.

If you're not busy?

Umm, no, not busy.

Would you like to?

Emm, that would be nice.

She suggests a pub and a time and I agree to everything she says.

She says, *Bye, see you soon.*

She jumps back on her bed. She is smiling. She is happiness.

What is going on?

I'm bewildered. What just happened? How could that have just happened?

I had no plan for that. Had no rehearsed responses. Should I have said no? Gut told me just to agree. This could be interesting. This could be where I should be heading. I've been interacting with Will and Laura. Seems to make sense that I should interact more with the person I know most about.

Won't be such an effort. We work together. We know each other. We're friendly with each other. Why did she call me, though? She has friends. Couldn't she meet one of them if she was feeling at a loose end? No, instead, she called me out of the blue. What does it mean?

This feels a bit spooky. She can't possible know anything. She can't suspect.

What if she does? What if this is some kind of trap? She'll be nice. She'll be charming. And, when my guard is down, she'll confront me.

Stomach lurches at the thought of that. Feel kind of thrilled at the thought too.

Maybe she won't be annoyed. Maybe she'll like that she is being watched.

Fantasy running my thoughts again.

No.

She doesn't suspect. She doesn't know. She wouldn't find it a turn on.

I WANTED IT TO BE MARION

I'm watching Marion get dressed.

She is getting dressed to meet me.

I am not feeling as happy as I should – nerves getting the better of me.

She is sitting in her bedroom, applying make-up. She has just had a shower, she has a long towel wrapped around her, the clothes she is going to wear are laid out on the bed beside her. She is taking her time. She is making the effort.

She's chosen something pretty. Not for me are the delights of her 'out-with-the-girls' clothes, the skimpy tops, plunging necklines and short skirts – her pick-up clothes. For me it is a long summer dress, all flowers and blossoms. Chosen a persona just for me.

I'm watching her on the screen but I'm feeling ill. I don't know what I'll say to her. We'll sit in the pub. We'll sip our drinks. There will be silence. Awkward looks. Stifled yawns. Surreptitious looks at watches. Then goodnights and shaking heads.

I don't know how to speak to her.

I can easily slip into conversation with Laura and Will. We have talked for hours about hundreds of subjects. I become that character when I'm with them and I feel natural, feel confident. With Marion, I have to be the work version of me. I have to be the 'out-with-my-colleagues' version of me. I don't think he can cope one-to-one with pretty girls. Pretty girls that he's seen naked, that he's seen shagging, that he's seen crying, that he's seen using her toys. That is too much intimacy for him to cope with. How can he pretend he knows nothing? How can he pretend innocence?

I go to the toilet and try to throw up. Nothing happens but retching. Cold water on my face.

I can do this. I'm not like the person I am at work. I'm me. I'm in control.

This is part of the process. I know so much about her so I can mould myself into the perfect companion for the evening. I know her interests, I know her mind. This should be easy for me. I've got all the pieces. I just need to place them the right way.

This is why I am doing what I'm doing. Moving beyond the still image. Moving into the interactive world. I know what the moves will be. Prescience. I have seen all possible scenarios and I can manipulate them to get the outcome I want. I become the master of fate. I become omniscient.

I am in control.

I am control.

I go back to the watching room.

Marion is almost ready. Her dress has buttons up the front. She looks into a mirror to see if it is working for her. She seems to approve. She looks down at her chest and pulls her bra up and inward giving the effect of a bigger bosom. She finishes buttoning the dress, then decides to undo one more button at the top. Yes – that amount of cleavage looks better.

She must find something likeable in my work persona. I've tried to make him bland but not boring, unremarkable but not empty. I've failed. Marion likes him. She's got dressed up for him – she wants the night to go well with him.

I should have seen this coming. I should have realised that night bowling when she was hovering around asking questions and being attentive to my answers – not just being polite like the others. I should have seen that it was disappointment on her face when I left Euan's flat that night without her.

Maybe I shouldn't have picked her. Maybe I shouldn't have thought that she'd be the perfect candidate. There's something in that.

What have I been doing? Of course she was the perfect candidate – I made sure she was. I twisted all my requirements to make her fit the profile.

Debbie had a vacant flat above hers. Better transmission. Better access to install the cameras. Floorboards could have been lifted, holes drilled. But she just wasn't as appealing.

I wanted it to be Marion.

I wanted it to be like this.

I'm where I want to be.

Marion is at her chest of drawers. I know the drawer she is opening. I know what she keeps in it. She takes something small out and puts it under the pillow. Just in case.

I know my future.

I can see it before it happens.

Meeting someone for a drink in a pub is probably the worst way to get to know them. Sitting across a table, lots of noise too making it difficult to hear. What you should really do is something that keeps you occupied – gives you an excuse not to talk all the time, something that can cover awkward moments. Next time you meet it will be much easier. But people insist on trial by fire.

Marion tries very hard to keep the conversation going for the first ten minutes. I just can't seem to do it.

We talk about work. I know the few words that I am saying are dull but I can't let go – I just can't perform tonight.

Marion excuses herself and goes to the toilet.

I can hear her talking to people on the phone or at work tomorrow. *He was just so boring. Hardly said a word. Had to cut the night short.*

Maybe it is for the best. It will help my anonymity at work if they think I am dull. What an opportunity to miss though. I should be able to do this. I need to try harder.

Marion returns. She is smiling but it is a forced smile, the type you use to cover disappointment.

I brought something to show you, I say. I open my bag and bring out a folder. *Some of my photographs.*

Perfect icebreaker. She seems really pleased that I've got some with me. Good thing I'm still storing all my files at the rented flat.

The images are a mixture from over the years. Lots of shots of interesting things I see wandering about the city with my camera. A few still lifes thrown in for good measure. I've also put in a couple of window shots. I know she'll ask me about them but I'll say it was for a project I was doing. A couple of friends posed for me and I took the snaps through their window, sort of commentary on where the world is going with the reality TV obsession. I want her to see these images, scrutinise her reaction.

She accepts my explanation for them with an interested nod.

It was a good idea to bring photographs with me. The chat starts to flow freely between us. I'm getting into the swing of it now. I'm saying all the right things. All the things that she wants me to say. I become her ideal man – the paragon of everything she is looking for. I share her interests, I share her hopes and her fears, I am sensitive, I am a decision maker, I just adore children and want to meet the right person soon and have a family.

She laughs and smiles. She is enjoying herself – forced smiles long gone.

Occasionally she puts a hand on the table and touches mine.

Would you like to come up for a coffee?

It seems strange to be in here again. It feels a bit surreal because I've become so accustomed to watching this room from a specific angle. It looks exactly as it does on-screen but it just feels different.

Set the videos for us coming back here. Looking forward to watching it later. Me on the screen, in Marion's flat. I resist the urge to turn to the ceiling above the curtains and wave.

Marion brings a couple of mugs of coffee through and puts them in front of me. She goes to her bookcase and brings the book on Weston nudes over. *I got this after you told me about him. His photographs are great.*

She sits beside me on the sofa and opens the book on her lap. *I'll show you my favourites.*

This evening has been weird up until now but this is just insane. I'm sitting with Marion – in her flat – being recorded by my own cameras. Marion right beside me, her leg firmly against mine, and she is showing me photographs of naked women.

I don't believe it. I'm dreaming. I must be making this up.

Marion opens to a photograph of Charis lying on sand. Her arm covers her face.

I really like that one. Do you like the one with the gasmask? It's funny.

I tell her that I have a wonderful Weston print in my flat and a Cunningham print.

I'd love to see them. She is looking at me. Looking right into my eyes.

I don't know what I'm doing.

She leans forward and her lips lightly brush mine.

She moves back and watches for a response. She takes my stillness as a positive sign and leans in again. We kiss. Lips. Her lips. So soft, so warm. I feel her tongue gently touching my bottom lip. Tracing a line. My tongue touches Hélène's.

She takes me by the hand and we walk to the bedroom. She kisses me. And then walks round the bed. I'm left standing. She sits on the bed and slowly unbuttons her dress. *Hélène undressing for Henri for those first photographs.* She puts her arms behind her back and unhooks her bra. She lets it fall to her lap. She sits just letting me watch. *Hélène's hands on mine pulling them to her breasts.* Marion touches the bed beside her. I can't move. She stands. Her dress falls to the floor. She steps out of it. I know what I'll see. She pulls her knickers and lets them fall. She steps out of them. She lets me look then slowly walks towards me. *Hélène under me – I feel her guiding hand.* Marion is in front of me. So close. She leans up and kisses me. Her hands move round my head. I feel her press against me. Will and Laura, bodies hard against each other. Marion's lips on my neck, on the top of my chest, hand unbuttoning my shirt, my eyes close with the rapture of her touch, Laura touching me, *Hélène touching me, her leg between mine gently rubbing against my crotch.* I turn from her, not sure if I should step away. She presses against my back, kissing my neck, hands at my waist, pulling out my shirt, she takes my hands and puts them on her buttocks, I'm touching skin, smooth, warm, her hands slide round my waist, she rubs at my thighs through the material, my hands grip hard, hers move to the top of my trousers, they slip slowly, slowly in, moving down.

My eyes open. I am in Marion's flat.

I look at the camera. I feel its lens on me. I feel myself on the screen.

Everything stops. Heart, blood, time. A moment of stillness.

I pull away from Marion.

I have to go.

I don't look at her as I leave the room.

She doesn't follow me.

Images backwards and forwards.

Play, rewind, play, rewind, play, rewind, play, rewind, play, rewind, play, rewind, play, rewind, play, rewind, play, rewind, play, rewind, play, rewind, play, rewind, play, rewind, play, rewind, play, rewind, play, rewind, play, rewind.

I watch them enter the bedroom. I watch her kiss him. I watch her going to the bed. I watch her undressing. I watch her go to him. I watch her kiss him. Touch him. I watch him turn. I watch her hands on him.

I watch as his eyes close. I watch her putting his hands on her. I watch his bliss. I watch his eyes open. They are my eyes. He looks straight at the camera. He looks straight at me. My eyes in that head, burning though the screen. I stare. All that I can see are those eyes. He leaves the room.

Press pause. Don't want to see what happens next. The story ends at that point.

I press rewind. Stop when they walk out of the room backwards. Press play. It starts again.

I take a few days off sick. Suspicion when I phoned in and spoke to Anne. She said that I have missed a number of days in the last few months.

I said, *I know.* And hung up.

I need some time. I need to understand what happened. I was so close to something there. I could almost feel it. Then it went.

I know I'll understand soon. I just need to think about it hard enough.

Something has changed. I'm getting very close to an answer, it's just out of reach, but I know that if I can just see it then I'll know what to do. I'll know how it ends.

Back to work. Marion was waiting for me to say something but, when I walk past her without even looking, I can feel her outrage. She goes into a sulk. I ignore Marion and she ignores me.

It is probably for the best.

I still don't have an answer.

Henri is a methodical man.

Henri is calm.

Henri takes the knife from the drawer.

Henri places it on the table and covers it with a cloth.

Henri sits at the table and places his open pocket watch in front of him. He stares at the inscription. Henri amour Hélène. He smiles at the words and, for a moment, he forgets that Hélène is with another man.

Henri is ruined.

Hélène has seen to that.

Everyone knows about his photographs.

Henri cannot believe the hypocrisy. The very same men that have their own private collections publicly denounce him.

Henri wondered why she would do such a thing to him. He only once complained that she slept with other men. The look that she gave him stilled the other accusations he had.

Henri thought that she would want to go back home. This time she could hold her head up high. The sun of his legitimacy would warm them both. What could be wrong with that?

He heard whispers at first. People were saying that he was a pornographer. The moral right lined up against him.

Henri realised that pillow talk started the rumours.

Henri realised it was Hélène.

Now Henri waits for her to come home. He waits for her to shout and rage at him again.

He does not mind.

It is too late for that now.

There is only one thing left for him to do.

Only one way to save her.

Henri moves Hélène's head back.

Her eyes on his. He sees the shock in them.

He sees the pupils dilate.

Henri goes to his camera. He does not have much time. Hélène will slip away any moment.

He needs to take the final image before then.

He knows that she will not die.

He knows that her heart will stop and the blood that weeps from her will slow and dry.

He knows that the flesh will end but the image will go on forever.

He knows that the world will not see her grow old – it will not see her wither.

He has preserved her.

Captured her soul in a final print.

His finger reaches for the button, slick with blood.

The shutter clicks.

He knows that she will not die.

When they found him he was sitting at the table with the body. He said nothing when they took him away.

At the trial the plea of a crime of passion was dismissed. If it was true, how could the deliberate taking of a photograph be explained? How could the posing of the dying woman's body be explained?

Henri was portrayed as a monster. A cold-hearted foreigner that killed his wife when she tried to escape from his pornography.

The newspapers made much of the fact that he held her against her will and made her pose for lewd photographs.

No one paid much attention to her being much younger in these images.

No one cared that she was not a prisoner.

Henri was expressionless when the sentence was delivered. Life imprisonment.

Henri did not look at the jury as he was led away. He knew he was guilty.

Henri's regret is that only the newspaper reports and court records will speak for his life.

A whole life reduced to words.

Henri is a methodical man.

Henri is calm.

Henri gently takes the rope he has made from his sheets and ties it to the bars of the window.

Henri thinks of Hélène and smiles as he kicks away the chair.

The last photograph of Hélène went missing from the evidence box after the trial.

For a hundred years it has been a legend.

FIRST SITTING

She gets ready for a night out.

Ritual of dressing. Lots of time spent wandering around in her underwear, selecting possible clothes then discarding them.

She puts on make-up. She dries her hair. She puts on her costume for the night. Friday night of fun with the girls. She is off tomorrow. I'm due in but I'll see how I feel.

I've started watching Marion again. I've been listening to one side of phone conversations with various friends. Plans were made. Drinking. Dancing. Happiness.

It has been a couple of weeks since our night together. We haven't spoken. She hasn't mentioned me to her friends – as far as I'm aware.

I think I have my answer. I know what to do. My plans rely on her coming back home alone tonight. Can't very well apologise if she's brought a shag with her. She did say on the phone last night that she was off men for good. But who knows if someone will catch her eye tonight?

She needs to be alone.

Running out of time.

Will is on a business trip soon. Timing couldn't be better. I've got some contingency plans but they'd be second best. Head filled with plans within plans.

Marion, at last, seems satisfied with the way she looks. Too much make-up for my taste but I suppose I've got no right to say much now. She takes a tiny handbag from her cupboard, transfers a few notes and coins to it from her usual bag and leaves the bedroom.

My cue to go. Already got my jacket on and car keys in my hand. Quick to the car. Boot already has my rucksack and sports bag in it.

I wait for her to pass on her way to the bus stop. Always takes a bus to the city centre if the weather is OK. She gets a cab home.

Hope she has a good night tonight. She's had a shitty few weeks one way or another. Needs a bit of fun.

I see her cross the road on her way to the bus stop. I wait until she's gone and then circle round to the main road and stop a couple of hundred metres away. Marion reaches the shelter. A few people are there already. Bus drives past. I wait until Marion is on before I pull away.

Friday evening traffic is heavy, heavy. Hundreds of people migrating to the city centre for a night of binge drinking, drunken fondling and vomiting – perfect start to the weekend.

I'm in town and looking for a space before the bus is anywhere near. I have the advantage. I know where she is meeting her friends. I go into a coffee bar diagonally across the street from it. I order a latte and manage to get a stool by the window. Pull out a paperback to disguise my observations.

Not paying much attention to the words. I'm thinking about the exhibition. Planning to have a little showing of some of my snaps. Not shown any of my work for years. This time it will be special. This time heads will turn.

I see Marion walking into the pub.

I have time to waste so I order another latte and watch the world go by. Boys and girls dressed for weekend *partee*. Boys in smart trousers, pastel or white pressed shirts, not tucked in. Girls dressed in next to nothing, all Wonderbras and deep cleavages, skirts short enough to see panties and far too much make-up. They all look tribal. Off to some mating ritual.

Feeling unsettled. Wonder if I should go back to my flat for a while – see what Will and Laura are up to? Maybe I should just go back and hang out there for a while? It feels like I've not spent much time at home recently. The rented flat is just too convenient. I'll have to decide soon if I want to extend the lease or not. Finances are looking a bit dodgy at the moment. I've bought a lot of equipment over the last few months. I've bought some other stuff too – for tonight. Expensive for what you get.

Maybe I should do what the caretaker suggested and go into business selling the footage I have of Marion and Will and Laura. He said we could make some good money from things like that. Seems a bit sordid, making money from my work.

Henri made money from his photographs of Hélène – nothing wrong with that. He wasn't exploiting anyone. Hélène wanted to be part of what he did and she shared in everything he got from it.

My hand is in my pocket, touching the little booklet I've made.

Photographs of Hélène. I would like to take them out and look at them. A coffee shop might not be the best place.

There is one photograph of Hélène that is worth more than you'd guess. Worth more than the supposed nude photograph of Wyatt Earp's wife. The image is the last one that Henri took of Hélène – the last photograph ever taken of Hélène.

For a small community on the web, it has become the Holy Grail of pictures from the 'classic' period. Every so often, you hear rumours of it surfacing and then disappearing into some private collection for an obscene amount of money. It has become mythological. I know that Henri took the photograph. Every fibre of me knows that it exists. I wonder if I'll ever get to see it.

I decide to go back to the car. Fight my way through the swaggering boys with their 'looking-for-pussy' expressions and clouds of after-shave. Many of them will get lucky. Many of them will wake up and look at the girl beside them and say *I must have been rat-arsed last night*.

I drive around for a while. Wandering. Following the road.

I might have to wait outside Marion's flat for hours tonight. Depends on what she ends up doing. Depends on how much fun she's having.

I drive along the street where Sarah's flat is. No lights on but it is not dark enough. She could be in. I've been phoning her office every week for a while now. I ask to speak to her and, when I'm told I'll be connected, I hang up. I phone on different days at different times. I've learned that she is going away with the gang during the summer – another week of sun and fun. Got plans for when she does.

I'm patient. I can wait for it.

Drive to the rented flat. I walk in and check the screens. Empty bedroom. Empty lounge. I call Marion's number. The phone rings out and clicks on to the answer machine message. *Hi, I can't come to . . .* I hang up. She hasn't come back early.

I think I should go there for a few minutes. Just get a feel of the place again. Work through what I'm going to do later. It is still light but it doesn't matter. I've been seen going into her flat with her now. As long as no one mentions seeing me to her, then I can come and go as I please. I'll do it.

Jog round. I take off my shoes when I get inside. I'll be back here in a few hours so I don't need to take too many precautions. I've also been here with Marion, any DNA or fibres are now legitimate. I walk to the bedroom – clothes on the floor and the bed from her dressing dilemmas.

I remember that night. Each frame imprinted in my memory from watching over and over. She was there on the bed. She wanted to be with him. She wanted to feel his skin against hers. She wanted to love him.

I don't know who that man was. I don't know if it was me. Head aches thinking about it. I see the footage. Forward, rewind. Forward, rewind. Stop thinking about that.

I've planned tonight in detail but it is good to be here to rehearse in situ. I look around the room. I know where everything will be. I can see every angle, every position.

I touch the bed. What would it have been like? How would it have felt to be him. I strip quickly, before I can change my mind and slip under the duvet. Soft touch of her sheets against my skin. I put my head on her pillow. I can smell her on the sheets, on the pillow. I breathe her in. I feel like Marion feels when she lies in her bed. I've watched her bed rituals every night. I know each gesture by heart. I copy them. I fill with understanding.

Back to that night. If he stayed? Feel her skin against me. Feel her sitting astride me. Hands on my chest. Slowly moving up and down. Eyes looking into mine. I am watching them through the lens. Up to the attic. Electromagnetic waves pulsing across space. Hitting the receiver in the flat. Translated to images. Watching us on the screen. Together. Loving. Like Hélène and Henri. Like Will and Laura.

I get out of bed and smooth the duvet. I place Marion's discarded clothes where they were. I'm not too careful – I'll be moving them again later. I stand there for a moment. Naked. Flesh before the lens. I dress.

Check the peephole. Back to the car.

Just need to wait now. See if I can capture it tonight.

I put on a compilation CD to help pass the time.

'What Difference Does it Make?' is the first track.

I've nodded off a couple of times despite the tension of the evening. I take a brisk walk to help me stay focused. No clouds in the sky tonight so it is cool. It will be cold for Marion coming home. Goosebumped flesh on the fake leather taxi seat.

Despite the streetlights I can still see stars. It has become a commonplace notion that we are made from stardust – that every atom in our bodies originated in some star. Matter in existence for eternity, changing form over time but always there. But I am still awed by the thought – it makes me feel small. It makes me feel part of the universe.

It would be a good night to be on the roof. It has been a few weeks since the caretaker incident and still no replacement for him. It is great from my point of view – no interference, full access. Still got chipboard panel over the caretaker's window. Still got black soot marks climbing up the wall.

I check windows as I walk back to the car. Curtains closed. Curtain open but room dark. Telltale blue flicker in some.

In the car, I take the set of laminated cards from my pocket. Each one has a scan of an Hélène image. Top left-hand corner of each card has a hole-punched circle. I've put a silver key-ring chain through the holes to keep the images together but also allow me to flick through them easily.

Some of these are going to be difficult.

Some of these are going to be impossible.

Not much use tonight.

I put the cards back in my pocket when I see a taxi turn into the street. Run over the dialogue in my mind as I wait to see if it is Marion. Hope she is alone. Hope she hasn't decided that a night of shagging will be the perfect cure for her boy blues.

The taxi pulls up outside Marion's flat.

I get out of my car and go to the boot, take out the gym bag and throw it on to my shoulder. Heavy. Rucksack on the other shoulder.

Marion is in the taxi. Alone. I watch her pay the driver and then get out. She doesn't look in my direction.

I lock the boot and start to cross the street before the taxi has pulled away. I catch up with Marion as she is putting her key into the security door.

Marion.

She jumps when she hears her name and spins round. Keys held up like a knife, eyes wide.

She sees that it is me and the fear goes. Flicker of smile on her face quickly replaced with a frown. *What are you doing here?*

Her face tells me I'm not forgiven.

What do you want?

I run through my practised speech. I tell her I am sorry. I tell her I was confused. I tell her that I wasn't thinking straight. I tell her that I've behaved badly. I ask her to forgive me.

She listens patiently. The stony set of her face slowly relaxing. I know that she wants to hear these words.

As I talk I see the dilation in her pupils. I smell the alcohol on her breath. I see the flushing on her cheeks and chest. I ask if I can come up for a drink. The bag bites at my shoulder.

She looks at me. I can't read her expression. I don't know what will happen next. Everything depends on what she does now. I need this to work. I'm running out of options.

Please agree. Please let me complete my task.

She turns without a word and opens the security door. She walks through it. As it swings closed, she throws, *You better come up then,* over her shoulder.

She walks up the stairs ahead of me. She says nothing.

I lag behind with the heavy bag and watch the top of her thighs rubbing together. She is not completely steady on her feet. Slightly drunk. It'll make things easier. Need to make sure she has another couple of drinks before I start.

She opens the door and holds it for me. I drop the gym bag in the hall and it makes a thump. She looks at it.

Been at the gym, I say.

She walks into her bedroom. *I'll be with you in a minute.*

I go to the lounge taking the rucksack from my shoulder. Need to work quickly. I open the bag and take a bottle of rum from it. Grab two glasses pour a generous measure in one of then and a splash in the other. Spiced rum is her tipple of choice and that helps me considerably. Take a cola bottle from the bag next and fill my glass before returning it to the bag. Second cola bottle in my hands.

I hear Marion closing the bathroom door.

I pour liquid from the second bottle into her glass and stir the mixture. I hold it up to the light. No traces. Perfectly mixed. It would be better if she has two glasses. It will work faster that way. Have to try and drink my glass in a couple of gulps and hope she does the same.

I take off my jacket and throw it on a chair.

I walk to the window. Curtains still open. I pull them closed. Don't need glasses or wigs or mugs this time. I'm here legitimately. If anyone sees me, they'll think I'm some new bloke. They'll think Marion is some slapper – a maneater.

Marion comes into the lounge. She's taken off her shoes but otherwise she is the same. Have to watch what she was doing in the bedroom later.

I hand her the glass I've prepared for her. *I've made us a drink.*

She looks surprised.

Hope you don't mind?

She takes it. She sips it. She sits on the sofa.

I sit with my glass and take a gulp. Cola. Just enough rum round the rim to give an alcohol smell.

I watch her taking a bigger sip. No reaction. She can't taste it. Good.

We sit watching each other.

I notice that her skirt got pulled up when she sat. I can see her underwear.

She's drinking to match me – Dutch courage for both of us perhaps. I get up and take her glass to refill it. Her finger brushes against my hand when I take it. Need her to have another drink before she makes a move on me. Don't know if I could stop it this time. But I'm counting on the fact that she'll think I should make the first move. She won't want to embarrass herself again. I'm hoping the alcohol hasn't made her annoyance with me go completely.

I make her another rum and Coke. She's watching me so I have to make myself one. Can't drink from my glass now as it is tainted like hers.

It is going to be a tricky few minutes while it takes effect. The stuff in her drink will make her lose her inhibitions somewhat. Mixed with alcohol, it should knock her out fairly quickly.

I sit down again and say that I want to explain things to her. Got to keep talking until it takes effect.

I can't help but notice she has both legs on the sofa now. Soles of her feet together, knickers clearly visible. I wonder if she is sitting like that on purpose.

I quickly look away to her bookshelf and look like I am thinking about how to begin. My eyes land on her Anne Hooper and Tracey Cox books – not the best place to look under the circumstances.

I start to stumble over words. I feign embarrassment at talking about my emotions.

She listens and drinks.

I waffle on for another few minutes trying not to look at her. Don't want to give her any signals that might be misinterpreted.

I stop.

There is silence.

I steal a look.

Her eyes are closed, her head down at her chest.

I wait.

I call her name softly.

She does not stir.

I wait.

I call her name again, louder.

Still no response.

I get up and walk to her side.

I gently push her shoulder.

Nothing.

I lean close and listen.

Her breathing is deep.

I gently shake her.

Nothing.

She's out cold.

I'm impressed with the effects. Quicker than I had hoped but she's probably got a lot of alcohol in her system and that will make it work more quickly.

There is a danger mixing it with alcohol though – risk of fatality. I'll just have to be vigilant.

The best side effect is what it does to memory. She'll have either no recollection of the evening or it will feel like a dream. If I'm careful enough not to wake her when I move her, she'll never know what happened. That is what makes this stuff so dangerous.

First things first.

I take her glass and rinse it in the sink with warm water. I put a generous squirt of washing up liquid into it and fill it with hot water from the kettle.

I check Marion again before I go and prepare the bedroom. She's completely unconscious.

I retrieve the gym bag and carry it into the bedroom.

I take the black sheets from it and spread them over the bed and part way up the wall by the headboard.

Next are lamps from the bag and then studio flash. It only takes a few minutes to set everything up.

I angle the reflective umbrella of the studio flash at the bed. Camera tripod next and then to the lounge to get my camera from the rucksack.

Quick check on Marion.

Camera on tripod.

I'll have to be careful carrying Marion through. Any sudden movements like banging her off doors could breakthrough the anaesthetic effects and it would be more than difficult to explain why her bedroom looks like a studio.

I lay her on the bed. I pull her dress up over her hips and then move her into a sitting position to pull it over her head. It is not easy manipulating an unconscious body. She is a dead weight.

I glance at the camera positions knowing that the videos are on preset and started recording a couple of hours ago on the off chance she got home early. I get to experience this first hand and then over and over again on the screen.

I lean her against me as I drop the dress to the floor and then reach round to unhook her bra. Cradling her head and shoulders, I ease her back on to the bed and slip the bra off her arms.

I don't spend time looking at her yet. Got a job to do.

I lift her from the waist and pull down her knickers. Lift her legs from the knees to take them off completely. I can't help but look at her now. Not quite a Brazilian but near enough.

I reach out and touch her skin –so warm. Trace of stubble. I run my fingertips over her body.

Lean close to smell her skin.

Stop now. This isn't sexual.

I place a pillow under her and move her legs apart.

Almost forgot. I take a sleeping mask from my bag and slip it over her head. Don't want the flash to register on her eyes.

I take the flip cards of Hélène from my pocket and select the first shot – classic reclining nude.

I look through the viewfinder and then move the camera and tripod into a better position. Perfect.

I add pressure to the button.

Flash

I've got two rolls completed. Ended up with many similar shots because I couldn't get her into all the positions I needed. I've got enough though.

Dressing her was harder that undressing her and I was scared I would wake her.

Everything packed away now.

I take a piece of paper from my pocket and put it on her bedside table. It says that she crashed out and I put her on her bed. I also wrote that I was happy she understood that I thought we should just be friends. I kiss her on the forehead and then check her pulse.

I gather up my bags and the bottles and leave her flat.

Only a few minutes and I can start developing at the rented flat. I'm shattered but I can't wait until morning. Might even watch the evening back on video.

I'll keep a live feed on though. Make sure she wakes up OK.

Finally got some Hélène-type shots – not quite what I need but close. Proved that it can be done.

Real thing next.

This was the practice run.

I just can't wait.

KILLING THE PAST

Make the call. Latest in a series every week for the last two months. Voice on the other end says that Sarah is not available and won't be back until a week on Monday. I hang up while I'm connected to someone else that can help with my enquiry.

I want to go round straight away. Do what I've been planning – if only my nerve holds. Can't rush into things at this stage. Need to be calm. Need to be methodical. Too much else going on to risk making an impatient mistake.

Can't be sure that she has not just taken a day off to pack and that she leaves tomorrow. I can't just wander in if she is still there.

I drive to her flat and watch it from the car and then on foot. No signs of her being home.

Inconclusive. Need more information.

I call her number. Answer machine picks up. I don't want to hear her voice, feelings still raw, but I force myself to listen until the beep is about to sound. Her sweet voice – makes me question if I'm doing the right thing. Harden my heart. I've got to do it. Need to have restitution.

Still not enough evidence that she is gone.

I go back to my flat and wait until evening.

I try her number again.

I'm sorry I can't get to the phone right now but . . .

I try a few more times. Problem is, if someone else tries to call her, I'll get the engaged tone. It'll make me think she's still here.

I call her after she would normally be in bed. Keep on ringing until the machine clicks on then hang up. I keep on calling, trying to make sure that she gets up in annoyance to find out who the hell keeps phoning.

No answer

She must have gone.

I'll do it tomorrow.

I look out everything I'll need. Practise. Plan.

I drive out of the city as fast as I can. Feeling dazed after the work I've done.

My body knows where I'm going. Drives on automatic.

It was a difficult today. It took some time to work up to it. But eventually I found the courage.

I got into Sarah's flat.

Found what I was looking for. Took as much as I could in the few minutes I allowed myself.

I had to mess up the place a bit, make it look real. Took her DVD player and some cash. Dumped the hardware in a skip and gave the money to a homeless guy. I'm not a thief.

When I stop I'm near the coast. Childhood holiday haunt. It will take about half an hour to walk across the fields and golf course before I hit the dunes. Few more minutes and I'll be in water. If I keep going? If the water engulfs me?

It would have been easier if I'd gone to the car park further along the beach. I don't want to be close to people. I'll go this way. The most direct route.

Golfers shout at me as I ruin their shots by marching in front of them. They don't dare take pot shots when they see the steel in my eyes. Walk on.

Don't stop for anything.

Grass gives way to sand and I shuffle over the dunes. It is a warm evening and the beach has a few stragglers left from a day of sunbathing.

I walk to the quiet end of the beach. I dump my bag on the sand confident that no one will steal it. I start to hunt for driftwood.

There is a group of young people going back the way I've just come. They have the same idea as me. They've already collected enough for a good bonfire but they are still searching.

I pass a couple of them. Arms full of wood. They laugh and talk and smile. Tanned legs and shorts and bikini tops and bare chests. They bump into each other as they walk. Deliberately touching. I see tartan rugs and lovemaking under the stars later.

By the time I get back to my bag with the lone armful of wood, their bonfire is lit.

I dig a pit in the sand, reinforce the sides with wood. Open my bag and pull out a newspaper, twist the pages into loops and drop them into the hole. I used to love making bonfires on the beach when I was younger. I would spend the night here watching the flames and listening to the waves. Heading back to the caravan as dawn broke.

I spray some lighter fluid on the paper. I know that's cheating. I pile on the wood. Pushed for time.

All the handy, washed-up crates to sit on have been taken by the group at the other end of the beach but I'm clever, I've brought a fold-down canvas stool.

I sit.

I pull my gym bag towards me. I open it. Ready for the treasures.

I open a box of matches. I drag one along the side until it flares and flick it towards the fuel-soaked paper. I'm being dramatic – just what the moment calls for. The match blows out before it hits the paper. I kneel down, light a match and hold it against the paper.

Fire.

Open the bag. I feel calm as I pull out the top album – like I'm in the eye of a hurricane, everything unnaturally still, just waiting for the storm to rage again.

If I'd had more time at her flat I would have searched everywhere, made sure I got every one of them.

I rub my fingers across the front of the album. Garish tropical sunset on the cover.

I open the book. Her childhood comes pouring out. Better than all the fantasies I've had about seeing these images.

I look at each one carefully, committing as much as I can to memory but soon there is too much in my head and I only see flashes of detail.

Baby in the bath. First day at school. Christmas. Birthdays. Holidays. Friends. Boys. Teenage years. Puberty. Adult. The gang.

Her life. A journey in pictures. Each image special. Every memory they evoke unique to her.

As the sun sets, I reach the last envelope. Beach scene. Multicoloured ball hangs in the air. Peter, no, Dave jumps for it.

I drop it into the flames.

I take the next print. It blackens and burns – top coating of plastic curls away momentarily from the other layers before it disappears.

Again. Again. Again.

Offer them all to the fire. Sacrifice and absolution.

I take the negatives last.

My hand shakes at the enormity of what I'm doing. No copies can be made if I do this.

Will she know it was me? I've left no traces so nothing can be proved. But there is vigilante justice. Dave and his meaty fists.

I'll think about that later. Too much to do. Can't be distracted.

I drop the negatives on the fire.

Those images lost to her forever.

I open each album, peel back the acetate, take out the memories and give them to the flames.

Face wet with tears as I finish.

All gone.

I feel sickened by the violation.

My heart goes cold.

She brought it on herself.

She is to blame. Not me.

I turn back to the bonfire when I reach the top of the dunes.

Flames dancing and flickering. I almost see the images in the smoke as it rises and is swallowed in the dark.

I hear a couple of the kids from the other bonfire. Probably the ones I saw earlier. They've snuck off to be alone. I hear whispers and moans in the dark.

I don't wait.

I go to the car.

SECOND SITTING

When it comes down to it, it is all about timing.

I've been preparing for the next few hours for months. Longer perhaps. Longer than I'll ever know.

A culmination.

Hélène is made flesh tonight.

Hélène leaves the print, becomes tangible, then returns to the immortality of image with a new face.

Will out of town on business. Not back until Sunday. That has given me choices.

Laura and I have made some tentative arrangements to meet up but we've kept our plans fluid. I've told her I'm waiting for some good news. I've been priming her for a few weeks. Hired the space for a photographic exhibition. Made it sound like I'm waiting to find out if I'm being offered the space. She's almost as excited as I am.

I watch her from the flat. She arrives home just after five. Flops down with a cup of tea in the lounge a few minutes after I see her going through the downstairs door.

I call her. I tell her to hold everything – not to make plans for the evening. *I'll be over in a while with a carry-out and some tequila. It's celebration time.*

She is happy for me and can't wait to see me. She thinks nothing of having me over when Will is away. Gay gambit worked perfectly. Mr Non-threatening. Mr Confidante. Women are so trusting of gay men – let their guards down too easily.

I wait and watch for a while. I'm supposed to be in the flat at the other side of the city so I can't just appear. I've got a carry-out on order and I've got the ingredients for many margaritas ready to go.

Laura has a shower and I watch her idly drying herself.

I set tapes to record the feed from Laura's flat and wait for the food to arrive.

Car is already packed. Duplicate keys in my pocket ready for when she's unconscious. Quick trip downstairs to retrieve equipment and then set up. I've been practising setting everything up quickly – will only take a few minutes.

I know exactly what I need to do with Laura. Every position planned and memorised. I know I won't even need to look at the booklet of Hélène images.

Knock on the door. Carry-out arrived.

I dip the rim of Laura's glass in a saucer of salt and pour her a margarita. I've insisted that I am the barman tonight although she protested we were celebrating my good news and I am the one that should be pampered.

She's in the kitchen getting the plates that are warming in the oven. I had planned to put an amount of the powder directly into her food. Strong curry taste would disguise it completely but I was scared that she might not finish her meal and that would lead to dosage problems. I also didn't want to risk her forcing me to share her food. Drinks again. Easy to do. Still the same risks but I'm willing to take them.

She's already had a half-dose in her first drink and the second one is ready.

We eat.

We chat.

She drinks.

By the time we're finished eating I can see the effects becoming apparent. Pupils are dilated. Slurred speech. Loss of fine motor coordination.

She's told me several time, *I'm feeling a teensy-weensy bit tipsy.*

I say, *I make a pretty strong margarita.*

The next quarter of an hour is a bit more drawn out than the time with Marion. Marion was already drunk and hadn't just eaten. The effect was quick.

Laura seems to be trying hard not to fall asleep. Eyes close, head nods to her chest then jerks up again. She apologises for being a lightweight.

I wait a full four minutes after her eyes close for the last time before I call her name.

Hélène.

I go to her and gently tap her shoulder.

No response.

I lean down and check her breathing.

I put my fingertip to her throat and feel her slow, steady pulse.

I go to the bedroom with my rucksack and spread the black sheet over the bed and headboard.

Gently carry Laura through and place her on the bed. I watch her as she lies on the bed, looking for signs of consciousness. Dead to the world.

I decide to undress her before going to the car to get the equipment. Don't want to move her too much once I've got everything set up.

Unbutton her top. Cotton against my fingertips. I've seen her naked many times but not directly with my eyes. Always been some artificial lens in the way before. Lift each shoulder as I take the top off.

Trousers have a tied cord instead of buttons. I pay attention to the bow although I know that she won't notice any difference when she wakes up. She'll still be groggy.

Slide one hand under the small of her back and lift while pulling them over her hips. My fingers brush across her skin.

More curves than Marion. More like Hélène. Natural look too – not the waxing that Marion goes for.

I look at her.

I touch her.

Hands and fingers exploring.

I leave her naked on the bed and go for the equipment. I've streamlined this time – only one lamp and no flashgun. I don't want her face to be covered so I have to be careful with sudden blasts of light. Could be enough to wake her a little. I'm using a faster film and longer exposures to compensate for reduced lighting. It will give such a nice grain to the prints.

Get back to the bedroom.

No change in her condition.

Set up quickly.

First position.

Eye to the viewfinder.

Perfect.

Snap.

It takes me almost two hours to complete the shots. I'm drenched in sweat by the time I'm finished – her body heavy to move.

I've gone past my allotted time and there is a danger that she'll come round. She might now only be in a deep sleep.

I pack the equipment and take it to the car. Night air making the sweat chill my body.

When I get back to the bedroom, the only evidence I've been there is my camera and Laura's nudity.

One last shot to take.

Flesh burns into silver salts then light burns paper to create the image.

Laura as Hélène as flesh as photograph. I'm just completing the circle.

The story ended a century ago. It seemed to be finished. I've brought it to life it. Resurrected Hélène.

I control the story now. I have become fate.

Every action from now on is my choice. I can see every possible future spreading out in front of me. Every detail alters every one that follows.

Henri was the victim of his own passion – I could see that in the first image he captured of Hélène. He was bound to her from that moment and together their end was sealed. I could read that print. I could see history in it. Death at his hands. He saved Hélène for eternity – preserving all those moments with a lens and a box and some treated paper – but he lost himself. Damned to a mortal's end. No full image of him ever captured.

Hélène lies on the bed. I've emptied her. Caught her soul on strips of negative.

Henri knew what to do once he realised he had taken all Hélène had to give. He knew how to stop her withering. They say he put the knife in front of her in the last shot. A reminder of the immortality he'd given her.

I sit on the bed. Camera at my side.

I take the knife from my rucksack and place it beside Hélène.

I can preserve this moment forever.

It is time to decide the future.

FINAL PRINT

Too much to do.

Early morning when I get back to my flat.

I go straight the bathroom – I've already set it up as a darkroom.

Head sore from lack of sleep. I'm supposed to be at work later but I'm not going in – too busy. So much to do and so little time to make sure I get through it all. I don't bother phoning in.

I fix the negatives and then hang them to dry. Impatient as I look at the reversed images.

These are good.

These are perfect.

The phone goes when I'm making prints but I ignore it. Could be work. I don't care. Don't think I want to go back. Want that life to be over.

Prints ready.

Exhibition starts tomorrow night. Cocktail reception to launch it. Wine and nibbles and expectations. The gallery staff are ready for opening. All I have to do is hang the prints. Let the world see my handywork.

Invitations went out last week.

Interested parties will be present – all but two.

I won't be there. I have somewhere more important to be.

Laura won't be there either.

If Will's flight isn't delayed, he'll arrive in time for the last drinks. He was so excited for me about the exhibition. He's been very supportive. He promised to come straight to it. I don't want him to go home first. That would spoil it.

I had debated having it while he was away – miss his reaction – but the timing of his flight was just too perfect and I was able to make it appear as a happy coincidence.

I wish I could be there when he sees the photographs.

Couple of video cameras there to record everyone else's reactions.

I decided on a title for the exhibition. *Window on the World* – pretentious but appropriate.

All my friends will be there captured in images.

It will be hailed as a masterpiece. A sharp commentary on our modern voyeur culture with an acknowledgement of where it all began in the section that is homage to early photography simply called 'Henri and Hélène'.

I wonder if they'll know the photographs are real? No actors, no posing. I wonder what they will make of the torpor of the women being Hélène? I wonder what Marion will think when she sees pictures of herself hanging in the gallery? Will she recognise herself?

Doesn't matter. She'd be happy that she posed for me.

WINDOW ON THE WORLD

Today was a rush.

Felt hassled all day long. Everything seemed to take forever to do. But the hanging prints looked good in the end.

Just made the last post with Marion's package. Little present for her to open in the morning.

One last thing to do.

I go to the window and point the camera at Will and Laura's lounge.

Switch on the monitors and press record on the video machines. See the views inside the flat flicker and settle.

Laura is putting on earrings. She's looking lovely.

She is waiting for me to collect her.

I stayed with Laura for a while last night. Undressed and lay next to her on the bed. I looked out the window at my flat. I watched the curtains part and saw myself looking at us on the bed. Bodies touching but still. Corpses on the slab.

I dressed Laura and then myself.

I went to the lounge to wait for her to wake.

I made my choice.

The only one I could.

Henri got it wrong. He saved Hélène but sacrificed himself. He left the story the moment she died. There was nothing left of him. Photographs taken when he was arrested were too late. The images in newspapers the same. There was nothing left of him by then. He was only shadow and words.

I heard her stir after six. Heard the slap-slap of her feet on the wooden floor when she went to the bathroom. Heard her groan and moan. A few minutes later she stumbled into the lounge. She looked terrible.

I asked her how she was feeling and she said, *Like death warmed up.*

I explained to her that she passed out. I told her that I didn't want to leave her alone. I told her that I thought we overdid the drinks and that curry was dodgy too. I pretended that I was sick during the night.

She told me that she didn't remember a thing.

I made her some breakfast and satisfied myself she was feeling better before I left.

Alcohol and the other stuff are a dangerous combination and I need her fit and healthy for what is to come.

There she is waiting for me to collect her for tonight.

She's sitting in the lounge. Pretty dress.

I pan down to the front door when I see the van pull up.

I watch as the driver walks to the door and pushes the intercom. On the lounge screen, I see Laura react. She goes out of shot and I see the man being buzzed into the building. He's carrying a box.

I turn on my angle-poise lamp and shine it on the window.

I watch as Laura comes into the lounge and sits down with the package. I knew she would come back in because she's waiting for me to call her and the phone is in here. Everything just as I want it.

She opens the box.

She doesn't know what it could be.

Lid lands on the sofa beside her.

Hand reaches in.

Inquisitive look on her face.

This is it. This is the moment.

Her head is down.

She looks into the box.

Lens only sees the top of her head but I can tell what she is thinking.

She stays motionless for second after second.

Then her hands shake.

Something else in the box.

It is a card.

I've left a light on for you if you look out your window. Come up and we can talk.

She walks hesitantly to the window and her eyes scan the tower block.

She sees the light.

Snap of the shutter.

I close the curtains.

I sit.

I wait.

Don't know exactly what will happen next. Left that to chance. Too many variables. As long as I get the ending I need, it doesn't really matter what the last steps are.

The ending is set.

The ending has been rehearsed.

My hope is that it is Laura who comes. She'll be scared by now. She might be making calls right now. She might not come alone.

Just have to wait.

Not long now.

No going back. Too late for that.

Everything is ready.

I don't know how long I've been waiting.

Knock at the door.

I don't move. I feel nervous.

Thumps at the door.

Calls to *Open up!*

I stand.

I am calm.

I don't rush.

I am methodical.

I go to the cameras behind my chair and switch them on.

Henri disappeared the moment that Hélène died.

Only words mark his time here.

I am not Henri.

There will be more than words.

I am smarter.

This story is about me.

I'm recording every detail.

I walk to the door.